THE NEW
ABBEY GIRLS

ELSIE JEANETTE OXENHAM

Girls Gone By Publishers

COMPLETE AND UNABRIDGED

Published by

Girls Gone By Publishers
4 Rock Terrace
Coleford
Bath
Somerset
BA3 5NF

First published by Collins Publishers 1923
This edition published 2008
Text and illustrations © HarperCollins Publishers
Introduction to the Abbey Series © Clarissa Cridland 2004
Elsie Oxenham and the English Folk Dance Society © Ann Mackie-
    Hunter 2008
From Rags to Riches © Adrianne Fitzpatrick 2008
Publishing History © Clarissa Cridland 2008
Design and layout © Girls Gone By Publishers

Typeset in England by AJF
Printed in England by CPI Antony Rowe, Chippenham, Wiltshhire

ISBN 978-1-84745-053-1

"Jen was dancing a morris jig."

CONTENTS

CONTENTS

INTRODUCTION TO THE ABBEY SERIES

The Abbey Series

Providing a list of the 38 Abbey titles is not as simple as it seems, since the order in which they were written and published is not the order in which they should necessarily be read. The list provided below is the reading order, with the original publication dates given in parentheses afterwards. Titles 4–10 inclusive are usually known as the 'retrospective' Abbey titles, since, although they were written after the original Abbey Girls had grown up, they take the reader back to the early days when Joy, Joan and Jen were schoolgirls. Titles 1–3 and 11–27 are generally known as the 'first generation' Abbey titles, and books 28–38 as the 'second generation' Abbey titles, featuring as they do the children of those original Abbey girls. Looking at the list, it should also be noted that *Jen of the Abbey School* was written retrospectively, being set during and after the events described in *The Abbey Girls Go Back to School*, and that *Maid of the Abbey* is set before *Jandy Mac Comes Back*, even though published two years afterwards.

The Abbey Series in Reading Order:

1. *Girls of the Hamlet Club* (1914)
2. *The Abbey Girls* (1920)
3. *The Girls of the Abbey School* (1921)
4. *Schooldays at the Abbey* (1938)
5. *Secrets of the Abbey* (1939)
6. *Stowaways in the Abbey* (1940)
7. *Schoolgirl Jen at the Abbey* (1950)
8. *Strangers at the Abbey* (1951)

9. *Selma at the Abbey* (1952)
10. *Tomboys at the Abbey* (1957)
11. *The Abbey Girls Go Back to School* (1922)
12. *Jen of the Abbey School* (1927)
13. *The New Abbey Girls* (1923)
14. *The Abbey Girls Again* (1924)
15. *The Abbey Girls in Town* (1925)
16. *Queen of the Abbey Girls* (1926)
17. *The Abbey Girls Win Through* (1928)
18. *The Abbey Girls at Home* (1929)
19. *The Abbey Girls Play Up* (1930)
20. *The Abbey Girls on Trial* (1931)
21. *Biddy's Secret* (1932)
22. *Rosamund's Victory* (1933)
23. *Maidlin to the Rescue* (1934)
24. *Joy's New Adventure* (1935)
25. *Rosamund's Tuck-Shop* (1936)
26. *Maidlin Bears the Torch* (1937)
27. *Rosamund's Castle* (1938)
28. *Maid of the Abbey* (1943)
29. *Jandy Mac Comes Back* (1941)
30. *Two Joans at the Abbey* (1945)
31. *An Abbey Champion* (1946)
32. *Robins in the Abbey* (1947)
33. *A Fiddler for the Abbey* (1948)
34. *Guardians of the Abbey* (1950)
35. *Rachel in the Abbey* (1951)
36. *A Dancer from the Abbey* (1953)
37. *The Song of the Abbey* (1954)
38. *Two Queens at the Abbey* (1959)

The Abbey
Although the fictional Gracedieu Abbey is set in Buckinghamshire, there is no real abbey to be found there, among the real Whiteleaf Cross and hamlets that still exist. The model Elsie used for Gracedieu was Cleeve Abbey, near Minehead, in Somerset. Cleeve Abbey is owned by English Heritage (note: the site is closed from 1 November to 21 March); EJO's Abbey fans make frequent pilgrimages to it from all over the world, and it is well worth a visit.

Clarissa Cridland

ELSIE OXENHAM AND THE
ENGLISH FOLK DANCE SOCIETY

The Abbey books from *The Abbey Girls Go Back to School* (1922) to *Queen of The Abbey Girls* (1926) contain a blending of real and fictional characters, as the leading members of the English Folk Dance Society (EFDS) of the early 1920s were brought into the fictional world of the Abbey Girls. Although Elsie Oxenham used nicknames for them, the Society's major figures were clearly identifiable to those who knew them.

Elsie was living in Ealing, a London suburb, with her family when she became aware of the existence of the EFDS and its sister club, the English Folk Song Society, and was thus easily able to attend their classes and parties as well as the vacation schools. The description of the vacation school which Cicely, Joan, Joy and Jen attended in Cheltenham in *The Abbey Girls Go Back to School* was an authentic portrayal of real-life vacation schools.

The English Folk Dance Society was founded by Cecil Sharp (EJO's 'Prophet') in 1911, and he remained its director until his death in 1924. Sharp was born in London in 1859 and educated at the well known public school Uppingham until the age of 15, after which he spent time with private tutors until he went up to Clare College, Cambridge. He came down from Cambridge in 1882 and emigrated to Adelaide, South Australia, where he initially worked in banking and law. However, his major interest was music and he was soon appointed assistant organist at the St Peter's Anglican Cathedral and later became conductor of the Choral Societies of both the Cathedral and Government House. He returned to England in 1892, marrying Constance Birch in Somerset a year later.

From 1893–1900 Sharp taught music at Ludgrove, a prep

school then in London, but he also held a number of other positions in the musical world in those years, including that of Principal of the Hampstead Conservatoire of Music from 1896–1905. He was so highly regarded as a teacher that he was appointed tutor to the Royal Household between the years 1904 and 1907.

While he and his wife Constance were spending Christmas with her mother in 1899, Sharp had his pivotal encounter with Morris dancing, which at that time was bordering on extinction. A group of Morris dancers, accompanied by their musician William Kimber, performed five dances in the village of Headington Quarry, near Oxford. Such was Sharp's enthusiasm that he asked Kimber to play the tunes again so he could notate and later arrange them.

In 1901 Cecil Sharp joined the English Folk Song Society, which had been formed in 1898. In 1902 he published *A Book of British Songs for Home and School*. While visiting Somerset the following year, he heard seemingly unknown folk songs and, as an experienced teacher, saw their educational potential. Consequently, in 1904 he published with Charles Mason the first part of *Folk Songs from Somerset*. Sharp and other enthusiasts such as Ralph Vaughan Williams travelled widely throughout the country, writing down the words and music of these songs so they would not be lost to posterity.

As a result of his reputation as one of the eminent collectors of traditional folk songs Cecil Sharp received a visit from Mary Neal in 1905. Miss Neal, along with Emmeline Pethick-Lawrence, had established the Espérance Girls Club in London in the mid 1890s. (They also founded the Maison Espérance Dresssmaking Co-operative to provide girls with better employment opportunities; conditions in the garment industry at that time were appalling: for very little money many women and girls did extremely intricate work in poor conditions which often permanently impaired their eyesight. A number of devout Christian men and women from affluent families were involved from the mid 1800s onwards in what became known as settlement work where clubs and co-operatives such as the Espérance were formed to improve the lives of the working poor.)

Mary Neal sought Sharp's advice as to whether the folk songs, which were becoming widely available thanks to the efforts of the Folk Song Society, were suitable for her girls. Sharp's response was most affirmative. The Espérance girls greeted the folk songs with great enthusiasm, and they and Miss Neal soon wondered if it was possible to learn dances to the songs. When she asked Cecil Sharp, he directed her to William Kimber and the Headington Quarry Morris men in 1899. Miss Neal then visited Kimber and invited him to the Espérance Club to teach the dances to her girls.

The girls first performed the dances at their Christmas party and so enthusiastic was the reception that a public performance of folk singing and dancing, with Cecil Sharp giving an explanatory lecture, was organised. Before long they received invitations to give demonstrations and classes around the country, including in schools. The School Boards became interested; and Sharp, in collaboration with Herbert MacIlwaine, the Espérance Club's musical director, produced the first Morris book in 1907.

Nonetheless, the relationship between Mary Neal, her Espérance Club and Cecil Sharp became strained and eventually openly hostile. This came about for two reasons: firstly, Miss Neal's support of the Women's Social and Political Union (the Suffragettes), for her girls danced at many Suffragette events. Sharp did not approve of the movement despite the fact that his sister Janet was an active member. Secondly, and the major reason for the hostility on Sharp's part, was that he believed that the dances should remain 'untainted' and be retained in the original form. However, Mary Neal had a much more relaxed approach, and he believed that this would threaten the integrity of the folk movement. Both used newspapers and magazines to put forward their views.

This led in 1911 to Sharp's founding the English Folk Dance Society, whose aim was to preserve and promote the traditional dance forms. By this time he had met Maud Karpeles (EJO's 'Little Foot-Page') who became his assistant and eventually his biographer. Maud (1885–1976) was of well-to-do, middle class German Jewish descent, and had studied piano in Berlin. She was a Fabian socialist—the Fabians believed in the gradual development of social democracy through gradual processes of reform and the education of the poorer classes. She became a voluntary social worker involved with the women's settlement work in Canning Town. The settlement's aim was to enrich the lives of these very poor girls with sporting and cultural activities.

In 1909, accompanied by her sister Helen (EJO's 'Mrs Joshua'), she had her first encounter with English folk songs and dances at the Stratford-upon-Avon Festival. Her enthusiasm for both the songs and the dances coupled with her musical knowledge led to her founding a folk dance club at the Canning Town Settlement and subsequently her meeting with Cecil Sharp. She shared his views and enthusiasm for traditional dance, and thus when he lectured on folk dances it was the Canning Town club who demonstrated them. In a short while she became his trusted assistant and secretary, even to the extent of coming to live with Cecil and Constance Sharp and their family.

When the EFDS was formed in December 1911, the Canning Town dancers made up the core of the Society along with the staff and students of the Chelsea Physical Training College. It was in this year that Sharp first met Douglas Kennedy (1893–1988; EJO's 'Joshua') who was later to marry Helen Karpeles in 1914 and

11

eventually became Sharp's successor. Kennedy, a biologist, was introduced to folk dancing in 1911 by his sister Helen (EJO's 'Madam') and soon became a regular in the male demonstration side which Sharp used to illustrate his lectures.

The first vacation school was held in Stratford in 1912. It was in this year also that an EFDS male side gave their first public performance at the famous Savoy Theatre. The Society flourished, with demonstrations, vacation schools, classes and dance parties in the two years before the outbreak of war in August 1914.

Prior to the founding of the EFDS, Sharp had begun researching the almost extinct Northumbrian Rapper sword dances and the Yorkshire Long Sword dance. This resulted in the publication between 1911–13 of the three-volume *The Sword Dances of Northern England*.

In 1914, arising from his reputation as the leading authority on English folk songs and dances, Cecil Sharp was invited to lecture in the United States and made his seminal visit to the Appalachian Mountains. These encompass eighteen states from Maine to Georgia and include the Blue Ridge Mountains of Virginia and Tennessee's Smoky Mountains. The landform is composed of heavily wooded steep ridges, about 4000 feet (1200 metres) with dense undergrowth which made travel difficult, and the soil of the traverse valleys cut out by the rivers is poor. The area attracted poor, uneducated immigrants from Britain as, from the seventeenth century, the land was either cheap or free. Communities remained isolated and this preserved the ballads and songs they had brought with them from the influences which arose in England as a result of the Industrial Revolution and the resultant urbanisation. Life was very hard and the people became very conservative, devoted to their heritage and their puritanical Protestant faith. As a result the songs and ballads their ancestors brought from Scotland, England, Ireland and Wales were cherished and handed down to the next generation. The ballads were usually sung unaccompanied by the women. Men generally played the dance tunes on the fiddle, although the Irish and the Scots brought their pipes as well.

The First World War meant that normal activities of the Society were curtailed. The men went to serve in the armed forces and many were killed in action. Douglas Kennedy was one of the few to return. The women undertook war work of varying kinds. However, the Society did contribute to the war effort, for some of the staff members of the Society took concert parties to France to entertain the troops behind the lines.

It was the decline in demonstrations and the accompanying lectures which led Sharp to accept invitations to lecture in the United States where he could earn the income needed to support his wife and family. His age, 55 in 1914, precluded any involvement in the war effort. The treasure trove of traditional music in the Appalachian Mountains was an added inducement. He left in 1916, accompanied by Maud Karpeles, his trusted assistant, on an extended trip which lasted until 1918.

The two members of the EFDS who featured most prominently in the Abbey books were Douglas Kennedy's sister Helen ('Madam'; 1889–1975) and Daisy Caroline Daking ('the Pixie'; 1884–1942). They are the dedicatees of *The Abbey Girls Go Back to School*.

Helen Dorothy Kennedy was four years older than her brother Douglas, who was to succeed Cecil Sharp as Director of the English Folk Dance Society. She taught dancing at the Stratford Summer School and was a founding member of the EFDS and a frequent dancer in the demonstration team. Helen Kennedy taught at Whitelands College, then in the King's Road, Chelsea. Whitelands was one of the leading teacher training colleges in the country; and it was the College's May Queen crownings, devised by John Ruskin in 1881, which gave Elsie Oxenham the inspiration for the Hamlet Club crownings. Folk dancing had soon become an integral part of the education system, and teachers were keen to add folk dancing certificates to their qualifications so they could obtain better teaching positions. Interestingly Helen Kennedy initially did not like morris dancing, until she learned its history. In 1917 she, like D C Daking, went to France with a concert party to teach folk dancing to the troops behind the lines. In 1920 she married Stanley North, an artist and picture restorer of high repute, who worked on the royal collection. However, she partially retained her maiden name, becoming known as Helen Kennedy North. In April 1922 she gave birth to a son, Roger. We know that Elsie Oxenham had visited their flat at 5 Bassett Road, North Kensington, which is described in *The New Abbey Girls*. In 1923 the Norths moved to larger flat in the same block. She was Elsie Oxenham's folk dancing teacher.

Daisy Caroline Daking ('the Pixie') was at various times called either Daisy or Caroline and to avoid confusion is normally referred to as D C Daking. Her early life was marred by the tragic death of her parents in 1888 when she was three and her sister, Molly, one. They were raised by their grandparents and family friends, the Maxwells, near Barnet in Hertfordshire. Little is known about her until 1914. However, from her poorly paid, unqualified jobs as an adult it can be surmised that she did not undertake further education, presumably due to lack of money; clearly, it was not through lack of academic ability, as in later years she had two books on psychology published—*Feed My Sheep* and *Jungian Psychology and Modern Spiritual Thought*. This theory is reinforced by her lack of a permanent home, indicating that her family had little money—her father had been a solicitor's clerk— and there was no house to be inherited. Also unknown is how D C Daking came to be involved with the folk dance movement.

In 1914 she was teaching folk dancing at the Oxford branch

of the EFDS. Her charismatic personality is clearly shown in this remembrance of her classes which Hilary Clare gives in her article 'The Pixie' in *The Abbey Chronicle* No 7, 1991:

> London born, deadly efficient, three-feet high, with classes so huge she had to mount a high chair to conduct them. Professors and biologists vied for her instruction; rowing blues sat on her doorstep enquiring whether their left foot back shuffle was really coming on. The folk-dancers became a club, and gave moonlight picnics up the Cherwell.

Tragedy was to strike again with the death of her sister in childbirth in February 1914. Monica Godfrey writes of the child in *The World of Elsie Jeanette Oxenham and Her Books*, p107:

> … after unhappy years with a stepmother, then in a children's home, the Pixie became his legal guardian and he lived with friends of hers in Oxfordshire.

Lack of money was no doubt the reason why she could not provide her nephew with a home.

At Cecil Sharp House they have her journal 'The Log of a Fine Companion', which detailed her five day journey with a friend by horse drawn caravan from Oxford to the EFDS summer school at Stratford-upon-Avon. Hilary Clare writes:

> 'The Log of the Fine Companion' is almost unbearable with its innocent pleasure in the English countryside, in friendship, and in folk dancing and music.
>> 'The Pixie', *The Abbey Chronicle* No 7, 1991

In September 1914 D C Daking travelled to Durham and

Northumberland. She was in Newcastle in May 1915 and one of her pupils was Catherine Ord (EJO's 'Miss Newcastle'). She was as popular there as at Oxford, for the Branch report for April 1915 says:

> As to Miss Daking's success, that may be attested by the compliment paid by one of her pupils: "Well, you'd never know she was from the South", and that, in a North-country mouth, means much.
>
> 'The Pixie', *The Abbey Chronicle* No 7, 1991

D C Daking travelled to France with the Lena Ashwell Concert Party, where she remained with the Army of Occupation for a few months. In 1918 she was appointed to the EFDS committee, a position she held until 1926. In 1919 she lived in Oxford and in 1920 she taught in Mansfield, Nottinghamshire. In was in this year that Elsie Oxenham met her.

In 1921 she was sharing the London flat in Theobald's Row, described by Elsie Oxenham in *The New Abbey Girls*, and teaching at Plaistow. At this time she was working in the West End making the hand woven frocks so vividly described in the books. Monica Godfrey believes the shop where she worked was Liberty's.

Other members of the EFDS featured in the books were May Gadd ('Dear Little Robin') and Elsie Avril ('The Fiddler'). Elsie Oxenham portrayed herself as 'The Writing Person'.

After 1926 the real members of the EFDS no longer appear in the books, and the most commonly held theory is that Helen Kennedy North and D C Daking in particular did not like this thinly disguised fictional portrayal of themselves, no matter how flattering.

Ann Mackie-Hunter

FROM RAGS TO RICHES

One of the major themes in the works of Elsie Jeanette Oxenham is the transformation of a heroine from dire poverty to undreamt-of riches. The poverty is not always financial, and nor, indeed, are the riches: emotional deprivation or lack of role, for example, are often tackled in this way. But the theme remains the same, as does the fairy-tale element in the transformation, due not necessarily to a traditional Prince Charming, but to some other benevolent person whose interest or friendship makes all the difference.

Eilidh Munro, of *A Princess in Tatters*, is the first of EJO's rags-to-riches heroines. Abandoned at birth—her mother dies and her father, Duncan, runs away, leaving the baby to be raised by an aunt who subsequently dies, the child effectively becoming the live-in servant to a poor family—Eilidh is a delightfully mischievous little girl with a determined streak.

When Eilidh is eleven, Bernard Raby arrives at Loch Ruel on a painting expedition and is very taken with the child all dressed in tatters. He arranges for her to be a model for his painting; but as their friendship grows, he realises that Eilidh is the daughter of his brother-in-law, who has remarried (after becoming a millionaire in America) and now has two children by his second wife. Bernard challenges Duncan Munro, who then tries to destroy any evidence of Eilidh's paternity, but is foiled in the attempt, and Mollie Raby, another of Duncan's in-laws, becomes Eilidh's guardian and teacher. Duncan dies in a shooting accident and Eilidh makes the leap from uneducated savage to heiress in need of taming and training.

Like Eilidh, Joy Shirley, first encountered in *The Abbey Girls*, is in a difficult position financially, though perhaps genteel poverty best describes her circumstances. Her parents are dead and she is being brought up by an aunt, a widow, along with her cousin Joan. Mrs Shirley is struggling to raise the two girls alone and finally turns to Joy's grandfather for help. Sir Antony Abinger had cast off his daughter when she insisted on marrying the man of her choice, and steadfastly refused to acknowledge his grandchild; but upon Mrs Shirley's appeal, he allows the small family to move into the abbey, where Mrs Shirley takes on the work of caretaker. She is still unable to afford to send the girls to school, so while their situation has been eased, it is by no means resolved. By the end of the book, Sir Antony has come to know the two girls, if only by passing acquaintance, and Joy inherits the Hall when he dies. It's unclear if she would have inherited anyway—there were no other relatives to do so—but the implication is that having met Joy, Sir Antony has become reconciled somewhat to the situation, and on his deathbed he welcomes Joy back into the family.

In *The New Abbey Girls* we learn that she has so much money that she could give away piles of it and never even notice:

> "It's the whole question of one's attitude to money," Joy said at last, when she had described the new feeling of responsibility which had come at the time of Jen's accident, her efforts to do what she could and give help where she saw it needed, and the new demands suddenly made upon her. "I can give it away; that's easy enough. I've plenty; I can give away a lot, and never feel it."
>
> p101

However, she sees the responsibilities of having great wealth as being more than simply distributing the money. As the Pixie remarks:

"… You can't give money to the point of feeling it, as most of us have to do. You've too much. But you must give somehow; you've got to *work* for it. Every one must do that … Your giving of money is too easy. *You* have to give yourself; in time, and thought, and trouble. You can do a *lot* for people, if you only will. You've made a very good beginning. I like your idea of finding girls who really need a holiday and seeing that they get it …"

p102

Her new riches do not consist in untold wealth alone. She tries to give appropriately and responsibly, but she also shares her house with those in need—for example, with Miss Macey's school in *The Girls of the Abbey School*, Mary-Dorothy and Biddy Devine in *The Abbey Girls Again*, Selma in *Selma at the Abbey*—as well as providing a home for Maidlin and Rosamund in this book.

Joy is not the only one to benefit from Sir Antony's legacy. Her progression from poverty to wealth is the more obvious, but Joan isn't left out. She is able to return to school with Joy the following term (having previously given up her scholarship to Joy in *The Abbey Girls*). And Sir Antony is so impressed by her knowledge of and love for the abbey that he leaves that part of the estate to her, along with sufficient funds for its care. In the series as a whole, the abbey stands for far more in the lives of many characters than money ever can.

In *The New Abbey Girls* EJO visits the theme once more as Maidlin di Ravarati suddenly becomes a 'person of consequence'. The aunt in Cumberland who has raised her is ill, while her other aunt—Ann Watson, caretaker of the abbey—feels completely inadequate to shoulder the task of preparing the girl for her new life as an heiress. At Ann's request, Joy takes on the responsibility—temporarily, until Maidlin's father returns from China; then after his death, permanently. Maidlin doesn't have a lot to unlearn, fortunately, but she has never before needed the social skills required by an heiress to a fortune. Joy, having been through it so recently herself, is considered to be the ideal person to help her make the transition. But Maidlin's story doesn't end there, for she turns out to have a Voice:

> … [Maidlin] had to leave her place again to sing the solo which was expected from her. She was never nervous where music was concerned, and the princess clapped in real appreciation of the song and turned to Miss Macey to say— "Surely a voice with a future before it! Is she being trained carefully?"
>
> *The Abbey Girls at Home*, p242

She goes on to become a well known singer, performing at the Queen's Hall and on the radio. So her riches are not just financial—indeed, she ultimately gives her fortune away. But she also finds success and fulfilment—identity, even—in her career.

Maidlin's 'twin', Rosamund Kane, comes from a well-to-do family, yet she too has her transformation. From a very ordinary, jolly schoolgirl, she rises to the position of Countess of Kentisbury. This path is not without its twists and turns. Rosamund's father remarries after the death of her mother; the new wife is young enough to be his daughter, much to Rosamund's horror. Rosamund herself has her allowance cut off, and the money left to her by her mother is insufficient to live on, so she must find a way to support herself. Although Joy would very happily provide everything Rosamund needs, that young lady is independent and proud and insists on finding her own way through.

When her father dies, leaving behind a baby boy who unexpectedly becomes next in line to the Kentisbury earldom, Rosamund fights for custody, believing that the young mother is more interested in having a good time than in raising a child who would be a suitable Earl. But she has to fight more than just the abbey girls (for her independence) and the young step-mother: the Earl of Kentisbury also wants to assume responsibility for the baby who will be his heir. Rosamund wins the right to care for her brother, but concedes to Kentisbury's needs as well by moving into the Dower House at Kentisbury Castle. During this time, she comes to know and to love the invalid Earl, and they marry. Rosamund never expects to have children—the Earl has been too ill for too long—but under her loving care his health improves and not only does Rosamund have a son who supplants her brother as heir, but she is blessed with two sets of twin girls. From jolly schoolgirl to fairytale princess—via a long and circuitous route.

Mary-Dorothy Devine is another who might not be considered an obvious candidate for the role of rags-to-riches heroine, yet her story encapsulates a different aspect of poverty—that of the spirit. When we first encounter her in *The Abbey Girls Again*, she is weighed down by the destruction of a dream and by the responsibilities of caring for a sister half her age. Mary wanted to be a writer, just like her journalist father, but he criticised her fledgling attempts and destroyed her self-esteem. (It's interesting to speculate how different things might have been between the two sisters if Mary had been able to fulfil her potential while Biddy was growing up. Instead of losing herself in an unhealthy fantasy world and thus becoming unable to cope with real-life difficulties, would she have been able to siphon off the creative energies in her writing and draw on her natural strengths in dealing with a teenager? But then there would have been no story!)

Jen recognises at an instinctive level that Mary needs something to restore her to life. She chooses to introduce her initially to the beauty of flowers, and then challenges her with music and dancing. Mary begins to use both her names in a reference to the dance 'The Mary and Dorothy':

> Mary read the names aloud. "… 'The Mary and Dorothy'; is that really a dance?" She looked up, a touch of colour in her face, and laughed. "I hope it's pretty! Those are my names. I never knew I was called after a dance!"
>
> *The Abbey Girls Again*, p34

She opens herself up to the healing magic of the new world into which the abbey girls have dragged her, finds her imagination stirred to fever pitch and has to turn to the written word. Before long she has had an article published in a newspaper, and is causing consternation among her many relatives in South Africa, who wonder at the transformation from stuffy person who penned duty letters to vibrant writer. It's a mystery that Ruth Devine (another person who has come into sudden wealth thanks to a newly discovered diamond mine on the family farm!) must solve when she comes to visit in *The Abbey Girls in Town*. To Ruth's surprise—she's expecting to have to take her young cousin in hand to ensure she has a good time!—Mary-Dorothy is full of life, not only dancing but *teaching* dancing, and is working on a novel. Instead of Ruth whisking Biddy away to have fun, the two girls creep out of the house to allow Mary time to write the next thrilling instalment. Mary-Dorothy goes on to become Joy's secretary, moving into specially decorated rooms at the Hall, and also develops into a highly successful writer of girls' novels.

The Girl Who Wouldn't Make Friends introduces another variant on the theme: Robin Brent, the god-daughter of Robert

Quellyn, inherits the entire Quellyn estate while Gwyneth, Quellyn's adopted daughter, has been left with nothing. Once again a very ordinary schoolgirl has been raised to a position of significance, while for Gwyneth it must have seemed like a reversal of fortunes in the negative sense! However, EJO prefers justice and happy endings so Gwyneth is adopted by the Brents and becomes Robin's sister.

Other examples include Belinda Bellanne, who achieves her dream of becoming a singer after Maidlin overhears her singing to Elizabeth and Margaret Marchwood; Cecily Brown, who is the pawn of international gangsters in *A Camp Mystery* but is adopted by the Guides; and Doranne Hardie, who inherits a massive estate after her great-aunt dies. (The extent of the inheritance comes as a huge surprise because the aunt lived modestly in a tiny little cottage.) Doranne embraces the responsibility that comes with such wealth and creates Rainbows Village where the Roses (more 'rags to riches' characters, suddenly gaining titles) come to live.

Then there is Damaris, who has a dream to become a ballet dancer. Her aunt disapproved and refused to allow her to continue her lessons, but she has kept up her dancing as far as she is able. While she and her sister Rachel are holidaying in France, Monsieur Berthelot, a great lover of ballet, sees her dance and insists on arranging for her to have lessons. She is accepted into the corps de ballet of *A Goose-girl* but is cast out because she can't help but add to the choreography. When the girl dancing the title role falls ill, Damaris is called in and is, of course, a huge success. It would seem that her dream is to be snatched away from her after an accident on stage injures her hip, but healing eventually takes place and Damaris returns to the stage— briefly: she has fallen in love and the family life that she has always craved alongside the desire to dance is to be hers.

So there are many variants on the one theme, but it seems clear that EJO loved above all to show girls who were deprived in one way or another being swept to fame, fortune or simply happiness through the intervention of others. *The New Abbey Girls* shows the beginnings of two such stories, and its heroines become part of that all-encompassing family which is the abbey community.

Adrianne Fitzpatrick

PUBLISHING HISTORY

The New Abbey Girls was first published in 1923. It had a colour frontispiece and two black-and-white plates by Elsie Anna Wood, all of which we have reproduced in this edition. It also had decorated boards (shown below left). We have used the front of the dustwrapper as our front cover, and have reproduced the spine of the dustwrapper on the back cover. The original is shown below right. There was a reprint of the first edition, which was identical in every way, except for the books advertised in the back, and from these this reprint can be dated to 1925.

In the late 1920s, *The New Abbey Girls* was reprinted at 3/6 in Collins' Boys' and Girls' Library. The book was slightly larger in format, and its boards were standardised (overleaf, top right) in what is known as the 'Blazer Girls' edition. The dustwrapper (overleaf, top left) had the same picture but with a slightly different design. A blurb specific to this book had been added to the front flap. We have only seen a partial copy of this—the end of every

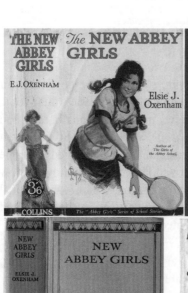

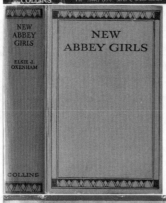

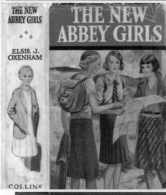

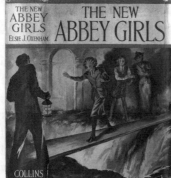

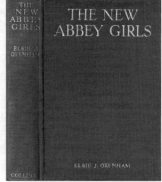

line has been cut off—but we have used this text, reconstructed to the best of our ability, on the back cover of this GGBP edition.

Very confusingly, Collins also used the series name Collins' Boys' and Girls' Library for a range of books they issued from the mid 1920s at 1/6. These were in a small format (6¾ x 4¼ x ¾ inches), and several titles by Elsie Oxenham were included. I have not seen an edition of *The New Abbey Girls* in this format, but I am told by several people that there was one. (For further details of the designs of this series, which were uniform, except for the actual picture on the front of the wrapper, see the GGBP editions of *The Abbey Girls*, *The Abbey Girls Go Back to School* or *Goblin Island*.)

In the mid 1930s *The New Abbey Girls* was published in the 'School and Adventure Library' at a price of 1/6. The boards are in a red and black design (opposite, centre left), and the wrapper (opposite, centre right) features two illustrations (on front and spine) which clearly were originally drawn for a different book, or even two different books. The frontispiece is that of the first edition, and there were no other illustrations. I have been told of a copy inscribed 1936.

Perhaps the best known and most reprinted edition of *The New Abbey Girls* is that commonly known as the 'fat orange', though it is worth noting that 'fat orange' can sometimes be 'thin orange'. The boards of the 'fat orange' editions were usually orange, though they could be beige or blue, and they had silver lettering (opposite, bottom right) but were otherwise plain. This is one of the few editions which was usually dated, and it was first printed in this edition in 1937 or 1938, and reprinted in 1940, 1942 and 1945 (getting gradually thinner). The confusion over the first 'fat orange' is because this printing wasn't dated, and the two different dates are listed in later printings. There may possibly have been other dates, but these are the ones about which

I know. This series was entitled 'The Abbey School Series' (very misleading) and was one into which Collins put most of their Abbey titles at this date. There was a dustwrapper with a wrap-around design by an uncredited artist (page 26, bottom left), the front part of which was used as the

frontispiece (above left) with the caption 'Jen nearly fell in'. By the time the 'fat orange' had become 'thin' the spine illustration had had to shrink (above right).

It would then appear that there was no other edition of *The New Abbey Girls* until it was published in a much abridged version under the Collins Children's Press imprint in 1961. (It should be noted that this Children's Press imprint was quite different to the 1930s Children's Press editions of some other titles—eg *The Abbey Girls*—which were not abridged.)

This 1961 edition of *The New Abbey Girls* was then reprinted in 1966, 1968 and 1970. The front (sometimes boards, sometimes dustwrapper) was identical for each of these editions and so is pictured just once (opposite, top centre). However, there were some variations otherwise. The 1961 edition had coloured pictorial boards, which were not laminated but were slightly rough (back and spine shown opposite, top left) and it was part of the New Challenge Library. In 1966, the book was given a dustwrapper, with a new illustration for the spine (opposite, top right). The boards of the book had a 'sporting equipment' design (opposite), which was uniform for all Children's Press titles at

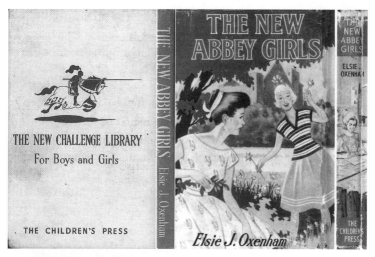

this time. The book was in the girls' section of The Boys' and Girls' Library. However, for the 1968 edition the dustwrapper was replaced by laminated boards and the back cover was given a new design to show the titles in The Boys' and Girls' Library. The 1970 reprint was exactly the same as that of 1968.

I have recently learned of a small size edition which has red boards with a girl's head outlined in black on the front and a girl in a tunic outlined on the spine. I don't have a copy of this to be able to include scans here.

It is interesting to note that *The New Abbey Girls* wasn't printed either as a 'small red Abbey' or a Seagull, unlike so many other of Collins' Abbey titles. One could speculate endlessly as to why, but it does mean that the full text has been out of print for many years.

I am extremely grateful to everyone who has supplied me

29

with details of their copies. There may well be other editions and reprints which are not included here. If so, this is because I do not know about them. It would be good to have details for use in any future reprints.

Text
For this GGBP edition we have used the text of the first edition, which contained a handful of punctuation errors—missing or misplaced full stops, apostrophes and commas—which we have corrected.

Clarissa Cridland

FURTHER INFORMATION

There are four flourishing Abbey societies, in Australia, New Zealand, the UK and South Africa. Each of the first three produces a quarterly or tri-annual A5 magazine.

The Abbey Girls of Australia (newsletter *The Abbey Guardian*)
Details from: Cath Vaughan-Pow (editor), PO Box 136, Jesmond, NSW 2299, Australia
e-mail: editor@abbeygirls.com

The Abbey Gatehouse (New Zealand) (magazine *The Abbey Gatehouse*)
Details from: Barbara Robertson (editor), 39D, Bengal Street, Wellington 6004, New Zealand
e-mail: born.robertson@xtra.co.nz

The Elsie Jeanette Oxenham Appreciation Society (UK) (journal *The Abbey Chronicle*)
Details from: Ruth Allen (membership secretary), 32 Tadfield Road, Romsey, Hampshire SO51 5AJ, UK
e-mail: abbey@bufobooks.demon.co.uk
website: http://www.bufobooks.demon.co.uk/abbeylnk.htm

The Abbey Chapter (South Africa) (no magazine but group meets regularly)
Details from: Rose Humphreys, 3 Egret Street, Somerset West 7130, South Africa
e-mail: dogrose@ballmail.co.za

Elsie Jeanette Oxenham website
There is also an excellent EJO website to be found at http://home.pacific.net.au/~bcooper/popular.htm

The
New Abbey Girls

ELSIE JEANETTE OXENHAM

ILLUSTRATED BY ELSIE WOOD

CONTENTS

LIST OF ILLUSTRATIONS

CHAPTER I

MORNING IN THE ABBEY

"I won't! I won't go! And if you ask her to have me, I'll run away!" and scarlet with anger, her face working with distress, Maidlin rushed away into the abbey and hid herself in a corner.

Ann Watson, the caretaker, turned to her washing with pinched lips and worried face. It was only a week since this tempestuous niece had come to stay with her, and had been allowed to live there by the mistress of the abbey on promise of very good behaviour, and because she was "not a boy and not a silly infant."

"Fourteen ought to have some sense!" Joan had said, in giving permission.

But what a week it had been! Maidlin had been quiet enough and even reverent in her attitude to the beautiful old ruins, loving them and wondering at them, and wandering much among them, fascinated by her aunt's stories of the white-robed monks of long ago. There had been no repetition of the tragedy of Joan's schooldays, when the wall of the chapter-house had been defaced by thoughtless Dicky Jessop. But so much had happened in that week of Maidlin's visit! Ann's brows puckered again as she thought over it all, and wondered what she must do now. For Maidlin had suddenly become a person of consequence, and Ann hardly felt able to cope with the situation. And what was worse, the child had unexpectedly developed a temper, which had not shown at first, and Ann felt very decidedly that she did not know how to deal with her.

Maidlin had no mother, and her home had always been with

her other aunt, who was married to a well-to-do farmer away in the north. This aunt's sudden illness had brought about the visit to Aunt Ann, who looked after Joan's Abbey of Grace-Dieu, and told visitors all about the Cistercians, and the destruction of the abbey, and its rescue by Sir Antony of the Hall. If Ann felt kindly towards the visitors, she went on to tell of Sir Antony's romantic behaviour in bringing his granddaughter and her aunt and cousin to live in the abbey, but keeping the relationship a secret; of the minuet danced on the cloister garth, which had awakened his interest in the cousins; of his death soon afterwards, leaving the Hall and all the property to Joy, the child of his only daughter, but giving the abbey to Joan, because she loved it so; and of the discovery of the secret passages and the hidden treasures of the abbey.

During the last few weeks Ann had added another chapter, for the benefit of particularly interested or promising-looking tourists, and had told how the cousins had gone, last August, to the dancing-school at Cheltenham; how, ever since, the Hall and the abbey had been haunted by a pair of lovers; and how, very soon, the handsome soldier who was such a favourite with every one and who had also gone to learn folk-dancing, was going to carry off the lady of the abbey and leave only Joy in possession. It was a long story, and took time to tell; but it thrilled those hearers who loved romance and who found a fitting setting for the tale of dancing, love, and treasure in the gray ruined arches of the abbey; and Ann found it worth her while to tell the story well, and had no scruple about turning her inner knowledge to account.

"Ann yarns about you and me and grandfather's will, no end! And now that Jack's come on the scene, she'll be worse than ever!" Joy had said many a time.

"Oh, well, it pleases her and it pleases them, and it doesn't hurt us! And anyway, we can't stop her!" Joan said philosophically.

"I guess Ann pockets some thumping big tips, all the same! I think we ought to claim a royalty! When you're married and done for, and I'm in charge of the abbey, I shall put my foot down heavily, and have no gossiping!" said the lady of the Hall severely. "I'm of age! I'm twenty-one! And I shall be very stern with Ann!"

"Good luck to you!" Joan laughed. "But remember, if Ann throws up the job, you'll have the fag of finding some one else as good, and then the worse fag of teaching her all about the abbey."

"All that history! Those stacks of dates! Help! I simply couldn't!" Joy moaned. "Ann shall tell any old person every old thing she likes! I'll never dare to give her notice! My dear child, I don't know it all myself!"

"I know you don't," Joan laughed. "You never did, did you?"

As she washed, Ann's mind ran over the familiar story and she glanced through her lancet windows at the sunny garth, her troubled eyes seeing in memory what they might never, perhaps, see again in fact—two bronze-haired girls dancing minuets or morris jigs on the turf. "Princess Royal," "Jockie," "Ladies' Pleasure"; Ann knew them all by name. But those days were over, she feared. For yesterday had been Joan's wedding-day, and the Hall had been astir with guests all afternoon. Now it was quiet again, the bride and bridegroom were far away, and every one was filled with sympathy for the lonely cousin left behind. What would Joy do without Joan? Even Ann wondered that. They had been together all their lives. Joy had always relied on Joan. What would she do without her now?

"She'll be lonely!" Ann said to herself. "Not at once, perhaps, because of Miss Jen. But when Miss Jen goes home"—and Ann shook her head doubtfully.

For Jen, three years younger than the cousins, but a friend of five years' standing, had claimed her right to be Joan's bridesmaid in earnest. At school she had been Joan's Maid of Honour in many a May-day procession, holding up her violet train and wearing her colours proudly—the "chief bridesmaid," in the language of the school, to the Violet Queen. Now that Joan had been a bride, Jen had naturally pointed out the position due to herself in the ceremony, and Joan had agreed warmly that she could not be properly married without her particular maid in her own rightful place. So Joy and Jen had been bridesmaids, and Jen had attended Joan throughout the ceremony as she had so often waited on her before. And though Joan had gone away with her soldier, Jen was still at the Hall, and would relieve Joy's loneliness for the first few days, and help to comfort Mrs. Shirley in her loss of her only daughter.

Ann knew Jen well, and had known her since Jen had begun her schooldays, five years ago, as a thirteen-year-old visitor to the Hall during its term as the headquarters of the school. She was glad Jen was to stay for a few days. Then her thoughts turned from weddings and the past to the problem of the moment, and she sighed and knit her brows again as she bent over her tub.

Three days ago the letter had come, from Maidlin's father in Italy. He was not in Italy just now, it appeared, but in China, and China seemed a very long way off, very much farther than Italy, which, to Ann, had always seemed far enough. And the letter, with its amazing news and its awkward suggestions, had disturbed Ann greatly. What to do about it, and how to start, she did not know. Only one solution had occurred to her, but she had thought it a very good one. But, as if the letter and its problems had not been enough, on top of it all Maidlin had most unexpectedly developed this "Italian" temper, unsuspected until now, and had flatly and very violently refused to consider Ann's solution of the difficulty for a single moment. It was very hard! Ann sighed

again, and thought and thought, but could see no other way. It
had seemed such a good idea!

From somewhere in the abbey ruins came a high, clear voice,
singing cheerfully an old jingle learnt the summer before.

"Cripple Creek girls, don't you want to go to Somerset?
Somerset girls, don't you want to go to town?
Somerset girls, don't you want to go to Cripple Creek?
Cripple Creek girls, don't you want to go to town?"

Ann smiled. She had heard about those Cripple Creek girls
before. "Miss Joy's keepin' up her spirits!" she said approvingly,
and looked out to see the singer.

From the old doorway of the tresaunt, the passage leading to
the abbot's garden and the gate into the grounds of the Hall,
another verse pealed forth, but a strictly unofficial verse this time,
and one Ann had never heard before.

"Girls of the abbey, don't you want to go to Cheltenham?
Cheltenham girls, don't you want to go to town?
Cheltenham girls, don't you want to come to see the abbey?
Abbey girls, don't you want to go to town?"

"Well!" Joy was talking cheerily to herself. "A good lot of it
has come true! We did go to Chelt.—dear old place!—and we're
going back, too, 'married ladies or not!' as the President says.
And the Cheltenham folks mostly came back to town. And some
of them have been here to see the abbey; and if things turn out as
seems likely at present, the abbey girls will be going to town. I
suppose that means me myself; I being the only original abbey
girl left. But, of course, we did take in Jenny-Wren and Jacky-
boy pretty thoroughly, so perhaps they may count too. But this

41

won't get my letters written! Bother weddings! Bother being an heiress and boss of an estate! It's more worry than it's worth!"

The broken arches of the cloisters had wide, low sills of gray stone. Joy spread papers, letters, envelopes and pad about, and laid a stone on each to keep them steady. From Joan's sanctum opening off the cloisters, in the early days Joy's own little bedroom, she brought a cushion, and throwing it down on the stone sat upon it, her back against the wall, and set to work, humming all the time about the abbey girls who wanted to go to town.

Ann, at her window a few yards away, smiled as she looked at her. "Miss Joy don't even begin to grow up! Now why that Maidlin should have such a spite at her is more than I can tell! There couldn't be a nicer young lady, unless 'twere Miss Joan herself—Mrs. Raymond, begging her pardon! A bit wild, Miss Joy used to be; but I'm sure these last few months she's been different somehow—kinder, and more gentle spoken like. But she don't look grown up this morning, and that's a fact!"

It was a fact. Joy's mane of ruddy-bronze hair was "up," because when it was up it was out of the way, and there was too much of it and it was too heavy to be carried in any other way with comfort. Otherwise it would have been down her back in a plait. In spite of her twenty-one years, to which she only referred when she wanted an argument for getting her own way, she was wearing the old blue gym tunic, reaching barely to her knees, which she had worn so happily for the month's dancing at Cheltenham. Ever since that time she had worn it occasionally in mornings, when the fancy seized her, or when she felt "dancey," and no remonstrance from her aunt or cousin had moved her.

"You never said it wasn't decent at Cheltenham!" she had argued many a time with Joan. "Just because you had on your own, and everybody else wore gymmies too! If it was decent there, it must be decent here. It's jolly comfortable! And anyway, it's only in the garden or the abbey. I don't wear it out in the road, or after twelve o'clock, when visitors might walk in at any moment."

So, writing-pad propped on the knees of her gym stockings, she leaned against the cloister wall and scribbled answers to the pile of letters, murmuring a comment now and then.

"Can't be done! No, my dear man, I couldn't think of it!—I'll consult aunty about this one.—Oh, what cheek! Begging letters are the limit! I will *not* give to everybody who asks, just because I've got the money! I'd have nothing left in three months! But this one—yes, I'll think it over. Sounds more the right kind. Oh, this is from Miss Macey. I wonder what the old dear wants? Perhaps it's just more good wishes for Joan, come rather late. No, it's for me all right. Oh—help!"

She read the letter from her old schoolmistress, her merry face growing serious; then laid it down and sat staring across the garth at the high refectory windows. "This needs some thinking about! *Dear* old Mackums! She's fearfully apologetic and all the rest of it, but she does know what she wants. I could do it for her, but it would be a fearful fag. Hi, Jenny-Wren! Come here and give me good advice! I know you're looking for me. Now don't begin cheering me up!" she threatened. "For I don't need it. I know you've all made up your minds to cheer me up, but you needn't bother, thank you! I can get along quite well without Joan!"

"I can't!" Jen came across the garth to join her. "I keep looking for her round every corner. The abbey and the Hall used to be full of Joan, and now they're horribly empty. I haven't come to cheer you up. I've come to be bucked up myself. I've no time to think about you! What do you suppose Joan's doing now? Where will they have got to?"

"They're doing the sights of Paris, my child, and have

forgotten our existence. You needn't be sentimental over Joan; you know what she's like when Jack's round," Joy mocked. "There isn't anybody else, if she's got him!"

"He's worse. Nobody else exists, if Joan's there. Of course, it's awfully nice, and all that; and I'm glad they've got married. They weren't any use to anybody until they did, anyway. But I do feel left alone and lost. Isn't the morning after a wedding a horrible time?"

"Let's talk about the weather!" Joy suggested kindly. "Isn't it wonderfully mild for March? Feels like June, doesn't it? Awfully fortunate for the wedding! But, of course, the abbey's sheltered by the hills; it may be cold enough up on top! We shall soon have the blossom out, at this rate!"

"Joy, you're a pig! And you do look a sight! You need Joan to look after you. Do go and get dressed!"

"Soon. I want to consult you on a matter of serious importance first. Business must be attended to, Jenny-Wren."

"I'm sure you can't do business in a gymmy!"

"I can do better business in a gymmy. The—er—freedom of my costume and—and of my lower limbs assists the free working of my business faculties, and stimulates the flow of my imagination, which is a great asset in dealing with business matters," the lady of the Hall assured her seriously.

"I shouldn't have thought it was. But get busy at it, whatever it is, for you'll have to go and dress, Joy, or at least you'll have to vanish from here. Tourists will be turning up to see the abbey, and you mustn't be caught looking such a sight."

"She talks as if a tunic were indecent, instead of only a little unusual!" Joy complained. "Look here, Jen, my infant! I've had a letter from Mackums."

"Oh! Does she want me to go over and see her? Why didn't she write to me?"

"It isn't about you at all. It's about quite another little girl, an infant of fifteen, called Rosamund Kane."

"Never heard of her. Who is she? And what about her?"

"She's left on Mackums's tender hands as a boarder, while her folks are abroad. Her relations live away up in the north, like yours, and aren't any use to this kid. And Wycombe doesn't suit her; she's lived in the north too, and it makes her all floppy, and she isn't well."

"Oh, but she'll get used to it! That's only for the first week," Jen said, from experience. "I always used to flop for a few days, and moon round with a headache, and say I'd never do any work. But it went off, and I was all right for the rest of the term."

"This kid has had two terms of it and it hasn't gone off, and Mackums is worried about her. Wycombe's so much among the hills."

"Yes, it's different out here. Better ask the kid—oh, is that what Miss Macey wants? Has she asked you to have the kid here?"

"That's exactly and precisely what she has done, Jenny-Wren. She's frightfully apologetic, and all that, but she knows we've heaps of room and maids and everything, and she says, could we possibly have the kid here for a few months, so that she could live in country air and cycle to school every day? Mackums thinks it would be the making of her. I dare say it would; but it's a bit of a fag, isn't it?"

"It would be topping for the kid," Jen said slowly. "I haven't forgotten how you took me in, in the dip. time, and were so awfully decent to me."

"Joan was, you mean. You told me so quite plainly. Don't you remember how you ticked me off?"

"I was a rude infant, then. You were both awfully good about it. It must have been a fag to put up with a kid all the time. And it would be worse now. What shall you do, Joy?"

"I don't know. I'm still thinking."

"You've been awfully good already, asking people here for holidays, because you thought they needed a rest in the country. Joan told me about it."

"I've had a queer feeling"—Joy began, and paused. "I'm going to tell you about it sometime. But at this particular moment, what about Rosamund?"

"You could ask Mrs. Shirley," Jen suggested.

Joy shook her head. "Aunty would say I must decide. You see, I was planning to go up to town quite a lot. There hasn't been time yet, with getting first Cicely and then Joan married. But now that we've cleared the air, and just for fear any one should feel lonely now and then, I'd made all kinds of plans, and I was going up to town quite often, to swot at music, and so on. But it seems to me that would hardly be fair, either to aunty or this kid. If she comes, I'll have to look after her, or she'll find it hideously dull; and she may worry aunty."

"It does need thinking about," Jen acknowledged. "I wish we'd got Joan; she always knew! Or Newcastle, from Cheltenham!"

"I could write for advice to everybody, all round the connection, of course!" Joy mocked. "But I think it would be better to decide for myself. If I let the kid come here, it's I who will have to take the worry of her. But it does complicate matters."

"Not half!" Jen agreed, and sat on the grass, leaning against Joy's knee and frowning over the problem.

At eighteen, she was tall and slim and lithe, moving with the unconscious grace of one who had been a folk-dancer since she was thirteen. The yellow hair she had always worn in long plaits had been cut short after her accident the previous summer, and, discovering the comfort of a crown of bobbed curls, Jen had stoutly refused, for the present, to let it grow again. She wore it caught back from her face with a slide, and was happy in the freedom of the prevailing fashion. In her jumper and short skirt she still looked a schoolgirl, except for her height. When this difficulty was pointed out to her, she was wont to say airily, "I had a serious illness, and one always grows in bed. I'm really only fifteen; and don't you forget it!"—and to omit to mention that it was more than a year since she had left school.

They sat thinking over their problem, Joy leaning back against the old gray stone of her cloister arch and nursing one knee, Jen propped against her sitting on the grass. Suddenly the clanging of the great abbey bell brought them both to their feet.

"Joy! I said you'd be caught! Fly! You've just got time!"

"I shan't, then," Joy pulled herself together. "That old thing made me jump; but it's only eleven o'clock. We aren't open till twelve. Ann won't let the idiots in. She knows she's got to reckon with me now, and that I'm not soft, as Joan used to be! Go and tell her to send them for a walk in the woods for an hour, there's a good kid!"

"Here she comes! She wants to ask you something."

"Please, Miss Joy, it's a lady, and she says she's a friend of yours and she knows as how you'd let her in, and she's been to the Hall to see you, but they told her you was in the abbey." Ann looked doubtful, with an apologetic glance at Joy's knees.

The girls looked at one another. "Who on earth—?"

"I'll go and see, shall I?" and Jen raced away across the garth.

Joy hastily began to gather up her scattered papers. "These interruptions to business! When one does try to do a little work! Whoever can it be? Is it anybody I'm prepared to receive in this— er—costume? There aren't very many! But Jen will know," and she withdrew towards the door of the private room in the cloister wall, ready to take cover, if necessary.

"Jen's excited about it, whoever it is. I can hear her shrieks from here. She always did give a yell and hurl herself on people," and Joy chuckled.

Jen came flying back. "Joy! Oh, you needn't hide! You really needn't! It's some one who saw you first in your gymmy! Guess!"

"Cheltenham?" cried Joy. "Who?"

"It's Madam!" and Jen collapsed in laughter on the grass. "Fancy hiding from *her*, because you're in your tunic!"

"Idiot!" Joy hurled at her, and went leaping across the garth, all long, flying legs, to the tunnel passage and the old front gate.

CHAPTER II

ENTER MADAM

"But we thought you were teaching in Oxford last night! You said so at the wedding yesterday!" Joy was remonstrating, as she gave joyful welcome to this, their first teacher at the Cheltenham school, and a friend now of many months—"In spite of the fearful dressing-down we got when she first saw our dancing, that we thought was so awfully good!" as the girls were wont to say mournfully.

"So I was," Madam said imperturbably. "I had classes all evening. But I thought I'd give you a surprise, and I wanted to see the abbey again. My first visit, at Christmas, was so very short."

"But we asked you to come, and you said you had to get back to town for classes this morning?"

"They've got measles in the school. So they wired me, and I've got the morning off. I can't go back till they're out of quarantine, of course."

"No, you go to schools too much. Oh, that's topping! Can you stop a few days?"

"Schools, or teachers' classes. Oh, I've a town class to-night; three, in fact; and a lecture by the Director afterwards, and I've got to sing. But I've the morning off, so I came back to give you a shock. I thought you'd let me in."

"You did it! Several shocks. But it's topping to have you here."

"Busy person!" said Jen. "She shall sing to us, to your piano, Joy. She can practise for to-night. 'Aunt Nancy,' I suppose?"

"No, *not* 'Aunt Nancy!' English songs to-night," Madam retorted. "'The Blacksmith,' if you really want to know, and 'Dabbling in the Dew.'"

"The President would say it was bad taste on their part not to have 'Aunt Nancy' and 'Cocky Robin,'" said Joy. "She's crazy about them."

"Oh, they'll have those for encores!" Jen assured her gravely. "She won't get off with only *two*!"

Madam laughed. "Are you trying to pretend it's last Vacation School, or preparing for next?" she asked of Joy.

"Oh, I often fly round like this in mornings. I'll run you down to Wycombe in Belinda after lunch. If you'll come with me, that is?"—there was a sudden touch of gravity in Joy's usually mocking tone.

Madam gave her a quick look. "Will you? I'd love it! The woods are glorious! But my bag's down at the station. I walked up through the woods, by the beech path."

"We'll pick it up as we go. I thought maybe you'd rather not, knowing I nearly killed Jenny-Wren!"

"She's fearfully careful now," Jen said anxiously. "I can't get her to put on any speed at all. It's hideously dull! We only crashed that time because we were all talking and laughing, Dick and Jack and the rest. 'Twasn't her fault more than anybody else's."

"Oh, yes, it was! Everybody's been awfully decent about it, but I know perfectly well how it happened, and I haven't forgotten," Joy said sombrely.

"I'd love to be whirled down to Wycombe, instead of going all the way round by train," Madam said warmly.

"You're a sport! I won't smash you up, honestly. I know I'd have to reckon with somebody if I did!"

"Where is he, by the way? What have you done with him?

You had a funny husband yesterday!" Jen said reproachfully. "Oh, *did* you see him, in the garden, after Joan had gone?"

"I was trying not to look," Madam said seriously, but with amused eyes. "He wanted to play singing games on the lawn, didn't he? Oh, he went back to town last night. We didn't know to-day was to be a holiday, or I might have let him stay. He has heaps of work on hand, so we parted at the station, and he went home to get on with it."

"He nearly killed me in 'Haste to the Wedding,'" Joy said reminiscently. "He and you ought to be sued for dancing to the public danger. I'm sure it's against the bye-laws. Anything wilder than you two when it comes to 'Partners swing and change,' I never saw. It's absolutely dangerous."

"He tries to take me off my feet. But he can't do it because I lean back. You're quite safe if you lean well back. It *was* a jolly dance!" Madam said yearningly.

"I shouldn't have thought he could ever pull you over," Jen remarked.

"Oh, you don't know! He's strong. I have to lean very well back!" Madam laughed. "He'll be wild when he hears I've been here again without him. He's simply dying for another look at your old books; he wants to spend hours examining them. You'd have to search him when he was going away, though; I wouldn't answer for him where early manuscripts are concerned. When are you coming to town to see his book? He's doing one, just like yours, you know."

They were crossing the garth towards the refectory; and Jen, with Joan in her mind, stood back and watched, for Joan still held that no one could walk or run quite like Madam, whether in a blue tunic or, as now, in a swinging gray cloak and short skirt and soft comfortable hat. Then she dashed after them, and caught them at the top of the dark winding stair.

"What do you mean? Nobody could make a book like these now," Joy argued, as they stood in the refectory by the big cases which held the manuscripts discovered in the secret chamber under the abbey.

"He could. He's doing one. You must come and see it. Of course, it will take years to finish it. I'd like you to see it. It's really rather good." Madam was turning over the leaves of a missal with careful fingers but critical eyes, her studiously-offhand tone holding only the faintest suggestion of pride in her husband's beautiful work. "He's been at it for years already. He's doing the whole thing, of course, the lettering as well as the borders and the designs and the illuminating."

"Just like an old monk in a monastery?" Jen marvelled. "I knew he was an artist, but I didn't know just what he did. But nobody has time for that kind of work nowadays!"

"Beautiful work for its own sake? Not many, perhaps; but I seem to have found one who cares to do it. I'd like him to show you his book. It's going to be shown at an exhibition soon, but if you come in time you shall have a private view."

"Oh, we'll come!" Joy said warmly. "I'm going up to town one day soon! And you'll show us your flat? Cicely raves about it. She's told us oceans about the day she went to see you."

"She didn't see The Book." Madam spoke in solemn capitals. "It was away on loan. Oh, I'll give you tea! Just let me know when you're coming. I'm out a great deal, you know."

"Would you consider me a fit and proper guardian for an infant of fourteen, to set it a good example and bring it up in the way it should go?" Joy asked suddenly, while they were still poring over the beautiful old illuminated sheets.

"The very last person in the world I should choose. Why?" Madam asked absently, intent on a fourteenth-century book of prayers.

"You always were crushing!" Joy wailed. "D'you remember, Jen?—'You're *all wrong*, you four! You're wrong every *single* time!'—and then she hurled herself off the form and came flying across the room at us, and we stared at her, open-mouthed and blank and terrified."

"Nonsense! You were never terrified, not one of you, for a single second!" Madam retorted swiftly. "You simply thought how funny I was. I saw that well enough. But you *were* wrong; dreadfully wrong!"

"Of course we were! We haven't stopped being grateful to you yet for pulling us up so suddenly." Jen was sitting on the table among the priceless manuscripts, swinging her legs. "And we were so frightfully pleased with ourselves; that was why it was so funny. But you didn't paralyse us; we just loved it— and you, from the first. How the President went on when we got home that night! She and Newcastle talked about you till after midnight. But you do paralyse some people, you know."

"I know. I can't think why," Madam said pensively. "There's a fearful story, that's never been forgotten against me, of some one finding two people shivering out in the passage, terrified to go into their class; and when they opened the door, it was *my* room. I've never been allowed to forget it. But who is the infant you want to be guardian to?" to Joy. "I'm not so sure; perhaps I'm wrong. I haven't seen very much of you lately," and she gave her a keen, thoughtful look.

"Oh, I quite agree with you! It's just how I feel myself. And I don't want to do it a scrap. But I've been asked to take on the job, and—well, when you can do a thing, you feel such a rotter if you say you won't."

"It would be a great chance for the child, of course. But it would mean some responsibility for you," Madam said thoughtfully, when she understood the position. "You could hardly leave her here on Mrs. Shirley's hands continually, if you wanted to come up to town for classes, as you spoke of doing."

"No, it wouldn't be quite playing the game towards aunty. She isn't at all strong. It all needs some thinking about—Help! What on earth is it?"

"Oh, you little wretch! How you made us jump!" Jen cried wrathfully, as a small figure fell rather than climbed down from the high niche which had once been the pulpit, or seat of the lay brother who read aloud during meal-times to the assembled monks.

"Is this your new ward?" and Madam, having recovered from the shock, turned to look curiously at the dishevelled little figure, dusty and untidy, with big black eyes and a cloud of wild black hair.

"No, it's the novelette girl!" Jen was beginning shrilly, when she was interrupted.

"The bell's gone! You didn't hear, you were talking so hard! They'll be up here in a minute; they always come here first. Visitor-people, to see the abbey. Aren't you going to hide?"—to Joy. "You always do, when people come. But I don't believe you've time, unless aunty keeps them at the gate. I'll go"—and she whirled past them and down the winding stair in the wall.

"Gracious! It *is* after twelve! Then we can't say anything! We shall jolly well be caught this time!" Joy groaned, glancing hurriedly at her wrist-watch.

"Oh, couldn't we hide, as the child suggested?" Madam laughed. "Where do you generally go? Perhaps she'll keep them at bay for a moment. I'm game; but where? I want to see your underground passages again. Couldn't we—?"

"Through the chapter-house!" Jen laughed. "We'll go home by Underground, Joy!"

"Come on!" said Madam, eager as a schoolgirl for a joke or a new experience. "Joy, as mistress of everything and head over all, you simply must not be seen running about in a tunic at this time of day! Lead the way, Jenny-Wren!"

"I suppose it isn't quite the thing! It's not usual, anyway. Come on, then, if you're sure you don't mind!" and they all three followed the tempestuous small girl down the narrow stair.

"Don't fall and twist your ankle! Not *you*!" Jen warned Madam. "It's awful to have to sit out and watch other people dance! You wouldn't like it at all. The steps are frightfully uneven. There! That's safe!"

They could not have crossed the garth unseen. Already Ann's voice could be heard, "reciting dates," as Jen murmured, to the tourists. But it only took a second for them all to slip into the chapter-house, which stood at right angles to the refectory. Joy, delighting in the freedom of her costume, took a flying vault through the low window at the inner end, and Jen followed as swiftly and easily. They both turned to give their hands to their guest, but found her already on the sill; she took Jen's hand and sprang lightly down, and they all vanished into the tunnel of the secret passage, through the old carved door.

"I'd forgotten your flying leaps on to forms and chairs!" Joy laughed. "I was going to apologise for asking you to climb through windows, but perhaps I needn't."

"Oh, don't trouble! But you abbey people are so unexpected!" and Madam paused on the steps to laugh. "I might have known I'd be in for something unusual when I came here! Have we a light? Or do we sit in the dark? I suppose you'll have to shut the door?"

"I keep a torch in a hidie-hole, for fear of accidents," and Joy burrowed in the dark, and flashed on an electric torch, while Jen closed the outer door. "It's not the first time I've taken cover here! I'm not keen on tourists. Do you want to see the crypt and the well again? Or shall we go straight home to lunch?"

"Oh, I think we might just have a minute down there. I'd like to see the abbot's tomb again."

"Right-o! I do know a little about this, if Joan left anything out when you came before," and Joy led the way down the steps.

CHAPTER III

"BE careful here!" and Joy paused in the passage behind the stairs. "Do you draw the line at planks over bottomless pits?"

"*What?*" Madam peered over her shoulder. "What has happened down here? There were no bottomless pits when I came in January."

"It went all boggy and squishy in that heavy rain just after the President's wedding, and we decided there must be an underground spring, like the one you fall into on the upper path. So Joan said it had better be drained, and it was a bigger job than they expected. It isn't finished yet. I don't say the hole's bottomless, but it's rather deep, so don't fall off the plank. Do you mind?"

"Not so long as there's a light," Madam laughed, and followed her across a couple of uneven boards bridging a deep chasm.

Joy held the torch low to guide her steps, and Jen offered her hand. But Madam disdained it and ran lightly across. "I shan't fall! Unsteady people might, though. It's a long plank. Do all your visitors come across?"

"They have to, if they want to see the hermit's church. Some funk it, of course. Now we have to find our way through hills and mountains," and Joy guided her carefully among heaps of clay and rubbish. "The men aren't working to-day. There are very few men we can get, and they've had to leave this for a more urgent job in the village. But it's only for a week or two."

"Tell me again the story of how Joan and Jen found the jewels!"

Madam demanded, when they had inspected the crypt and ancient well, the inscriptions and the tomb of the first abbot, and were standing before the rough carving in the wall—"Jehane III"— which had given the clue to the position of the buried casket.

Instead of the story, Jen gave a shriek of dismay. "Joy! The torch is going out!"

"Help! What on earth shall we do?" gasped Joy, and stared helplessly at the light, which gave a last feeble flicker and went out.

"I've always said that would happen sooner or later!" Jen groaned. "Torches are beastly things! You never know how much is left in them."

For a moment there was silence in the old church, the blank silence of underground—"Of a tomb," as Jen said later. Then Madam's laugh rang out. "*Well*, Joy Shirley! Of all the ways to treat your visitors! Didn't I say you abbey people were unexpected? I suppose you know your way out by this time?"

"Oh, I know my way!" Joy said gloomily. "And I'll get you out, if I have to go on my hands and knees all the way. But it won't be easy; *you* can't crawl across planks!"

"I'd forgotten the bottomless pit!" Madam sobered hastily. "That's another story. You can't cross those planks without a light, Joy. I won't allow it. We'll wait—"

"You and Jen must wait, of course. We're not all three going to crawl! But I'm going to get out somehow and bring back a light for you."

"Joy, you can't!" Jen expostulated. "It won't help us for you to fall into the hole! And you'll break something, if you do; it's quite ten feet deep."

"My dear kid, I'm not going to sit down and do nothing!" Joy said brusquely. "I've got to get you out somehow. I brought you here."

"Joy, don't be silly!" Madam's voice had its old note of authority. "There are visitors in the abbey. Won't the woman bring them here? Surely she'll have a light?"

"Saved!" Jen cried dramatically. "Of course she will! So you needn't do tight-rope gym stunts, after all, Joy! We've only got to wait!"

"They're sure to come here, aren't they?" Madam insisted, as Joy still hesitated. "Very well, then. We'll wait. It would be awfully risky to try to cross that plank without a light. I dare say we could all do it if we had to; I'd try it in a moment, if I got too hungry! But if your woman is likely to turn up with lights and visitors within half an hour, we won't do anything ridiculous. Where's that tomb? We'll sit by it and wait. I never felt anything so solid as this blackness!"

"You always say you can see in the dark, Wild Cat!" Jen mocked to Joy. "Lead us to the tomb! I say! Doesn't it sound awful?"

"I'm frightfully sorry!" Joy apologised abjectly, as she guided them carefully through the blackness of the crypt. "Here you are! Here's Michael! He's something to hold on to, anyway. I'm sure he'll be pleased for you to sit on him. I say!" to Madam. "We don't often do this with our visitors!"

Madam felt her way carefully to a broad step, and with equal care sat down upon it. Then she leant back against the big square table-tomb and began to laugh, and laughed till she nearly cried. "I'll *never* forget it! Fancy losing your visitors in the depths of the earth! Do you often mislay people like this? I wonder how long we shall sit here! I *never* expected to be buried alive! Joy Shirley, you'll never hear the end of this!"

"I know," Joy agreed ruefully. "I never shall. Cicely and Joan will simply scream. Every one will ask me if I've buried any one lately!"

"I nearly *died* when the light went out!" and Madam went off into another peal of laughter. "Jen's shriek—and the last glimpse of your horror-stricken face—and the picture of you crawling along those planks—and the silence and darkness you can *feel*! It's simply priceless! *Can't* you feel it? It's as solid as a London fog! And neither of you ever thinking about the visitors we've run away from!"

"They may not come," Joy said gloomily. "Perhaps it's only some old ladies. If Ann tells them about the pit and the planks, they won't trouble to come down."

"Then you and I will eat Jenny-Wren, and then one of us will eat the other, and then the survivor will have to crawl! But we'll only go as far as that if we really have to."

"Oh, I think they'll look down, whoever they are, and we'll all yell together at the slightest sound!" Jen argued. "Besides, there's a man. I saw him as I scooted into the chapter-house. He won't mind planks! He'll want to see where the jewels were found!"

"It's frightfully ignominious to sit waiting to be rescued by a strange man!" and Madam's voice shook.

"Now don't you go off again!" Jen pleaded. "Do you ever have hysterics?"

"No, *never*! But I've never been buried alive before. Anything may happen! Joy, don't you really think it's funny?"

Joy surrendered, and began to laugh. "Oh, if you don't mind! If it were only Jen, I'd not care a scrap. But I am awfully sorry—"

"No, you never did care what you did to me, did you?" Jen mocked.

"That's playing with fire, Jenny-Wren; a dangerous game!" Madam said seriously, as there was ominous silence from where Joy sat. "You deserve to be put in the hermit's well for saying that."

"Joy knows I'm only ragging. I'll put *her* in the well, if she can't take a joke!"

"All the same, it's a sore subject, and one you'd be just as well not to joke upon. I can't see Joy's face, but I know just how she looked when you said that."

"I know too. That's why I said it," Jen said defiantly. "Just because I didn't mean it; don't you see? It's a—a course of treatment I'm giving her. She's so silly; she's daft! She will go on thinking it was her fault I tipped out of Belinda that day, and bashed my head; and everybody knows it was all an accident. So I make a joke about it whenever I get a chance, just to teach her. I can't see her either, but I know how she looked too—glum! She always does. But it's good for her."

"Jenny-Wren, you're a little beast!" Joy pulled herself together. "And I'm an idiot. I know you were only ragging. But how you understand!" to Madam. "You only see us for a few minutes once in a month or so, and yet you know all we're thinking and feeling!"

"Oh, but she always did!" Jen argued. "That was one of the very first things Cicely said about her; that she understood people so awfully well!"

"You've got to amuse me!" Madam said peremptorily. "I'm not going to sit here in the depths doing nothing! Tell me something interesting! What did you mean by what you said in the refectory, Jenny-Wren, when that child fell out of the pulpit on to us like a bomb? You called her 'the novelette girl'?"

"That's what Joy calls her. Her name's Madalena di Ravarati."

"I say! Really? But who or what is she?"

"Our good caretaker is her aunt," Joy explained. "Oh, we don't call her all that! Ann calls her Maidlin, and so does everybody else; I believe it's old English for Magdalene. She's lived with another aunt in the north, who always called her Maidlin."

61

"Maidlin! It's pretty. So is she, I should think, when you see her properly. She had beautiful dark eyes, and a lovely clear skin. Surely she's partly Italian?"

"That's the novelette bit, of course. About twenty years ago Ann was nurse in a swank family in London; and she had a little sister, heaps younger, who came up from the country to be a housemaid in the same place. And this sister, Mary, was very pretty; Ann says so, and anyway, you can guess it from what followed, and from Madalena herself! A visitor at the house, a 'foreign gentleman,' apparently an Italian, fell in love with the pretty housemaid; the mistress thought he kept coming to see her daughter, who had money, but was getting on in years. He knew his family wanted him to marry some one at home, whom he didn't want a scrap; and, since he was a very decent chap, he was in a hole. Finally he and Mary went out one day and were married, and then went back and told Ann they had done it. He took Mary away to the other sister, in the country, the one who has brought Maidlin up, and wrote to his people to break the news. They were furious, and told him to come home at once, but not to dare to bring his wife. He wouldn't go without her; but it got on her mind, and at last, after some months, she begged him to go and try to get things settled up more happily. He gave in and went, meaning to be back, whatever happened, before the baby was born. But Mary was taken ill suddenly, and she died, and he never saw her again. Maidlin was a tiny scrap of a thing, and her aunt had hard work to save her life. Her father came to see her, but he couldn't forgive himself for having gone away at all, although he had only done it to please Mary. He didn't know what to do with the kid, so he left her with the aunt, who was married to a farmer but hadn't any family, and sent money quite regularly for her to be properly brought up, though Ann says he hadn't very much himself, so he couldn't have her sent to expensive schools or anything like that. His folks had heaps and heaps, but they wouldn't forgive him unless he would marry again, and it was to be somebody they chose this time. He never forgot Mary, so he wouldn't, and so they kept him awfully short of money, and it was some time before he could find any way of making any for himself. He'd never expected to need to, you see."

"I think it was topping of him," Jen remarked. "You could understand him giving up everything for Mary, while she was alive. But to stick to her like that, when she's been dead for fourteen years, is awfully fine, I think."

"Yes, I like the father," Madam agreed. "And is he still alive? Does he ever come to see the child?"

"Ann says he's got some kind of post abroad. I suppose he had to take what he could get. He does come, but he hasn't been for some years now. Just at present the Cumberland aunt is ill, so Maidlin is stopping with Ann. And we call her the novelette girl. Do you wonder?"

"I don't blame you! And she'll go back to Cumberland when the aunt is better?"

"Oh, yes, I guess so! I say, aren't you getting chilly?"

"A bit," Madam assented. "Sit up close, both of you. We'll huddle together to keep warm. This is most pathetic! Hasn't anybody any chocolate? I've a whole packet in my bag at the station; and a pound of apples!"

"A lot of use that is!" Jen jeered. "I haven't a crumb, and Joy hasn't even a pocket."

"Joy ought to keep a secret store down here, if she means to bury her visitors often. You should have laid in provisions before you cut off our retreat, Joy."

"I shall never hear the end of it!" Joy groaned.

"No, you never will. I shall tell everybody; every single person I meet! It's far too good a story to be wasted! Get up, Joy!" Madam said peremptorily. "You've sat there long enough. I forgot you hadn't a skirt on. Tunics aren't made for sitting on damp stones in."

"No, it's coming through," and Joy stood up and shook herself. "But what can I do? Jump?"

"You might do capers," Jen began to laugh. "Try uprights, Joy. Your kick-jumps are still awful. Don't kick us, though! Pity Madam can't criticise! It's such a waste to have her here and not get any good of her!"

"Do 'Princess Royal' in the dark!" Madam suggested, laughter in her voice again. "Not the half-capers, though! Don't go careering round among the pillars, or you'll break something or somebody, probably yourself! We're quite warm; we're dressed, you see!"

"It serves you right, Joy!" Jen teased.

"I'll do 'Princess Royal' on the spot. Sing the tune for me!" Joy demanded.

Madam, really anxious lest she should have taken a chill, complied, and criticised the sound of the feet at the end. "You lost your rhythm once or twice. And your step isn't clear enough even yet, after all my teaching. Are you warmer now?"

"You bet! Trust a morris jig for that. I've done 'Princess Royal' a good many times, but never in quite such a queer place before!"

"In church, too!" there was mock reproof in Jen's tone.

"Well, that's all right. Morris dances have been done in churches before now. What about York Cathedral?" Madam argued. "Now 'Molly Oxford,' Joy! That's almost all on one spot. But don't galley into us."

Joy defiantly began to dance again. "I wish you could see! I'm really doing a very beautiful jig! My galleys are superfine. And my side-step—"

"Oh, I can hear what that's like! I know all about your

side-step!" Madam laughed. "I'll give you a lesson as soon as we get back to daylight!"

"Wonderful person!" Jen teased. "She doesn't need to see you, Joy! It *must* be bad!"

"You won't give anybody lessons. You'll come straight home and have a very big lunch. What an age they're taking to get here! Ann must be reciting every date she knows! Or else they're asking streams of questions, and she's yarning on about us no end."

"All about the wedding yesterday! And she hasn't an idea we're waiting to be rescued," Jen laughed. "Won't she be upset?"

"You'd better have a go too. It's awfully warming! Let's each take a corner, and do galleys for all we're worth, till we're as hot as hot," Joy suggested.

"What a picture for our rescuers!" Madam began to laugh. "No, we'll be the orchestra. What would you like now?"

"Sing me 'Trunkles.' I want to practise my galleys," Joy demanded.

Madam, with a suppressed chuckle, was complying when Jen gave a wild yell. "Help! Help! Come to the rescue! We're buried! Come and save us, *please*!"

"At last! And I was just doing such a *beautiful* galley!" Joy said resentfully. "Coo-ee!" and she shouted through her hands. "Shall we go to meet them?"

"And break our necks or sprain our ankles among those rubbish-heaps? No, thanks! I'm going to wait to be rescued properly. There's no fear of them not coming after those shrieks," and Madam sat on her step, elbows on knees and chin on hands, and waited for the rescue party, her lips twitching with amusement, her eyes full of laughter.

Ann, bewildered by the shouts and not recognising the voices in the enclosed space, came first across the planks, looking distinctly frightened. Joy and Jen were upon her in a moment, explaining at express speed what had happened, both talking at once, forgetful of everything else.

Madam's amused eyes found the astonished visitor in the background, as she still sat "waiting to be rescued properly." He was tall and grave, and his questioning gaze went from one to the other of the excited girls, and rested longest on Joy, in her very short tunic and the rolled-up hair which announced the fact that in spite of appearances she was more than fifteen. The bright bronze hair betrayed her as plainly as a label, for every one had heard of the red-haired girls who owned the abbey and the Hall, and he had just heard the whole story from Ann.

His look was so incredulous that Madam chuckled again. Then she rose and went forward with the dignity she knew so well how to assume. "Thank you! We were without a light, so had to wait till you came. Now, Joy, perhaps you will lead the way. I shall soon have to hurry for my train. And you—you have to dress"—her voice was suspiciously unsteady.

"Oh!" Jen's eyes had just fallen on the stranger.

Joy became conscious of his presence at the same moment. "We'll go home to lunch. Perhaps you will hold the light while we cross the planks," she said haughtily. "After that we can manage quite well."

"Allow me! We will come with you to the entrance, of course," and the stranger took the light from Ann, and, crossing the plank, turned to give his hand to each as she followed.

Madam accepted his help graciously, with calm dignity and no sign of inward amusement. Joy stalked across haughtily, not seeming to see the offered hand. Jen, with an admiring eye on Madam, tried to imitate her gracious manner, clutched his hand, and nearly fell into the hole.

"Gracious, Jenny-Wren! You might as well have crossed in

the dark!" Madam mocked. "Don't go and fall in now, after waiting nearly an hour to be rescued!"

"Had you been imprisoned there so long?" the tourist turned to Joy in dismay. "Then I urge you to hurry home, and take something hot to drink. It was most unsafe to stay so long in such a vault."

"We'd have stayed longer if we'd fallen into the pit!" Joy retorted.

"We'd been there about a week," Jen informed him. "We were dancing about to keep warm; Joy was, at least."

Madam's hand on her arm restrained her from more indiscretions. "Thank you! We can have no difficulty now. Here are the steps. Joy, I think, after all, we won't go by Underground to-day!"

"I never saw anybody so—so dignified! How do you do it?" Jen whispered, as she followed Madam up the steps to the welcome daylight. "Joy tried, but she only managed to look cross! It wasn't the poor man's fault. He was quite nice about it! How do you manage to look so regal?"

"I'm hungry! I shall eat grass in a moment! Aren't you going to feed me, Joy? You said something about a very big lunch. And I agree with our friend about hot drinks. Couldn't we run?" and Madam cast dignity to the winds, and raced, with Jen leading the way, across the garth to the tresaunt entrance and so to the old gate into the gardens of the Hall.

Joy gave a despairing look round, then followed, all long legs and flying girdle. "I don't suppose you two lunatics saw that severe old lady sitting waiting in the cloisters? No, I thought you hadn't! Horrified disapproval wasn't in it with the way she looked, when first you two and then I went flying across the garth. She'll spread the most awful stories of lunatics at large in the abbey. Why couldn't you be dignified for two minutes longer?"

indignantly to Madam. "You can put it on so jolly well when you like!"

"No, really? An old lady? I never saw her. Shall I go back and apologise, on your behalf?" Madam teased.

"It would only be you she disapproved of, Joy. Oh, don't let's go back! I'm simply dying of hunger," Jen wailed. "I believe it was about a week! Mrs. Shirley will have sent out search-parties!"

"I suppose you know the President has given you a new name since you got married?" Joy queried, as she locked the garden gate behind them.

"Me? No, what?" Madam demanded. "And why since I got married? I haven't changed!"

"Oh, yes, you have! You're much nicer!" Jen teased.

"Well—! In what way, please?"

"She calls you The Duchess," Joy said grimly. "Because of the grand manner you put on now and then. Says you look as if you ought to have pages walking backwards before you, bowing, and others holding up your train."

"Well, she does look duchessy when she goes about swinging a big cloak! It's the way she walks, somehow! I can't think how she does it!" Jen sighed.

"Not when she's tearing madly across cloister garths, I suppose!" Madam teased. "I'll tell the President what I think of her next time she comes to see me. And when you come," to Joy, "I shall be very forgiving and do my best not to lose you underground!"

"Seeing that you live in a top flat—!" Jen mocked.

"I shall never hear the end of it!" Joy sighed, as they reached the house. "Aunty, dear! We've brought The Duchess home to lunch!"

CHAPTER IV

THE NOVELETTE GIRL

WHEN Madam, laden with almond-blossom and daffodils for her London flat, had been tucked into Belinda's sidecar and whirled away down to Wycombe to catch the afternoon train, Jen, at Joy's request, returned to the abbey for the letters and papers left there in the morning.

Ann had them in safe keeping; as she handed them over, she asked anxious questions about the morning's adventure, and Jen explained just what had happened, breaking into irrepressible laughter again at thought of their dilemma, of Joy's jigs in the dark, and Madam's unhesitating criticism, and of their ignominiously helpless position until rescue came.

As she talked, Ann listened in dismay and tried to express her regret that they had had to wait so long. The gentleman and the old lady had been greatly interested in the ruins, it appeared, and had asked questions which had seemed endless. They had left a card, with a request that it be given to Miss Shirley, so Ann handed it to Jen, whose lips pursed in a whistle of dismay as she read the names.

"Help! Those people! Joy won't like that!" she said softly, under her breath. "And I suppose Ann told them every single scrap of gossip she could think of! She would, of course. And we thought they were only ordinary tourists, whom we'd never see or hear of again! Well, that was bad luck! Joy will be mad! And wouldn't Madam have been amused! We'll have to tell her sometime."

"I was wanting a word with Miss Joy," Ann's voice was nervous and hesitating as she broke in on Jen's worried thinking. "Would it do if I came up to the Hall to-night, Miss Jen? 'Tis—'tis important business, like."

"Help! Is Ann going to give notice? What next? Poor old Joy! Everything's going wrong at once!" Jen's lips tightened again. "That will be all right, Ann. She's only gone for a run on her bike. She'll be home to tea," and she turned to cross the garth soberly. "I wonder what's up with Ann? She's been here for years and years. And she's always seemed so fond of Joan and Joy! Between Miss Macey's school kid, and these new people turning up at such an awkward time, and Ann giving notice—if that's what she wants with Joy!—things don't look like being so awfully flat, after all. Everybody said Joy would be so dull without Joan; and the day after a wedding is supposed to be frightfully stale. I haven't exactly felt the staleness of it yet, I must say. Oh, there's the novelette girl!"

She paused beside a little figure curled up in a corner, in an angle between two gray walls. Maidlin's black eyes had been on her with a touch of suspicion from the moment she appeared. She pushed back the thick, untidy black hair which lay in a mane on her shoulders, and looked up at Jen without moving. Jen was not the mistress of the abbey!

Jen was still too near her schooldays to expect to be treated with deference, however. She stood over the child and said warmly, "Thank you for giving us warning this morning! It was jolly decent of you to think of it. It wasn't your fault we got caught, after all, and in a much worse place! Did you try to keep them back while we escaped?"

"I said to aunty I'd pick up the letters on the lawn. Miss Joy had dropped some. What's she been saying to you?" suspiciously.

"Who? Your aunt? Nothing. We spoke about this morning,

and she said she wanted to talk business with Joy and she'd come to the Hall this evening. That was all. What did you expect her to say?"

"I knew she would!" and Maidlin was on her feet with a bound. "I told her!"—and she sped across the garth and hurled herself into Ann's little kitchen.

"Well!" Jen murmured, and stood staring after her. "What on earth's the matter with the kid? Ought I to go and help? She looked as if she might tear Ann limb from limb! I'd like to know what it's all about! But perhaps I'd better not. They seem to be shrieking at one another," at sound of raised voices from the other side of the garth. "I hope no visitors will come till they've got the row over, whatever it is! That Madalena hasn't half got a jolly old temper! Who'd have thought it? She's looked quiet enough up till now! She is like a novelette, more and more!" and she went home by way of the tresaunt and garden, pondering this strange development in their guest.

"The row seemed to have something to do with Ann's business with Joy, so perhaps we'll hear all about it to-night," she said hopefully, as she laid the letters on the big table in the lounge hall, and sat down to write the story of Joan's wedding, for the benefit of Cicely and her husband in Ceylon.

"I say 'Traveller's Joy!'" and at the first sound of Belinda's horn, Jen went flying to the door. "Come in here at once! What umpteen years you've been, just running Madam down to Wycombe! I've three thrilling things to tell you! Did she like Belinda?"

"Loved her. Wants to engage me to take her to all her classes, so that she won't have any more trains to catch." Joy tossed her motoring-cap into the side-car with her big gloves, and came stalking in in her leather coat and breeches. "Come and undress me, Jenny-Wren! Three thrilling things! How many times can you say it quickly? I've had adventures by the way, too. We had to go to the station first, to pick up My Lady's bag and music-case. Then coming home, just outside the abbey gates, I almost committed murder; or perhaps it would only have been called manslaughter. No, on second thoughts, I think any jury would have acquitted me *this* time, anyway. They'd have brought in a verdict of suicide, probably whilst of unsound mind, considering the rage she was in."

"What are you talking about, silly?" Jen laughed, as she knelt and unbuttoned the leather gaiters. "Did you run over a hen?"

Joy, sitting on the big oak settle, said scornfully, "Hen? No, my child. I nearly killed Madalena di Ravarati. What do you suppose the father in Italy would have said?"

"Oh!" Jen sat back on her heels and stared up at her. "This is getting interesting! What did you do that for? Oh, was she flying out of the house in a rage?"

"In a towering temper—a real Italian passion, I should say. Never saw me coming, of course, but dashed headlong into the road. I just managed to avoid running her down; then, when I turned to swear at her, I saw she was galloping down the road at about a thousand miles an hour; no hat—slippers—overall on— hair all flying; looked a perfect lunatic!"

Jen chuckled. "I once ran up that road undressed! With my husband, you know; Jacky-boy! The time we got locked in the abbey, and couldn't get back to school in time for dinner! I suppose you went after Maidlin?"

"Rather! She tried to dodge, but of course I got her, and dumped her in the car and brought her back, and tried to find out what it was all about. But by that time she'd collapsed, and was crying herself sick; I really thought she'd be ill on my hands. So I raced her home and handed her over to Ann, and said I'd hear all about the row later on. She was quite done in, far too shaky to fight me, though she tried it on at first. I guess Ann would put her straight to bed. Best place for her, too! But fancy having a temper like that!"

"I know," Jen had attacked the gaiters again. "I saw the beginning of it. I don't know yet what the row's all about, but that's one of my three thrilling things—Madalena's Italian temper. I spoke to her on the garth, and she flared up, just like gunpowder! But you'll know all about it soon, Joy, for Ann's coming along to talk business with you after closing time; that's the second thing. I thought at first she was going to give notice, but by the way Maidlin went off with a whizz-bang when I happened to mention it, I think now perhaps it had something to do with her. She said— 'I knew she would! I told her!' and went flying off to have a scene with Ann. I heard them at it, but I didn't go to help. I suppose Maidlin got the worst of it, and went tearing off down the road in a rage."

"And barged into me and Belinda! What a queer business!" and Joy sat looking worried. "I hope Ann won't give notice! That would be about the limit! Losing Joan and having to adopt strange girls is bad enough; but if I'm left with the abbey on my hands too, I shall simply have to go out and commit suicide, as Madam says when things get really desperate!"

"It isn't quite the last straw, though," Jen said ruthlessly. "I hope you can stand one more shock. Who do you suppose those people were this morning?"

Joy stared at her amazedly. "Who? Oh, the tourists in the crypt?"

"Yes, but they weren't tourists, unfortunately. That's the point." Jen handed her the card. "The new people from the Manor! Such a way to get introduced to your new next-door neighbours! Isn't it disgusting?"

"What?" Joy stared at the card, then hurled it from her across the hall. "Oh, I say! That is rotten luck! What will they think of us? I don't care for myself, but I know Joan and aunty wanted to be friends. They won't like it. That old lady sitting glowering in the cloisters didn't like the look of me in a tunic at one o'clock in the morning; afternoon, I mean!"

"You wanted to be friends, too!" Jen pointed out. "You wanted to go boating on their lake, and skating in the winter!"

"Of course I did! We've used that lake all the time the house has been empty. I meant to go on using it still. But that old lady will never like me now. That was rotten luck!" Joy said mournfully. "And all because of an idiot of a torch! Why couldn't it say it was nearly run out?"

"It is annoying!" Jen said soothingly. "But we can't alter it now. Come and have some more tea, Joy. What we had with Madam was too early. And after that you've got to write your letters, and I must finish mine to Cicely. What shall you say to Miss Macey about her kid—Rosamund, isn't it?"

Joy frowned. "I'll wait till I've seen Ann before I decide. If she should give notice and leave the abbey on my hands, I don't see that I can take on anything more till I've fixed up with some one else. But if it isn't that, or if Ann's got any more worries for me, about Madalena or any one else—well—"

"You *will* go out and commit suicide?" Jen asked gently.

"No, I shall burst into tears! There'll be nothing else to do. And after that I shall be driven to take a very drastic step!" Joy said dramatically. "I was thinking about it when I nearly ran over Maidlin. I won't tell you what it's going to be yet, but I'm coming to see it's the only thing to do."

"O-o-o-oh!" Jen said admiringly. "Are you going to Paris after Joan? Or are you going to wire to Ceylon for Cicely? Or send for dear old Newcastle?"

"Neither, my child! But I shall act, and act in earnest, if things get much more tangled."

"Complications ensued, and a consultation of eminent specialists was held!" Jen murmured excitedly.

"Just that. If things get any worse, you'll see!"

CHAPTER V

THE big lounge hall of Joy's house was a very attractive place, with its oak-panelled walls and family portraits, big stained-glass windows, polished floor, big rugs, Joy's beautiful piano, and daffodils on each of the old tables in big blue bowls and vases. Mrs. Shirley was resting after the excitements of the last few days, and preferred to stay in her own little sitting-room upstairs, but the girls loved the hall and used it whenever they were indoors.

Each annexing a wide window-seat, they spread their papers on little tables at their sides, and tackled their letters in earnest, with many a sigh from Joy, and the silence of absorbed concentration from Jen, who dearly loved to tell a story, and in Joan's wedding found one greatly to her mind.

"Yes, Ann? What is it?" Joy's voice roused Jen to sudden interest.

She laid down her pad. "Is it business, Ann? Shall I go away?"

"Sit down, Ann. Pull up that big chair. Now tell me all about it. Jen said you wanted to see me." Joy had laid aside her writing with relief. "No, don't budge, Jenny-Wren. I may want your support, if the worst comes to the worst. Ann, put me out of my misery, do! You aren't going to say you want to chuck up the abbey? I thought you liked the job so much!"

"It's about Maidlin, Miss Joy," Ann began nervously.

"Oh! Well, I guess I can stand it! What's the worry, Ann? How can I help?"

"There's a letter from her father, miss, and—and I don't right

76

know what to do." Ann's nervousness increased as she went on.

"Oh? Well, I'm sure you'll be very glad to hear from him," Joy said vaguely. "That's very nice, Ann. Why has it worried you so?"

"He do say, Miss Joy," and Ann's correct English forsook her in her excitement, "he do say as how his old father and mother be both dead of the 'flu, it being very bad in them Italian parts just now. And all the money, what they wouldn't let him have any of, because of him getting married to our Mary—you'll remember the story, Miss Joy?"

"Yes, Ann, I know all about it," Joy assured her impatiently. "Well, what about the money?"

"Oh, Ann, dear, do go on!" wailed Jen. "Did they disinherit him, or has he got it all now?"

"It's all to belong to our Maidlin, the money, and the houses, and the horses and carriages and the motors, and the pictures, and all," and Ann gazed at Joy with incredulous, half-frightened eyes. "'Tis all written in the letter, Miss Joy. I've read it a many times these last three days, but 'tis all there, as plain as print."

"To Maidlin!" gasped Joy. "But why? What did the funny old things do that for? I thought they didn't love Maidlin so awfully much!"

"The novelette!" Jen murmured ecstatically. "Oh, how priceless! It's going on just like a book! Oh, I do hope nothing will spoil it now! Of course, Maidlin had to turn out to be an heiress in disguise! How simply tophole!"

"'Tis some old will," Ann was fumbling in her pocket for the letter. "I'll show you what he says, Miss Joy. I thought you'd tell me what to do."

"It would be an old will!" Jen chortled happily. "Was it hidden in a loft, or something? Does the property have to skip a generation once in every hundred years? Quite an original idea! Another romantic story for Joan's abbey! How pleased she'll be! As Madam says, aren't we unexpected people?"

"'Twere written when he'd been and married our Mary," Ann was explaining breathlessly. "His father said he'd leave him out of the money altogether, so he made it that every mortal thing must go to his grandchildren, for he'd got two, a boy and a girl, as he were bringing up, their parents being dead; and our Maidlin not being born then, nor thought of, you understand. But the girl, she died at school; and the boy were killed in the war; and there aren't any more, nor any one left to say it isn't fair."

"And the will was never changed! They'd never seen Maidlin, of course, and they were getting very old, and they forgot her existence," Joy said excitedly. "Probably they hardly realised she did exist! Very likely the old man was never quite the same after the shock of the grandson's death in the war; and so he never made a new will!"

"And so it all comes to the pretty housemaid's kid!" Jen murmured, and sat clasping her knees and gazing happily at Ann. "What a perfectly gorgeous story! It's simply priceless! And how it jolly well serves them right! For they were pigs about the marriage!"

"Well, Ann, what are you going to do now?" Joy asked briskly. "Is he coming to fetch Madalena? For if she's a great heiress, she'll want educating, and all kinds of things. She's not ready to take her proper place in society yet!" and a vision rose of the wild, untidy little figure, shaking with rage and sobs, who had almost met a sudden death under Belinda's wheels a few hours before.

"No, Miss Joy, that she be *not*! And that be my trouble," and Ann's strange nervousness returned, and she stammered and hesitated. "Her father, he writes as he can't come home all at once, for he's away in Chiny, and the folks there, what give him a job when he needed it bad, they be in the middle o' some work o' some kind, and sort of depending on him, and he says 'twould ruin it if he come away just now, and he can't chuck things up all at once. He'll come just as soon as he can get away, he says, but things is difficult and unsettled in that part o' Chiny, and he don't know quite when 'twill be."

"I see. It is awkward for him," Joy agreed. "He won't let them down, of course. He always does seem to have done the decent thing and stood by people properly. Well? What does he want done with Maidlin in the meantime? Are you to send her to Italy?"

"That would be awfully hard on the kiddy!" Jen urged. "She can't speak a word of French, let alone Italian, for I asked her. And she wouldn't know a soul."

"That's what he says, Miss Jen," Ann spoke eagerly. "He says 'twould be too hard on the child to send her there alone. No, he says, will we keep her till he can come and take her home himself; and if anything should happen to him out there, 'tis all written to a lawyer-man in London what's to be done with her then, and the name's in the letter here. And he says, could we send her to a good school for a little while, or—or get her a place to live with— with nice people, who'd know what she ought to learn, and teach her, so's she'd be ready when he comes."

"That's a very good idea," Joy said warmly. "Yes, that's quite the best thing to do. Not a school, though, I think. She wants people who will take more interest in her than that. In a school she'd only be one of a crowd of girls. But a nice family, where they knew the story and understood just what she needed;—yes, that's what you want. How will you find the right place, Ann? You must be very particular where you send her. Everything depends on that. Advertise? It's hardly good enough. Could I make any inquiries for you? Miss Macey might—"

"Joy, don't you see?" Jen spoke softly. To her eyes, gifted

with insight which Joy had never learned, it was plain enough. The pathetic pleading in Ann's eyes spoke for itself. Her helpless bewilderment was obvious, and so was the way out of the difficulty, as it had presented itself to her. Jen saw plainly what was in her mind, but how Joy would take it she was not sure. "Joy, she wants you to have Maidlin here. It's a frightful compliment, really, if you look at it in the proper way."

"My hat!" gasped Joy. "I hadn't thought of that! I say! What—what thundering cheek!" and she stared aghast at the caretaker.

"I—I know I hadn't ought to think of it, Miss Joy," Ann faltered. "But 'twould be the making of the child, and—and I don't know what to do. *I* ain't fit to look after her now!"

That was obvious. Joy sat biting her lips and staring out at the lawn. Jen watched her anxiously.

"Well, neither am I!" Joy burst out at last. "Fit to look after her, I mean. I'm about the last person you ought to choose, as Madam said this morning! But that—Miss Macey's girl—was only a question of letting the kid live here and go to school every day. This is quite different. You want me to take your kid, who knows absolutely nothing, and train her for you till she's fit to take her proper place—"

"No, only till her father comes home!" Jen put in quickly. "He'll come quite soon, Joy. It's only to start Maidlin properly. But I'm not saying you ought to do it. Of course, it would be a gorgeous thing for her, and all that, but there's no reason why you should fag to do it, if you don't want to. If you could help Ann to find some other place, wouldn't that do just as well?"

"I could do that, of course. I know heaps of people. I'd make all the inquiries for you, Ann. But I really don't feel I'm the proper person to bring Maidlin up for you!" Joy spoke eagerly and hopefully.

"I do ask your pardon for thinking of it, Miss Joy. I hadn't any right to say it. 'Twould be a trouble to you, I can see," Ann faltered apologetically. "But I'm wanting to do my best for the child, and I'd ha' liked her to come to you better'n to anybody else in the whole world. I can't bear to think o' sending her to strange folks. Her be a queer child, and sometimes I'm that worried by her odd ways I don't know what to do. How she'll get on wi' strange people I don't know. I doubt they won't have patience with her."

Ann's eyes wandered over the beautiful hall, and she sighed wistfully, with thoughts of all the empty bedrooms and corridors upstairs. A whole school had slept here once for two months! There was room and to spare for one small girl. It was such a beautiful house; and Joy, who had known what it was to come into an unexpected inheritance, had seemed such an ideal guardian for the ward who had suddenly become a person of such importance! Joan and Joy had always been ideals to Ann, fairy-tale girls, with their gifts, their wealth, their beauty; she had admired and adored them humbly, and she could have hoped for nothing better for Maidlin than to be cared for by one of them for a time. It had seemed such a good idea! But apparently it had been too much to hope for. She sighed regretfully again, and began another apology for her presumption.

Joy cut her short. "I'll think over all the likely people, and see if any of them could help, Ann. What about the aunt who has been mothering her, by the way? Won't she expect to be consulted now? Or is she still too ill?"

"Her be still very bad, Miss Joy, and they do say 'twould ha' been months before Maidlin could ha' gone back to her, in any case. 'Twere a stroke, and a bad one, and have left her all helpless like."

"I'm sorry it's so bad. We mustn't worry her, then. I'll come down and see you about it all in a day or two, when I've had time to think. In the meanwhile you'd better keep an eye on your heiress. I suppose you know I nearly killed her this afternoon? It wasn't my fault! She ran right out and into my bike. But I'd have been sorry. She couldn't have inherited her Italian estates if she'd been a mangled corpse under my wheels. What was the matter with the silly infant? Does she often get in fits like that? You'd better chain her up. What had you done to set her off?"

Ann, very red, would or could give no explanation. Maidlin was a silly child; she did not know what was good for her. She had a very bad temper; her mother had never had a temper, so it must have come from her father.

Jen watched the woman keenly, and Ann shrank under her penetrating eyes, and escaped with relief as soon as she could, leaving the letter from China for the girls to read.

As the door closed behind her, Jen burst out again, "Joy, don't you see? Maidlin doesn't want to be sent here. That's what she was so mad about this afternoon. She knew Ann was going to ask you to have her."

"Oh!" Joy said slowly. "Well, that settles it, of course. I wouldn't dream of having her if the very thought of coming here could put her in such a rage. But why, Jenny-Wren? Why should she hate it so? You see through people pretty well. What's the matter with her? Why won't she come here? Isn't the house good enough?" with a touch of indignation, as she in her turn looked round the hall.

Jen sat staring at her, her eyes very thoughtful. "I don't know. I don't know her well enough to say. But I know how I should feel in Maidlin's place. I might not rage as she does, for I'm not half Italian. But I know I'd feel bad."

"Oh? And why? Because you'd come into a fortune?" Joy raised her eyebrows. "I don't see why. I didn't! It's quite a jolly feeling! Why would you feel bad about it?"

"Not about that. She won't realise that yet; she can't understand it, anyway. But if I thought some one was going to be asked to have me; if I were Maidlin, and knew my aunt was coming up here to ask you to take me in; well, I should simply hate it, that's all."

"Oh, I see!" Joy said slowly, and stared back at her with knitted brows. "You think that's what was up with her? Well, if I say I won't have her—can't have her! That sounds better!—she'll be quite pleased, and it will be all right."

"I suppose so," Jen spoke doubtfully. "That depends on whether she really wanted to come or not."

"I thought you just said she'd hate it!"

"I never did! I said she'd hate knowing her aunt had *asked* you to have her. She might be dying to come all the time. That would make it all the worse. If she felt you didn't want her, and she'd been shoved on to you, I should think she'd feel simply sick."

Joy pursed her lips, and stared out into the garden. "It's awfully hard on the kid! You can't wonder if she's all worked up. And she has nobody who can really help her. Ann isn't a bit of good. Fancy going to Ann for help, when everything seems to be collapsing about you, and your whole world has crashed, and everything is going to be different! I had aunty and Joan, and they pulled me through, but I remember still how lost I felt. It *is* rough on the kiddy! And she's only an infant. She hasn't even got the aunt who's been like her mother to go to. She jolly well needs somebody," and she sat staring out at the lawn, and the almond blossom over the old orchard wall, the glimpse of the abbey ruins behind.

"Of course, I could do it … Joan would have done it," she said at last.

"Yes, I think she would," Jen agreed. "But she wouldn't have

THE NEW ABBEY GIRLS

taken on the job unless she'd meant to do it properly, Joy. I mean, if she'd agreed to have the kid here, she'd have done an awful lot for her. It's a very big thing to ask. And you have other things to do. I really wonder Ann had the cheek to suggest it. I never could have done it!"

"Oh, Ann! She never sees beyond the end of her nose. Any one can make a fool of Ann. She'd only think how nice it would be for her and Maidlin. She'd never feel it was cheek."

"It was cheek, all the same. And I believe Maidlin feels it was cheek, and that's why she's been so funny about it."

Joy lapsed into worried silence again. At last she spoke, and very definitely. "We'll tell aunty, of course; but she'll say I must do what I think right. She won't say I must do what I like, you notice! I think I ought to have the kid here, and do the proper thing by her, but I don't want to do it. And I'm not sure if I really ought to, after all. It's only the horrid feeling of being able to do something for somebody, and refusing because it's too much trouble, that worries me. I'm always coming up against it. It's the same about Miss Macey's girl, Rosamund; but Maidlin's a much bigger proposition. Much more work and worry for me!— There's nothing else for it! I've made up my mind! I'm going up to town to-morrow; you can come too, if you like! I'm going up to town to have a heart-to-heart talk with the Pixie!"

"Oh!" Jen gave a subdued shriek of delight. "Oh, Joy, of course! Why didn't I think of it? What a gorgeous idea! She'll talk some sense to us!"

CHAPTER VI

A DUMPING-GROUND FOR GIRLS

"You'd better ring up the Pixie and make sure she's in town," Jen suggested. "Half the time she isn't."

"She was getting back to-day. That's why she couldn't come to the wedding. She was awfully sorry about it, because she says it was all due to her—Joan's wedding, I mean." Joy was absent and preoccupied.

"Well, so it was. She simply flung them at one another. Do you remember?—'You'll look after him for me, won't you? You like looking after him, don't you? Yes, of course you do! That's nice! Gracious! Are there two of you?'—when she saw you, and we nearly died of laughing and enjoyed every minute of her, and Joan and Jack simply didn't know where to look. Ring up Jacky-boy, too, Joy, and say we'll stay the night with her. Then"—Jen's eyes kindled—"we could go to classes with her at night; she goes every Friday. Madam will have a fit if we turn up without any warning, especially after yesterday!"

Joy laughed. "She'll ask me if I've buried any of my visitors lately. I know her!" she said, and went to the telephone.

"That's all right," she said presently. "Jacky-boy says our room is always ready for us, any old time we like to come, and there are classes. And the Pixie says, 'Good! Come to tea at my flat! *Won't* we talk!' So to-morrow's all planned out."

That night she drifted into Jen's bedroom, in her dressing-gown. Jen, in the little room which had been hers when she was thirteen and was still hers whenever she came to the Hall, was already in bed; but she switched on the bed-light again at sound of the opening door, and Joy came in, brush in hand.

"May I sit on you? I want to talk."

"You may even brush your hair over me," Jen laughed. "When don't you want to talk, 'Traveller's Joy'? That will be more worth telling me! It's only at bedtime I'm sorry I've bobbed my hair," she remarked, lying watching while Joy brushed out her long bronze mane. "I love the comfort of it for everything else, and most of all for dancing or running, or riding in Belinda! But at night I do sometimes wish I had something to brush. Especially when there's anybody to talk to!"

"It's at night and in the morning most people would be glad," Joy was postponing the deeper matters which had brought her there.

"Oh, I'm glad in the morning!" Jen laughed, understanding very well, and wondering what was coming. "But I'd like to have something to brush at night; I miss the feel of it. Some day I'm going to let it grow again. It wants to, of course; I have to argue with it severely all the time."

"It's all your fault, Jenny-Wren!" Joy shook the shining veil over her face, and spoke vehemently.

Jen did not try to turn her off, now that she was ready to speak. "What's my fault? I'm sorry! What's the worry, Joy?"

"That I can't just say no to all these bothering people, and be done with it. I'd have done it a year ago, without thinking twice."

"Oh? But I don't see it! My fault? Why?"

"For nearly getting killed by me, and making me think about things seriously for the first time."

"Oh!" Jen said slowly. She sat up and clasped her knees, shaking back her yellow curls. "Tell me some more! I'm afraid I don't *quite* see it yet, Joy."

"I nearly killed you when I flung you out of Belinda, and at first we didn't know if you'd live or die," Joy said vehemently. "Then we didn't know if you'd ever be right in your head, or if your brain would never wake up, and you'd lie there for ever and never know us again. Then, when you did wake up and grin at us, we didn't know for days if you'd ever walk again, let alone run and dance. I suppose you know I nearly *died*? I nearly went off my head. Joan was busy with you, and Cicely wouldn't speak to me, and I had time to think, and I couldn't stop thinking. And good old Newcastle talked to me like a mother! Straight, you know; asked me if I were thinking of myself or you, and I said I'd never thought of any one but myself all my life; and I knew it was true."

"It wasn't as bad as that, Joy! They'd spoiled you, that was all. I'm so sorry you had such a rotten time. And I came quite all right again, after all."

"I was just a spoiled baby, up till that hideous time. Joan and aunty had been far too good to me, and I'd had all my own way. I saw what a useless thing I was, and I knew how everybody liked you; you can say you don't know why they should, but the fact remains that they do. And I thought if *I* had killed *you*, what an awful thing it would be. If I'd been killed myself, it wouldn't have mattered to anybody, but you——"

"Oh, Joy, *don't* be *silly*! If you're going to be sentimental, I shall begin saying things in earnest!"

"And when you began to get better," Joy said swiftly, "I said to myself such a time should never come again. I'd been forgiven for that time, and the worst hadn't happened; I'd been given another chance, and I'd use it properly. I'd do something worth while, and make people feel it was worth having me round, instead of being no use to any one and just pleasing myself and having a good time. I felt as if it were I who had come back after a dangerous illness, not you. And because I was so awfully grateful that you were alive, I meant to be different and do decent things all the rest of my life. The more you got better and stronger, the gladder I felt, and the more grateful. And now when I see you racing about, as if you'd never been ill, and dancing jigs as well as anybody, I remember what might have been, and how you might have been crippled and paralysed, in your spine or your brain, and yet have lived on for years and years; and sometimes it almost hurts me, I'm so thankful! Don't think I've forgotten, for I haven't. I can still feel what I felt that day, when dear old Newcastle had to take me in hand, because nobody else had time to think about me, and I was just going out of my mind because I was so frightened. I'll never forget, and I'll never stop being thankful."

"Joy, it's just awfully *nice* of you!" Jen dared not be what Joy would call sentimental, but her voice was shaky with sympathy, and she groped under the long red hair falling on the quilt till she found a hand, and drew it to her and laid her cheek on it. "It's a funny thing!" she said. "Of course, it was always Joan I was crazy for. She was my Queen, and I was her Maid, and she mothered me when I first came to school. I liked her better than any one else. You used to tease me when I was a kid. But to-night I like you *just* as much as I ever liked Joan, 'Traveller's Joy'!"

Joy gave a little laugh. "Call me that sometimes, there's a good kid! There's nobody left to do it now but you. It was Cicely and Joan who called me that. Jenny-Wren, ever since that time at Cheltenham last August, I've been wondering what I could do that would be worth while, because of my gladness at your coming back. I've heaps of money, and of course I want to use it well. And I've this gorgeous house, and it all feels too good for me. I'd never done anything to deserve it; it just came. I'm ashamed to be a worthless, useless, good-for-nothing, just pleasing myself."

"Joy, you aren't that! You've done heaps of jolly things for people. Joan told me, and said how glad she was about it. She was surprised, I think; but she said you thought so much more for other people than you used to do."

"I've tried," Joy said swiftly. "I can't see anything else to do but to use the money and the house and everything for people who need help, to give them a good time. I've wondered if I could do any very big thing in music, that would be worth having lived for; but that seems such cheek, even to think of it. But—"

"I don't think it's cheek. I believe you will, some day. Some of your own music is lovely!"

"But that's an extra," Joy said restlessly. "That would be all right if I found I could do it. But the money and the house are here, and must be used somehow. Seems to me the first thing is to use them properly. And I suppose 'properly' would be for other people. I may be all wrong, but that's how it looks to me."

"No, I think you're all right. But you have thought a lot about it, Joy!"

"I've been thinking all winter. I've talked a little to Joan and aunty, but not very much. I felt I ought to see it through for myself."

"Those people you've had here and given jolly country holidays to," Jen said tentatively. "You were trying to use your house properly then, Joy? Joan told me how awfully grateful they'd all been."

"That was one little way I thought of. I saw girls at Cheltenham who were working too hard; dancing all through their holidays— and the school holidays are short enough, when you've fifty infants in your class all the year round!—because they could get a better position if they had their certificates. I saw them when we said good-bye, going back tired with the hard work in the holidays. Just two or three, who weren't strong enough for it; most of them can stand it all right. But some went back tired, and it was the beginning of a long winter term! I got their addresses from headquarters, and if they were anywhere near, I asked them out here for long week-ends. And how they loved it! It's an awfully silly little thing to do, but it does mean a lot to some of them."

"Then it isn't a silly little thing!" Jen retorted. "And thinking of it wasn't a silly little thing, either. I think it's just a tophole thing to be able to do, Joy."

"I felt I could do it, and I'd be utterly mean, and a downright rotter, if I didn't. And really and truly, that's how I feel about Maidlin, and Miss Macey's girl, too," and Joy tossed back her hair and faced Jen defiantly. "I'll feel I'm a slacker if I refuse, and since last August I've tried not to be a slacker. But I may be all wrong. I don't feel sure of myself; I've never had much sense. I *don't* feel the best person to bring up an heiress! I want some advice. So I'm going to town to have a heart-to-heart talk with the Pixie, for she's got the biggest share of matter-of-fact business-like common sense, mixed with the biggest supply of plain ordinary goodness and kindness, that I've ever met in anybody. She'll tell me what's what, and just what I ought to do. After I've talked to her I shall know where I am. I'm going to consult her on the whole question of the responsibility of riches. Now go to sleep, Jenny-Wren, and forget all my silly talking. But I wanted to unload it on to somebody; and I wanted you to know it was all your fault. Thank you for listening! I feel better!"

"I shan't forget a single word!" Jen vowed, as Joy switched off the light before bending to kiss her. "Joy, I think you're a perfect sport, and I do like you awfully! Don't laugh; it's rude! I love you for thinking it all out!"

"Think! I thought till I was silly, that night you nearly died, Jenny-Wren!" and Joy fled.

She was up early next morning, to make preparations for the

trip to town. But Jen was even earlier, and met her in the entrance-hall, in her fur cap and coat, her arms full of willow-twigs covered with silvery balls. "I've been robbing your woods! If the Pixie lives at the top of a London house, as I've been told, don't you think she'd like some pussy-palm to remind her of the country?"

"The Duchess loved it yesterday. Yes, let's take all we can carry. And daffodils from the orchard, and some almond in bud."

"My Jacky-boy will want some, too. Harley Street isn't exactly full of daffodils. We'd better take a good lot," and Jen went to examine the letters on the round table.

"One for you from home. The usual stacks for me," and Joy dropped on a window-seat in the early sunshine with her budget.

A cry from Jen made her look up quickly. "What's the matter? Anything wrong?"

"Father isn't well again, and—it's awfully hard on you, Joy! I know you won't mind, but it does seem as if everybody were making you a dumping-ground for girls all at once! Mother wonders if you could put up with me here for two or three weeks, because he may have to come up to London for treatment, and it's a pity for me to go home and have to come back again. He'd stay in town for some months, if he came. Can you put up with me? I'll try not to be too much bother! How many more girls can you make room for?" and Jen stood looking down at her with a comical expression of dismay and apology.

"Cheers! Oh, cheers! I hope you'll stay for years and years, and umpteen years! You know I'm glad to have you, Jenny-Wren! I'm sorry about your dad, and all that, but it will be gorgeous to have you here. How long will he need to stop? Will you stay with me all the time?"

"Oh, no! Only till they get settled somewhere in town. Mother will come with him, and there won't be anybody left at home. I'm sorry about my classes for the village kiddies; the children loved their dance-evenings so, and the boys' morris was getting quite good. And they're crazy for sword-dances! But I couldn't live there all alone, and mother and father will want me to be with them. But till they get settled, Joy—!"

"Keep them unsettled as long as ever you can, Jenny-Wren! I shan't consider them settled till they've bought and furnished a house in town. I can't have you living in hotels! Well, I am glad! I need you here jolly badly."

"And I'll see how you get on with the novelette girl, and Miss Macey's kid! They'll be able to amuse one another, anyway, Joy. People always say it's easier to have two than one. It's not a surprise about daddy, you know; we knew it might be necessary, but we hoped he'd pull through without having to come to town. It's so fearfully lonely at home, out among the moors, that if he wants specialists, or any particular treatment, he simply must come to town; our own doctor spoke of it months ago. But they hope he'll get quite all right in time. Mother's going to tell me definitely in a few days if they are coming, but she wanted me to consult you."

"Tell her I'm delighted, and overjoyed, and honoured; and the longer you can stop with me the more delighted and overjoyed and honoured I shall be. But if you chuck me and go and stop with Jacqueline in town, I won't forgive you in a hurry!"

"I know Jacky-boy would have me," Jen laughed. "If you and I quarrel, I can always run away to her. But I do love the abbey and the Hall; and I quite like you, 'Traveller's Joy'!"

"You stick to that, Jenny-Wren!" Joy said warmly. "I'm just frightfully glad to think you'll be here a little longer!"

CHAPTER VII

CONSULTING THE PIXIE

"WE'LL go in Eirene," said Joy, at lunch-time. "It seems rude to dear Belinda not to let her have a run to town, but considering the amount of pussy-willow and daffodils Jen's taking along with her, Eirene seems necessary."

And when the girls set out, in the little car which for longer journeys had taken the motor-cycle's place in Joy's affections, the back seat was heaped with flowers and catkins and blossom.

Jen was warm and picturesque in a round fur cap and big coat, for after the few days of sunshine which had been so convenient for Joan's wedding, and had turned spring into summer, the March winds had come back, and there was a threatening touch of north in the air which hinted at showers of sleet. These met them half-way to town, and the girls stopped to cover their flowers, and then crouched behind the wind-screen as they sped eastwards. Joy, in her leather chauffeur's suit, cared nothing for any kind of weather; she would have gone through the storm gaily on Belinda's exposed saddle, and was sheltered and comfortable behind the screen. She, too, had a big coat over the leather jacket and breeches she always wore on her cycle, and with a cap fastened under her chin could face any gale. The streets were glistening with rain as they raced through Uxbridge and Ealing and the West End, the wind whistling with a scream down side streets and across commons and open spaces.

"Nice, warm, cosy, sheltered spot, London!" Joy murmured. "Why did we leave our abbey under the hill? Did we really sit out on the garth yesterday? Are you all right, Jenny-Wren?"

"Ker-wite all yight, sank 'oo, mummy!" and Jen snuggled down under her rugs. "Where are we going first, Wild Cat? To get rid of some of the cargo, and see if my husband's all right?"

Joy glanced at her watch. "No, Jacky-boy must wait. The Little One's expecting us early. She said 'three o'clockish,' and it's three now. We're not to be late, for she has to go out. So we're all out for the Pixie's flat."

"Right-o! I'm dying to see her again. Have you seen her since that evening in the barn at Christmas, when you were her man in the Running Set, and you wouldn't let me dance?"

"She came to the President's wedding, the following week. I haven't seen her since. Now, don't chatter, my infant! I've got to keep an eye on the traffic. I don't want to kill you a second time."

Jen subsided, and watched in admiring silence as the strong hands gripped the wheel, the keen eyes watched carefully.

"You're an awfully good driver, Joy," she said seriously, when they were held up for a moment by a policeman at Oxford Circus.

"I've had the fright of my life," Joy said grimly. "I don't want another. It's a marvel to myself I can drive at all. Old Newcastle did that. She made me take her out that very same evening, before I had time to get nervy. If she hadn't, I don't suppose I'd ever have gone on Belinda again."

Jen glanced at her quickly. "*Made* you take her out? Wasn't it rather horrid?"

"Beastly. I was all shaky; not afraid of anything more happening; I knew perfectly well how it had happened! But frightened, simply scared to death about you. But it was good for me; I might have funked it if I'd had time to think. She made me go out to do things for you, you see—send telegrams, and fetch Jack from the cottage where she'd fainted, and tell them at the school, and so on. And, of course, I'd have done anything if I'd thought it was for you. Now we're off! We're almost there."

"You did have a rotten time!" Jen said sympathetically. "And I didn't know anything at all about it, for days and days! Oh, does the Pixie live here?" as Eirene pulled up before a block of high, straight-fronted houses in a wide, quiet street just off a busy thoroughfare, filled with trams and buses, motors and wagons.

"Shares a flat with two more, but she said they'd be out. Come and disentangle your pussy-palm! Its fingers are all tied up in knots."

"It looks awfully dull, and—and gray, and uninteresting!" Jen said doubtfully. "And she loves pretty things. I always think of lovely colours when I think of the Pixie—greens and blues and yellows and grays! This is so—so flat!"

"You wouldn't ask her to have her house green and blue and yellow outside, would you?" Joy mocked. "Perhaps inside it's more like her. Let's go up! I'll tootle to give her warning," and she woke the echoes with Eirene's horn.

The bare stone staircase, of wide, shallow steps, up which they climbed flight after flight to the top, depressed Jen still more. "It's cold and dreary and lifeless! It's not good enough for her! She's so much alive. I'm shivery!"

"I say!" a voice hailed them from the upper regions. "*Isn't* it nice to see you here! I am glad you've come! I *say*! You've got new coats! Oh, what a nice one, Jenny-Wren!" and the Pixie, four foot ten and a half, but looking very tiny, hung over the top railing to welcome them.

"Well, don't you think we need new coats?" Jen laughed. "Of all the dismal, chilly, wet, clammy places to live in, London's the worst! Why, we've been sitting out, in the abbey!"

"It isn't really. Only in March. You mustn't say rude things about London; I love it! I'm never quite happy away from town.

"'Isn't it nice to see you here.'"

Theobald's Row is just heavenly;" there was defiance in the Pixie's tone.

"That crowded street we've just crossed, with the trams and things? It's not exactly my idea of heaven!" Joy laughed.

"Oh, but I love a London crowd! It's different from any other crowd! Are those flowers for me? Oo-er!" with exaggerated emphasis. "All for me? Aren't they lovely? What's this?— almond? How my men at Plaistow will love it! Come and put it in water; this way!" and she hustled them through rooms and into the kitchen, without time for a glance about them.

"Oh, but I want to see!" Jen remonstrated. "I believe you've got a lovely room there. I want to see it. I didn't think there could be a pretty room in such a cold-looking house! It looks so business-like from the outside. Like offices, you know! Can't we see everything?"

"Of course you shall! Go and put your coats off; I want to see your frocks! That's my bedroom we came through; all our rooms open out of one another! My bed's the little one in the corner."

"Please, I haven't a frock on," Joy said meekly. "I'm Thomas, the chauffeur, to-day. Do you mind?" and she threw down her coat and stood in the doorway in breeches and gaiters.

"No, I like it," the Pixie looked up from her willow-buds and cast a quick glance over the neat figure. Then her eyes twinkled. "Going to classes to-night? Just like that?"

"Oh, no! We're going to change at Jack Wilmot's. Wouldn't Madam be surprised if I went to do morris like this?"

"I'd be sorry for your morris, in those boots. And for the boots, too. Oh, aren't these lovely?" as she arranged the daffodils in a bowl. "I shall take some, and the almond, down to Plaistow to-night; do you mind? They don't get flowers like these there. I'll say they've come straight from the country."

"There are a thousand million daffies in our orchard, under

the apple-trees, so you can say it safely. You're not to give them all away, though," Joy remonstrated. "We brought them for you."

"Oh, but I'll get the good of them there. And my men will love them so!"

"If there are men in the case, of course we needn't say any more! She'll give them all away to her men!" Jen mocked, coming from the bedroom. "What's on at Plaistow? And where is it, anyway?"

"I've got the loveliest classes. You must come and see them one day, but not yet; we've only just got started. We're only finding ourselves. At the big Y.M.C.A. Club, you know; men and girls—such dears, all of them! And we have big parties, and enjoy ourselves no end."

"It sounds all right! I'd love to come to a party!"

"You shall. I'll ask you some day. Now come and have some tea. Oh, I like your frock, Jenny-Wren! Have that for the wedding? You're to tell me all about it. *I* made that wedding! I was so sorry I couldn't come, but I had a big party in Nottingham that night. What did you want to see me about?" to Joy. "You said there was something important. Is it something Moral?" in anxious capitals. "Or only folk-dancing?"

"I'm afraid it's Moral. Do you mind?" Joy looked down at her hopefully. Everybody looked down at the Pixie hopefully, sure of help and sympathy.

"No, I'm glad. But what made you think of asking me? And what is it all about?"

"I'll tell you after tea. The wedding will be better for tea-time. There didn't seem to be anybody else," Joy said simply. "I couldn't think of any one else to go to; aunty always tells me to do what I think right, and to decide for myself! And I do want to talk to somebody in earnest, somebody who'll tell me what to do! I know you will. You see things so clearly."

"It's awfully nice of you," the Pixie said soberly, as she lifted the bowl of daffodils and led the way through the bedroom again. "Aren't they lovely?" she murmured, her eyes on the blaze of yellow. "*How* they'll love them down at Plaistow!"

"Oh! What a gorgeous room!" Jen stood on the threshold to gaze. "I'd *never* have believed you could find a room like that inside a house like this!"

"It's so big and square." Joy, the lover of the open air, looked round the lofty room with approval. "Nice big windows! It isn't stuffy, if it is in town!"

"And the colours!" Jen's tone was full of deepest satisfaction. "Oh, I am glad we came!"

The room was deep blue, and black, and dull blue-gray, in walls and carpet, big couch and easy-chairs; here and there was a touch of vivid flame-colour, in cushions, curtains, or china. The walls had tiny water-colours in gilt frames; the corners were full of shadows, and the Pixie, in her loose hanging jumper of green and blue silk, stood in the doorway with the glow of the firelight upon her, holding the bowl of daffodils, and looking up in delight at their approval. Jen treasured the picture for her next letter to Joan.

"It's an artist's room; I love it! Oh, we only rent it, but isn't it beautiful? I do think we're lucky! The others are out all day, you know. Brown's a typist, and she gets home about six. Parr's in the Women's Police, and she gets in at all hours, and just rolls into bed without waking anybody. I'm only odds and ends, of course, just here at odd times; for weeks I'm rushing round the country. But I may be a bit more settled at Plaistow. There's a lot of work to do there; a big chance, if we can only seize it. Yes, I love this room! Your daffodils shall stand here. Look at that beautiful blue bowl! My Nottingham class gave me that, the dears! Wasn't it lovely of them? Now come and have tea! Choose your chairs; Jenny-Wren, pass up the hotters! The kettle's boiling."

Jen lifted a plate of hot scones from the hearth. "These? I never heard them called hotters before."

"Oh, that's Oxford! We always called them hotters. Now tell me all about the wedding! What did you all wear? I love to hear what people wore. Was Joan's frock pretty? She'd look lovely, of course; she couldn't help it. And he didn't get married to you by mistake?" with a twinkle of amusement at Joy. "Gracious! You did give me a shock that day, when I found I'd got two of you in my class! I've never got over it. D'you remember?"

"Remember! You wanted me to go straight out and dye my tunic green, so that you'd know us apart."

"You aren't so much alike as I thought at first;" the Pixie studied her face thoughtfully. Joy had discarded her motoring cap, but perforce remained boy-like in her breeches, which she wore with great enjoyment. "But you're getting more like Joan, I do believe. What have you been doing to yourself lately?"

"I've thought that too," Jen said swiftly. "She is more like Joan than she used to be! It doesn't matter now that Joan's gone, but it's as well she didn't start getting like her before, or Jack might have got tied up in them."

"He never showed any signs of it coming on, that I could see! Have another hotter, aunty!" and Joy flourished the dish before the Pixie. "Oh, I've heard them call you aunty! It's because you mother everybody, I suppose. The cheek of you; that size, and mothering great hefty men!"

"They come to me about their shirts and socks, the dears! The Plaistow men are just beginning; I do feel so pleased about it! It feels just like being in France again. It's your expression that makes you more like Joan," the Pixie decided, still eyeing Joy carefully.

"It was only their expressions ever made them any different. Except for that, they always were as like as two pins," Jen remarked. "You're quite right, of course, aunty! I've noticed it myself."

"But tell me all about the wedding!" the Pixie demanded hungrily, and Joy plunged into the story, and ended with a laughing account of the morning adventure in the abbey, of Madam's visit, and her amused horror at being "buried alive."

"She'll never forget it against me, of course. I know that!" she ended ruefully.

"But she just loved it!" Jen added.

"Of course she did. She'll never let you forget it, though. I wish I'd been with you when you were buried! Has everybody had enough tea? Now, Joy, what's the trouble? It *is* nice of you to come to me about it!" and the Pixie pushed away the table with a business-like air. "Pull in your chairs to the fire! Shall I switch on the light?"

"No, firelight's cosiest," Jen took the corner of the big sofa, and retired into the background, but watched Joy's face, and then the Pixie's, continually; as the one talked, the other listened thoughtfully.

Joy sat on the fender, nursing her knee, and soberly repeated what she had said the night before. The Pixie, on a low stool before the fire, listened curiously, finding in the new thoughtfulness of Joy's face the explanation of the unexpected likeness she had just discovered.

"It's the whole question of one's attitude to money," Joy said at last, when she had described the new feeling of responsibility which had come at the time of Jen's accident, her efforts to do what she could and give help where she saw it needed, and the new demands suddenly made upon her. "I can give it away; that's easy enough. I've plenty; I can give away a lot, and never feel it. I do try to give sensibly, but I don't give to every old person who asks! They do ask, you know. I get shoals of begging letters."

"Of course you will. But you have to sift them. In some cases you'd do more harm than good by giving money. Your part is in taking trouble to make sure you are using the money well. You can't give money to the point of feeling it, as most of us have to do. You've too much. But you must give somehow; you've got to *work* for it. Every one must do that," the Pixie said, very definitely. "Your giving of money is too easy. *You* have to give yourself; in time, and thought, and trouble. You can do a *lot* for people, if you only will. You've made a very good beginning. I like your idea of finding girls who really need a holiday and seeing that they get it. I could find you heaps; East End girls, who'd almost die with joy at such a chance. Why don't you run a little hostel in the village? Not in your own house, for your aunt is there, and Joan will want to come back; and anyway, your work is cut out for you there with these two children. But a little house in the village, where you could have parties down all summer; and a nice woman to mother them?"

"That's a topping idea!" Joy said swiftly. "I like it! Go on, Pixie! And you do think I've got to take in these two infants? I was afraid you would. I knew it all the time, inside of me."

"Of course you will. Your work is waiting for you there. The schoolgirl may not bother you very much, but the heiress is another matter. You can just be the making of that child, if you will."

"Madam said I was the last person in the world she'd choose as a fit and proper guardian for a girl!" Joy said pensively. "Isn't she brutal sometimes?"

"But she took it back afterwards!" Jen's voice came out of the darkness over the Pixie's shoulder. "She said she wasn't so sure, after all."

The Pixie dismissed Madam and her sweeping judgments with a gesture. "She doesn't understand. You hadn't told her all this?"

"Help, no! It never came into my head! Besides, I didn't know about Maidlin then."

"Then she couldn't possibly judge. Of course, you can do it beautifully. You've been through it. You know just how she feels; about the fortune, I mean. And you've got big ideas; you'll put them into her. It's a chance, and you can do it better than any one else. And it's a chance to give service where it's needed; to give real personal help and trouble, the kind of thing no money can buy. That's what you rich people have got to do, besides using your money properly. If you just give away a little, and enjoy yourself on the rest, you'll feel a slacker. Isn't that what you've been feeling?"

"Yes," Joy said slowly. "Yes, I think it is. I knew you'd be definite, and go straight to the point!"

"Oh, but you had seen it for yourself! Let me know how you get on, won't you? I shall want to hear. And if ever you want girls in need of a holiday, just ring me up; I know plenty of them, poor things! Now I've got to run, you know, or my classes will be waiting for me. I *am* so glad you came! It *was* nice of you!"

"Couldn't Thomas the chauffeur, who's fearfully grateful to you, run you along to Plaistow?" Joy asked, standing on the rug in the firelight and looking down at her. "I haven't an idea where it is, but I'd find it all right. I don't like you racing round in tubes and buses; and isn't it the crowded time? You're too tiny to have to fight! Couldn't I take you along? I feel like a man when I'm with you; I want to take care of you!"

The Pixie bubbled with laughter, at thought of her years of roughing it in France during the war.

"I had such a *nice* thing said to me the other day! It was one of those dear men at Plaistow. He came up to me, and said, 'I say, miss! If your young man ain't good to you, you send 'im along to me!' Now wasn't that *beautiful*?"

"I know just how he felt!" Joy declared. "He wanted to be sure somebody was taking care of you. I know you don't need it; you spend all your time taking care of other people. But I feel just as he did. Can't we take you along?"

"No, of course not. I've just time to do it, and you couldn't find it in the dark." She switched on the lights, and Jen clapped her hands softly as a bright orange glow filled the blue room.

"What pretty shades! And I suppose it's wet and cold outside! I'd forgotten the wind and sleet. Aunty Pixie, it is so nice to have seen you at home! We only knew you in class-rooms before. Some day we're going to have tea with Madam, and get a pretty background for her too! I shall always think of you now as a tiny spot in this big, warm, blue room, with firelight on you, and yellow flowers!"

"Quite poetical, Jenny-Wren!" Joy mocked. "*I* shall think of her as even more business-like than I did before!"

The Pixie chuckled. "Come into the kitchen for three minutes! I want to put on the potatoes for Brown's dinner, and make her a fruit salad, so that it will be all ready when she comes in tired. She's due in twenty minutes. No, you can't help. Just sit on the table and talk to me," and she peeled potatoes at the sink in the diminutive kitchen at express speed. "Shall I tell you a perfectly awful thing that happened once? It was one morning. I was making some soup for their supper; I was going to sleep at Plaistow, as I shall to-night. I put it on to boil, and never thought of it again till I was on a bus and half-way to Canning Town! And it was about eleven o'clock then, and no one would be in till six!"

"Oh, I am so glad you can do that kind of thing!" Joy sighed. "It's such a relief to hear it! It's just exactly the kind of thing I've been doing all my life! But I never supposed other people were like that too. Not you, anyway!"

Jen chuckled. "What did you do?"

"Got out and took the first bus back. The flat was full of blue smoke, and the saucepan was done for. Now make up some of those flowers in a bundle for me, will you? My men will just love them. And get into your coats. We'll all have to run."

"Yes, or Jacky-boy will have gone to classes without us! We're hoping to give Madam a surprise."

"Oh, give her my love! I never see her, but I love her just the same, you know! And let me know how you get on with your heiress! I really want to hear. It *was* nice of you to come to me!" was the Pixie's last word, as she hung over the top railing and called good-bye after them while they clattered down the big stone steps.

CHAPTER VIII

JACQUELINE, or Jacky-boy, the "husband" of Jen's schooldays, came flying out to hurl herself on her better half, at the first sound of Eirene's horn before her door. In this partnership, the husband was the smaller, slighter person, nearly a head shorter than the tall wife, with bobbed black hair, and at the moment, in preparation for the evening's classes, she looked supremely childish in a short blue tunic and long legs.

"How late you are, Jen! Has Joy been talking somewhere? Come on; you've only just time to change! But it's topping to see you again!"

"Well, that is a nasty one!" Joy said indignantly. "I'm sure I don't talk *much*! Is there anybody who'll put Eirene to bed, or shall I go and tuck her up myself?"

"Oh, Parker will do it! There's heaps of room in beside father's car. Mother's out; you'll have to see her at night. Father's always out, of course! Come along and get ready! Have you had tea? Come up at once, then," and she ran before them upstairs to a big bedroom. "Now tell me everything while you change! I'll undo your straps; you get undressed. How did it go off on Wednesday?"

"Quite all right; and we've had a card from Dover from Captain and Mrs. Raymond," Joy said solemnly, as she unbuttoned her big leather coat.

Jack, sitting on the floor and struggling with locks and straps, looked up at her. "Is that Joan? Help! How funny it seems! As funny and impossible as when Madam got married, and we had to begin calling her something else!"

"We'll tell you about the wedding in bed to-night," Jen interrupted, hurling her coat and frock aside. "Give me out my gym blouse and tunic, quickly, husband! Now tell us all about to-night. That matters more just now. Who's teaching? What are you doing?"

"First there's half an hour of swords with her—Madam. We're doing 'Earsdon,'" Jack said importantly.

"Rappers! You little swank! And we've never tried them yet! That's what comes of living in town!" Joy said enviously. "I'm dying to try rappers! I will, too, at Cheltenham next summer!"

"How do you like them, Jacky-boy?" Jen had paused in her hasty toilet. "Aren't you frightened? I think I should be. They scrape and clash so, like huge knives. But I'd love to try them, even if I were frightened."

"My dear, I was terrified!" Jack said solemnly, as she tossed a blue tunic to each of them. "I never dreamt it was a rapper class! I'd got the half-hour to spare, before morris; so I thought I'd go. I supposed they'd be revising 'Sleights' and 'Haxby,' which is what I need. I didn't even know who was teaching. But suddenly Madam blew in, and said we'd do 'Earsdon.' 'Earsdon!' That miners' dance! I nearly *died*! And when we started, I was simply scared stiff! She seemed to think we'd done 'Winlaton,' or something; kept saying, 'It's just like "Winlaton"'—which it isn't, I believe. Anyway, she didn't seem to realise that I, at least, had never touched a rapper before, but had always looked at them with awe and respect from a safe distance! I didn't know where I was, or what we were supposed to be doing, or where anybody else was, or ought to be; I really was terrified! I thought my head would be cut off every minute. And she kept yelling at me because

I was wrong; of *course* I was wrong, all the time! Then she'd say, 'Don't look so worried, Miss Wilmot!' Worried! I was nearly dead, panting and gasping a thousand miles behind her! I nearly threw my sword at her. Then she'd get frantic: you know her way"—the other two laughed and nodded—"and she'd shout, 'Clockwise, Miss Wilmot!'—as if I could think which was clockwise, with those things buzzing round my head! I couldn't even remember which was my right hand, let alone clockwise. So I'd turn counter-clock, and we'd be all tied up in a knot, and she'd come flying down the room at me, and forget all about 'Miss Wilmot,' and say, 'It's *you*, Jacky-boy! You're wrong every time!' and the other four wondered if I was a lunatic, and they've never called me anything but Jacky-boy since. Oh, we had great fun for the first week or two!" Jack said pensively. "Now it's better, of course. I know what I'm supposed to be doing. We do have fun sometimes! Madam's funny husband comes to the class, you know."

"And joins in, do you mean?" Jen asked, with interest. She had forgotten all about hurrying, and was sitting on the bed in her blouse and gym knickers.

"Rather! He's trying to learn 'Earsdon,' and he can't do it a bit. It's rather priceless sometimes; of course, he always is a scream. He fools about, as he always does, and tries to make us laugh; and she pretends she doesn't see, and tries not to look, and then goes and tells him he's *all wrong*, just like the rest of us. And he argues that he must be right, and, of course, he isn't; and says it can't be done her way, and she ups and does it, and he's squashed—for the time being. They're always funny, even each one of them alone, but when you get them together they really are a treat! I say, are you coming up for the party next week?"

"Didn't know there was one. Oh, we can't come up once a

week, Jacky-boy! Unless any important business turns up, of course."

"Well, couldn't you make some?" Jack pleaded. "I'm dying to go, but father and mother are going to be away, and they say I mustn't go unless I've got company. It's silly; it's just round the corner! As a rule, father comes to take me home. Oh, couldn't you come and stop for a night or two? I'll be all alone! *Do!* Then we could go to the party together! Think what fun we'd have!"

"I'd love to go to a London party!" Jen looked at Joy wistfully.

Joy shook her head. "Don't see how we can, unless—well, if that should happen, of course we might have to come! No, I won't tell you what I mean! It's only a vague idea. I'd love a party too, of course. But there are things to do at home, Jenny-Wren! I say, hadn't you better be getting dressed?"

"Well, you might spare me Jen for a night or two, if you can't come yourself!" Jack urged.

"Help! What would be the good of that? You two infants couldn't chaperone one another! Jen needs me to look after her! What happens after swords this evening, Jacky-boy?"—neatly catching and returning the pillow Jen had hurled at her.

"Madam runs along to another hall and takes morris and country for an hour each, and I go there too, for it's revision for the exam, and I'd like to take it this summer. But that's too easy for you two; you've passed your Elementary! You'd better stay and join in the Advanced class; you'll know a lot of the girls. I saw them at Chelsea; it's all the same crowd."

"Who's teaching?" Joy asked. "Madam can't take two sets at once! I'd rather stick to her. You always have a good time with her."

"They're doing rather thrilling dances in the Advanced class, though," Jack remarked. "I watch for a minute or two sometimes. They're doing 'Bledington' just now; I'm sure your kick-jumps need practice, Joy! We're only at 'Bampton' and 'Headington' things."

"They do!" Joy laughed. "They're the limit for badness! But I'm out to enjoy myself to-night. I shall come with you to Madam's class."

"I shall stay and watch the Advanced lot, if it's some one new teaching them," Jen decided. "I don't say I'll join in, even if they'd have me; my morris has had a long rest since Cheltenham, and I'm not really up to that grade. My jumps are worse than Joy's! But I do love watching classes, and whoever she is, she'll be a good teacher. They all are!"

"She'll ask what you've got your tunic on for, if you don't mean to join in," said Jack. "You can't pretend you're going to join in the swords, you know."

"Now, husband, don't swank!" Jen said severely. "Remember you have advantages we poor country cousins haven't! I shall take my shoes along, in case I'm wanted to make up a set."

"It's only five minutes' walk," Jack explained, as they set out. "But come this way first! I want to show you something. I do this every Friday before classes, and I never get tired of it. I consider it one of the sights of London!"

She led them into Portland Place, to an island under a lamp-post. "Stand and look down towards Regent Street. There! Isn't it pretty?"

The wide road glistened in the wet like black ice. A long row of bright lights, in beautiful perspective, made a fairy chain on each side, and each was reflected in a long unswerving shaft in the shining pavement below. Here and there were ruby lights on retreating taxis, or blazing headlights on rushing cars; one or two vivid lights hung above the rest, like low stars. The three girls leaned on the posts and gazed enthralled, as cars rushed at them out of the blackness, swung past, or swerved round the corner, dazzling them for a moment with their brilliant lamps, then leaving darkness, and the long twin chain of stars, and the tapering fingers of light below.

"Yes, that's rather wonderful, Jacky-boy!" Jen said softly at last. "Are there many streets as beautiful as that?"

"I love the London streets at night! It's part of my Friday evening, just to stand here for a moment and look at those lights. It's even finer at the top end, where the taxis sweep round out of the Crescent, and you feel you're going to be killed every minute. The cars make beautiful curves round the island up there, like the curves we're told to make in country dancing! Now come on, or we'll be late, and my set will have got another Number Three. I couldn't possibly be anything but Three, of course! We'd better run!" She led the way, and Joy and Jen raced after her through the damp, quiet streets.

CHAPTER IX

OLD FRIENDS AND NEW

A BUSY thoroughfare, with mud, and traffic, and many small children playing in the doorways of small shops; a quieter side street, down which the cutting north wind blew drifting showers of sleet; then an iron gate, giving entrance to a dark tunnel; and here the girls stopped to pant after their run through rain and wind, while Jack led the way to a big doorway. "Come on! I don't like being late!"

"Is it in here? I thought you'd only dropped in to breathe!" and they followed her through the swing door.

In a dressing-room were girls in all stages of undress; girls changing shoes, girls changing stockings, girls changing blouses, girls one and all getting into tunics and saying their worst about the weather.

Jack, throwing greetings right and left, went to look through the inner door, unbuttoning her coat as she did so.

"She's here!" briefly, to Joy. "You two had better go and explain yourselves. We *are* late!"

"Why, it's Miss Shirley!" "Why, Joy!" "And Miss Robins, from Cheltenham!" one after another recognised the new-comers.

"I say, Shirley, this is an unexpected pleasure. Where have you dropped from?" A round-faced, jolly-looking dark girl came up, tying her girdle. "Where's Joan? Isn't she with you? And what's become of Hobart?"

Jen, in the background, rocked with laughter. "I didn't know you'd been adopted as thoroughly as *that*!" she told Joy afterwards. "I nearly died! I've never thought of the President as 'Hobart'!"

"Married, both of 'em," Joy assured the plump person solemnly. "Isn't it sad?"

"Oh, I say, Shirley! And you never asked *me*?"

Joy laughed, and left her still remonstrating. "Come and explain yourself to Madam, Jenny-Wren!"

"Why, it's little Robins! Where have you all come from? I say, are you all right again, Robins?"

Jen laughed and nodded, and followed Joy. "Isn't it jolly nice to be remembered?" she murmured.

The inner door opened on a big hall, with cleared floor, a piano on the platform, a dark girl tuning a violin, and Madam, in a bright green sports coat over a blue tunic, sitting on the hot water pipes to thaw herself.

"Where is everybody? They're all very late to-night. Or I'm very early—for once."

"Quite a mistake on your part," the violinist jeered.

Two girls were playing leapfrog to warm themselves; two more were strenuously practising morris steps, coached by a third; others were handling the swords waiting on the platform, or selecting the particular morris sticks they fancied.

"I think we'll start. It's time. Are there any more out there?" and then Madam saw the visitors, and her eyes widened in surprise. "Hal—lo? Why, Joy? Jen? Where on earth have you come from? What do you mean by it?" in mock indignation. "You never said anything about this yesterday!"

"Oh, we didn't know! We just decided to spend a night with Jack, and so we came along. Do you mind?"

"Have you buried anybody lately?" Madam asked accusingly, and a laugh from the fiddler showed that she had heard the story.

"Not since you. One a day is about as much as I can manage,"

Joy retorted. "Do you mind if we watch? Jacky-boy wants us to see how clever she is. She's swanking fearfully about having learnt rappers before either of us."

"Won't you dance? There's sure to be some one away, on a night like this. Aren't you perished?" and Madam shivered and hugged the pipes again.

"Oh, but we've never touched the things! No, thanks! We'll look on," and they subsided into a corner, and watched the evolutions of the "Earsdon" dance with keen interest.

"Now I'm going with her to have some morris!" Joy sprang up eagerly, when the sword class was over. "In another hall, Jacky-boy says, but only ten minutes' walk. Aren't you coming? Jack says they're doing 'Bampton'—'Glorishears' and 'Bobbing Joe.' You know your 'Bampton' needs rubbing up, Jenny-Wren! Don't be a slacker!"

"It does, but you needn't call me names! Go and rub up your own 'Bampton'! I'm going to stop here. I love Madam too, but I like watching new people. Tell Jack to come back for me; I couldn't possibly find my way home alone. I'll be lost in London for ever, if she doesn't come and rescue me," and Jen stuck to her corner beside the hot water pipes.

She thought better of it, however, and while the morris class was assembling she approached the girl who had taken command, and who, conforming to the fashion of the evening, was also sitting on the radiator, rubbing her hands and making scathing comments on the temperature to the violinist.

"Do you mind if I watch for a little while, please? We're only in town for one night, but we're awfully keen, so we came along with a friend."

"Oh, I mind frightfully! I think I'll turn you out," and she smiled. "Aren't you going to dance? Are you quite all right again?"

"Oh!" gasped Jen, utterly taken aback. "But you don't know me? I mean, I've never been in your class? And you haven't seen me since last August, anyway; nine months! And I must look quite different with my hair bobbed! I didn't think anybody would know me! How can you remember?"

"If you will distinguish yourself, as you did, and upset the whole school on the last morning, of course you must expect to be remembered," was the retort.

Jen retired to her corner stunned, and watched the first dance still in a state of incredulous amazement, which increased when the teacher turned to her to say, "Don't you want to dance, Miss Robins? There's room in that back set."

"She even knows my name!" marvelled Jen's mind, while she explained limply that she had never learned "Bledington Trunkles." "I've done no morris since Cheltenham; I wasn't quite up to it at Christmas," she added. "I'm quite all right now, but I don't want to put the rest of the set out."

Curled up in her corner, her big coat on over her tunic, one hand on the radiator, she watched in absorbed interest, for the teaching was very different from Madam's. There were about thirty girls in the class, all in tunics, mostly of blue, though a few were green or brown; and a few men in flannels. They were all enjoying themselves; that was obvious; but they were very much in earnest, thinking only of their work and trying hard to satisfy their teacher—not an easy task, for her standard was high. She had many original ways of helping them to reach it, however, and Jen's eyes widened in surprise, and then danced in amusement, when, at the end of the 'Bledington' dance, after a few pointed remarks on kick-jumps, the girl on the platform bade everybody take two chairs and practise jumps between them. At the sight the hall presented for the next five minutes, Jen collapsed in politely-suppressed laughter, hugging herself in silent glee, and longed for Cicely. Some jumped steadily, with stern determination and grimly-set faces, their eyes on the positions of their feet; others were too helpless with laughter to do much; some, after a few attempts, placed their chairs together and sat perched on the backs of both, or lay at full length on the seats and flatly refused to do another jump. The teacher walked up and down, and round the room, with comments and suggestions and criticisms, and the prostrate forms came to attention at her approach and had one more try.

"I loathe 'Bledington'!" a tall girl collapsed on a chair near Jen. "I shall never do kick-jumps, I'm sure of that!"

"Did any one say it was a cold night?" another laughed. "Aren't there any more windows we could open? Oh, look at that silly kid!"

"She'll have pneumonia," and the tall girl went to remonstrate with a little friend, who had climbed on to the sill of an open window and was sitting in an icy draught, a picturesque silhouette against the lights outside, with bobbed wavy hair, and slim neat neck and shoulders.

"Well, I always sit there in the summer!" said she, in an injured tone; but yielded to the forcible arguments of her friend, and descended to a less dangerous position.

A girl in the lighter blue of a well-known training college, with white belt and shoes, was sniffing her hands disgustedly. "Ugh! I loathe massage! I smell of disinfectant still!"

"Been at hospital again?" asked somebody.

"Yes, all afternoon. They always save up the worst cases for me. I wouldn't go if I could help it."

"It's part of your course, isn't it? You have to do it?"

"Rather! Can't get out of it. I say! Give me a dance at the party next week, will you?"

"I'd love to. Are you doing 'Newcastle' with anybody?"

"Haven't booked anything yet. Right-o! We'll have that. Thanks awfully! What are you going to do with me at the party, Morgan?"

"Morgan" turned and laughed. "Anything you like, old sport. You choose!"

"Let's 'Whim' together—swim together—I mean! Shall we?"

"Wish we could! I'm dying of heat. All right! I'll put you down for that."

"Are you going to the Easter School, Russell?" asked another, fanning herself vigorously with her big handkerchiefs and lying back exhausted in a chair.

"No, I'm saving up for Cheltenham. Can't manage both!"

"Oh, I can't stand Cheltenham! Too hot! I'm going at Easter instead!"

Then they were called to make four lines for a 'Bledington' jig, to show what progress the difficult step had made, and all sprang eagerly to their places, heat, exhaustion, everything forgotten.

Jen in her corner had been unnoticed. They were all absorbed in the enjoyment of the moment. She watched the teaching of "Lumps of Plum Pudding" with deep interest, her eyes going continually from the class to the teacher, as she gave little demonstrations of the various movements, and particularly of the side-step.

"She's interesting, isn't she?" and at the end of the dance some one sat down rather breathlessly beside Jen; she had been watching her absorbed face, and now spoke sympathetically.

"Awfully!" Jen turned quickly. "Oh, weren't you at Cheltenham?"

"Yes. I knew you by sight. I'm afraid I'm bad at names. I was in Room C with you the first week, and moved on with you and all your crowd to Naunton Park. After that we were in different classes."

"Oh, then you know Madam and the Pixie!" Jen said joyfully. "Aren't you the one Cicely calls the Writing Person? Don't you write girls' books?"

"Well, I do. And I do know Madam and the Pixie. Are you quite well again?"

"Everybody knows all about me!" Jen said, in a tone of mournful satisfaction. "Quite, thanks. Isn't it thrilling?—writing books, I mean?"

"It's very interesting!" the Writing Person said sedately. "So are people! I was frightfully interested in all your crowd at Cheltenham! Then your accident happened, and I didn't like to go round bothering your friends, to know how you were getting on; but I wanted to know very badly. Of course, I asked as soon as the autumn classes began, and was told you'd gone home and they thought you'd be all right in time. You look quite all right again!"

"Oh, I am! I could do morris jigs, if I happened to know them! But the less said about my kick-jumps the better, and I'm quite aware of it. I have tried them, but that's all."

"Oh, they're brutes! But you can't have 'Bledington' without them, and 'Bledington' as a whole is too good to live without, so the kick-jumps have to be thrown in somehow."

"You're frightfully keen on the dances, aren't you?" Jen asked, with interest.

"I'm frightfully interested! When I get introduced to a new tradition, and find out all its weird points, and just where it's peculiar, I feel as if I'd unearthed a hidden treasure, or come into a fortune. I want to go and thank the person who gave it me; but, of course, you can't."

"Why not? I don't see why. I should think she'd be pleased."

"*I* can't! I should think she'd think I was a lunatic! But it's how I feel, all the same; as if I'd been given an unexpected present.

Last term we did the 'Longborough' dances; they were all new to me, and I was a bit scared of them at first, but it's gorgeous to feel I understand them at last! I could hardly restrain myself when I found we were really going to do 'Princess Royal' to that wonderful tune. I wanted to get up and cheer."

Jen laughed. "Well, why didn't you? Oh, is that the tune that sounds like 'Princess Royal' gone drunk?"

"The first time you hear it, yes. But it grows on you tremendously. Are you thinking of the lecture at Cheltenham last summer, when the Director played it to us?"

"Yes! And the whole room laughed; it was so weird, after the one we know so well. It's one of the funny modal things, isn't it?"

"It's Dorian. I love it! When we were beginning to learn it, and were standing listening to 'Once to Yourself,' somebody in the class gasped 'Oh!' when the first E natural came out; and you can believe the rest of us laughed! But I felt like a millionaire when I went home that night and played it, knowing the steps that fitted the music. I'd never dreamt of such luck!"

"And you didn't go and tell her how glad you were?"

"How could I? Of course I didn't. But I really was awfully grateful. Now she's going to make us have another go at 'Lumps.' Won't you come and try it?"

Jen shook her head and laughed. "No, thanks! I know *all* about how bad my R.T.B.'s are! I'll watch you instead."

"I'd very strongly advise you to watch some one else! I only play at it, I'm afraid," and the Writing Person went to take her place.

"I'm glad I stayed to watch," Jen said, at the end. "It's better fun than dancing."

"It's as good, anyway. And not half so hot!" her new friend conceded, sitting down again rather breathlessly. "No, I will *not* practise kick-jumps, or anything else! I know mine are very funny, but I'm half-dead!"—this only for Jen's benefit, however, as the class were advised to work at their weak points, and the more energetic proceeded to do so.

"She'll be at you in a minute," Jen laughed.

"No, she won't plague me; she's been awfully nice to me. She doesn't worry me to do things I can't. Oh, time's up! No more morris! What a blow! I'm always sorry when it's over for another whole week."

"Do you come every Friday?" Jen asked with interest.

"I wouldn't miss a Friday for any money!" the Writing Person said fervently. "My work would simply stop. I couldn't carry on without Fridays to buck me up to it."

"Oh, do you find it helps?"

"It's the only thing that keeps me going, sometimes. I always get a fresh start after Fridays."

"How funny! Oh, here she comes! She must be after you. What have you been doing?"

"'Headington' circles in a 'Bledington' dance, probably. Or something equally childish and infantile. If there is an awkward way to do a movement, I'm sure to find it; and if there is an elementary mistake to be made, I make it."

"How did you get through the exam?" Jen laughed.

"I never took it. I knew better. I just moved myself up. Madam said I might," and the Writing Person awaited the comments with expectant eyes.

It was Jen who was wanted, however. "Come along, Miss Robins! You've embraced that radiator long enough. Haven't you the courage to join in 'Chelsea Reach'?"

"May I? I'd simply love it!" and Jen laughed and sprang up, throwing off her coat.

"I was beginning to wonder what you had your tunic on for!"

and stepping on to the platform she announced the dance. "It would be *very* nice if we could have the second figure right the first time of trying!" she added pensively, and several laughed in anticipation of the muddle to come.

"I danced the whole hour of Country!" Jen informed the rest, as they sat down starving to supper. "They do have topping teachers! And they're doing wonderful new dances in that grade. We had a gorgeous thing called 'Spring Garden'; I'd never even heard of it, but wasn't it appropriate for March? I danced a lot with that Writing Person; she asked me to be her 'man,' as her regular partner wasn't there. The partner's father has been very ill, and she's afraid he may be worse, or they may have gone to see him at the hospital. So I danced with her several times."

"We had the usual kind of jolly old time you always do have when Madam's in charge, and all enjoyed ourselves no end," said Joy. "I don't know how she does it, but she does make you love it! I think it's because you can see she's having such a good time herself. She's frightfully infectious, of course."

"Sounds nasty," Jack remarked. "She's tremendously alive, anyway."

"*I* had a perfectly gorgeous evening!" Jen said loftily.

CHAPTER X

THE HEIRESS IN THE PULPIT

"Now we've got to face our problems!" said Joy, as they sped westwards next morning. "It's been a jolly little holiday, and I feel heaps fitter and fresher, and more able to deal with school kids and heiresses! But it can't be put off any longer. You're very quiet, Jenny-Wren! What's the matter? Did you dance too much last night? Too much 'Spring Garden'?"

"No, but I'm having a big think about last night. I'll tell you later, Wild Cat," and Jen sat in absorbed thought as Eirene left the Uxbridge rivers and bridges behind, and sped towards the commons and wide roads of Beaconsfield.

At the gates of the big day-school in Wycombe, Joy paused to leave a note, written the night before, assuring her old head mistress she would be delighted to welcome Rosamund as soon as convenient. "May as well do the thing handsomely, since it's got to be done! I wonder what kind of kid she is!" she said, as she handed in the note and came back to Jen and Eirene.

"You aren't going in?"

"Don't see any need to. I hardly know a soul here now, except Babs Honor. No, I want to get home, and square things with Ann and Maidlin. If the infant really doesn't want to come, we may have a breezy time, considering the Italian temper!"

"Perhaps she'll have run away again!"

"Not if she only did it because she didn't want to come to the Hall!" Joy said swiftly. "I thought of that. But I told Ann definitely I couldn't think of having her; so if that's the trouble, the kid's mind will have been easy about it. She'll be waiting for me to find her a nice family to board with."

"As if there could be a nicer family than you and me! I do wonder whether she really wants to come or not!" Jen pondered. "It's obvious she didn't want to be shoved at you, but then nobody would. I'd like to know how she really feels."

"So would I. But I don't suppose we ever shall."

As soon as lunch was over, and Joy had changed from her leather suit to more usual costume—a pretty brown house-frock, to be correct—she slipped on her coat and went bareheaded through the garden to the abbey, to have her talk with Ann. Although it was Saturday afternoon, there were no tourists in the abbey, the bitter March wind being distinctly discouraging for country rambles.

"It was just exactly this kind of day that Cicely and the Rambling Club first came to the abbey, and made friends with Joan, six years ago," she said to herself. "I was out tramping through the woods, being 'Wild Cat that Walked by his Wild Lone,' and leaving Joan and aunty to do all the work—as usual! I was a little slacker! Fancy if any one had told us then all the things that were going to happen in this old abbey! And Joan and Cicely are both married! I can't quite get used to the idea, even now!"

She found the caretaker sitting over the fire in her little front room, the room in which Joan had entertained the schoolgirls and told Cicely her ambitions, and where Miriam had sung during the storm, on that long-past day. Maidlin was nowhere to be seen.

"Oh, Ann!" Joy plunged into business at once. "I just blew in—literally! I was blown right across the garth!—to say I think it will be best if your Maidlin comes to us, after all. I'd like to have her for a little while, anyway, and see what I can do for her. If I find I'm not making a good job of it, I'll find some better place. But at present it seems simpler for her just to come to us.

Jen is staying for a while, and there's a girl coming up from school every day, so we shall be quite a jolly little party. It will keep me from being lonely!"

Ann had risen, and was clasping her hands in nervous excitement. "Oh, Miss Joy? Do you mean it, really? I'd rather the child went to you than to anybody in the whole world! And—and to live at the Hall! She can't help but turn out good, living there! And with you, Miss Joy!" and then, in her delight and relief, she broke down and cried.

"Oh, Ann, dear, don't be an idiot!" Joy said brusquely. "There are thousands of better places for her, and I'm a very bad person to look after her. But I do happen to be on the spot. She'd better come to us, and then you can see her all the time and be sure she's all right. Where is she? Will she be willing to come, by the way?"

"She's in the abbey, Miss Joy. She's there whenever she can slip away from me. She don't do no harm, ever."

"I'll find her and have a talk with her. I oughtn't to have asked you if she'd come. Of course she'll come!—when I've talked to her! Now, Ann, since she's out, we'll talk business for a few minutes! What about money? She'll want clothes and things. Shall I advance it, till her father comes home?"

"There's the gentleman in London, Miss Joy. 'Twere in the letter, that he'd give us all the money we needed for her."

"I remember; a lawyer. Give me the address, and I'll write to him and explain the arrangements we're making. I think I'll take Maidlin up to see him, and to do some shopping. I shan't send her to school at present," Joy spoke as if she had suddenly become the mother of a schoolgirl daughter, which indeed was how she felt. "I don't suppose she's ready for the tip-top kind of school she'll have to go to. I think it will be better for her just to come and live with us, and get into our ways, and go about with Jen and me for a while. I'll take her up to town a few times, and begin giving her new ideas. When she seems ready for school, we'll think about it, if her father hasn't come home by that time. Now I'll go and find her. Do you know at all where she'll be?"

"She—she climbs up to the pulpit, Miss Joy," Ann faltered. "I've told her she didn't ought to, but she don't do no harm, so she says."

"She fell out of it, almost on to my head, two days ago," Joy laughed. "No!" she said to herself, as she crossed the garth and climbed the dark refectory stairs, "poor dear Ann isn't quite the proper guardian to bring up an heiress! I doubt if I am, either; but at least I shan't teach her to say she 'didn't ought to'! Now I must be *very* tactful and gentle! Why isn't Joan here? She was the tactful, gentle one! I *never* was!" resentfully.

Deliberately, she climbed up the little steps to the reader's pulpit, and confronted the defiant eyes of the small girl curled up there with a book. "Is there room for two? Will you let me in? Have you decided this is the nicest spot in the whole abbey?"

Maidlin's eyes fell before hers, in confused remembrance of that last meeting out in the road. "The refectory's the best, and you can see it all from here. People don't see me when they come with aunty. They only look at the books and jewels in the cases."

"Have you been along the secret passage to the Hall? But I suppose not. Ann would only show you the beginning of it."

"She wouldn't let me go. She said the door at the other end was shut. And I hadn't a torch."

"Or you'd have gone without her? But it has to be kept shut, you know. We can't have people wandering about inside our walls while we're living there. But I can open it with my key. Would you like to go? Suppose you come back through the tunnel, and have tea with me? You're going to live with me, aren't you?"

"No!" burst explosively from Maidlin, and she sprang up, ready for another wild flight.

But Joy barred her way. "If you push past me, I shall fall off the steps and break my neck, or sprain my ankle! That would be rather an unkind way of refusing an invitation; don't you think so? Why don't you want to come? The house seems so empty without Joan; and Jen isn't going to stay with me very long. Make room for me up there, and we'll talk about it. Why don't you want to come? The house is really rather nice, and I don't think I'm so very awful. Nobody ever told me I was! I'm asking you to come. Now what's the row, kid?" and Joy sat on the top step, since she was really too big for the small amount of space Maidlin would spare for her.

The child's head was bent, her long black hair hiding her face. Her shoulders shook. "Aunty asked you to ask me! You had to do it! I don't know how she could! You feel you've got to have me! It—it isn't fair!"

For a moment Joy longed wildly for Joan. Then she pulled herself together, and spoke seriously, though very gently. "It's difficult to know what to say! I'm afraid I'm not very clever. Maidlin, your aunt has made it hard for both of us. It's difficult for me to make you believe I'm in earnest. She did ask me, of course, and she did it without giving me time to ask you on my own account. I said I'd rather not, because I didn't feel good enough. Perhaps," unkindly, "that's how you feel, too? Of course, if that's so—"

"Oh!" It was jerked out of Maidlin by her indignant surprise. "I'd *love* to come!" she panted. "It's only—only—"

Joy's eyes gleamed. But she only said quietly, "I thought you hated the very idea, and I supposed perhaps I wasn't good enough, for some reason. Look here, kiddy!" and at a restless, impatient movement of distress from the child, she caught both the excited little hands and held them firmly, "don't let's have any more nonsense about it! I've thought it over, and I really want you to come. I can only ask you to take my word for it. I'm not the best kind of guardian you could have, but perhaps I'll do for a time, just to go on with. But I am used to having people like me. Somehow they always have done; I can't tell you why. It's very mysterious, of course; but there it is. It hurts me when you shy, and say you won't come, when I've asked you. If you can't bear the sight of me, say so straight out. I don't want to make you miserable. But if it's only Ann's asking me that's worrying you, then let's wash it all out!—*bother!* I mean, let's forget all about that, and her, and go ahead and please ourselves. I'm frightfully interested in what's happened to you. It's so exactly what I fell into when I was about your age. I'd simply love to help you to pull through, for, of course, you need help. You know that as well as I do. *I* needed help, and I had it. Now if you'll let me, I'd like to help you. I'll enjoy doing it. Can't we call it square, and leave it at that? Cut out all the rest, and never worry about it again. I'll do the best I can for you; but *don't* go and make me feel I'm not good enough! Unless you really think so, of course. I'd rather know the worst."

Maidlin was shaking with passionate sobbing. "I'd rather have you than anybody in the world! But—but I thought you didn't— you couldn't really—"

"I guess that's good enough!" Joy said quietly. "Now, kiddy, listen to me just for a minute! You're going to begin a new kind of life, right now. There are heaps of things you'll have to forget. I'm not telling you to forget your aunts. They've been awfully good to you, and taken your mother's place. You'll never forget that, and you'll always love them. Your father will want you to. But there are things they've taught you that you may have to forget. You're old enough to understand that. Everything will be so different now. And this that your Aunty Ann did, when she asked me to have you, is one of those things; a thing you'd never

THE NEW ABBEY GIRLS

have done yourself, and that made you mad. Let that be the first thing you forget. Never think about it again! Most of all, don't let it worry you. We'll put it away; and there will be other things. You'll go on being as fond of her as ever; it makes no difference to that. And your mother-aunty in Cumberland must come here to see you as soon as she's well enough; or if she can't, you must go to her. Now we're going to start afresh. Is it all settled?"

Maidlin looked at her dumbly, with bewildered, half-frightened eyes. "I—Miss Joy—I don't know—"

"That's the next thing you're going to forget, of course!" Joy said briskly. "You'd better start at once; there's nothing like taking a plunge and getting it over! You're coming to live with me, and we're going to be friends. After all, I'm only seven years older than you! But I suppose to you I feel like a middle-aged aunt!" mournfully. "Well, never mind; that won't last long! You'll soon lose all respect for me, every atom you've ever had, if you come to live at the Hall! Wait till you see the way Jen and I go on sometimes! You'll get a fearful shock; we're perfect infants. Now, never let me hear you say *Miss* Joy again! It will hurt my feelings dreadfully. If we quarrel, you may say it, but not till then, unless you're trying to have a fight with me. See? Now, say, 'Yes, Joy dear, I quite understand!' like a good kid."

Maidlin looked at her, growing red, then white. Then a spark lit in her dark eyes. "I quite understand, *Joy dear*! But I—I think it would be rather fun to have a fight with you! Are you—are you nice when you fight?" rather breathlessly.

"I'm perfectly dreadful," Joy assured her solemnly. "But I'll pillow-fight you to-night, if you like. I say, kid, shall I tell you a secret?" and she scrambled on to Maidlin's ledge, feeling that their relations had now reached a stage when such close quarters were possible. "Yes, there's just room; I'm hanging on by my teeth. *Don't think I'm grown up;* that's all! Because I'm not. Of course, I pretend to be. Your aunt thinks I am; and my aunt thinks I am! But Jen knows better; and I'm letting you into the secret, too. I'm a perfect kid, nine-tenths of the time; I may as well confess, for you'd find it out before bed-time. Are you shocked?" as Maidlin chuckled happily. "Now come away home through the secret passage. Aunty and Jen are expecting us to tea. I want to tell you all my plans for you; some of them are quite thrilling! I've been thinking about you all the way home from town this morning. Don't you want to hear all about it? Oh, are you shy?"

"I won't know—what to say," Maidlin hung back.

"How funny it must feel to be shy, and funnier still not to know what to say!" Joy said reflectively. "I've never felt troubled in either way myself. I try to make people think I'm shy, but they never seem to believe it. Now, Maidlin, my child, it may feel funny, but you'll find it very inconvenient, so the sooner you get out of it the better. You'll have to meet heaps of people; friends of your father's, and so on; and you won't want him to think you're awkward—"

"I'm not shy!" Maidlin protested vehemently. "But I don't know the proper things to say!"

"If that's all, you can easily pick them up. Come along to tea, and don't say a thing more than you want to, except when you're asked a question. Most of all, don't ever say things you don't mean. Just come and have tea with us, and listen! I believe I talk quite a lot; I'm always being told so! I know Jen and I yatter and babble for hours at a time, and all about nothing. You probably won't be able to get in a word when you want to. You don't think we're going to stop talking because you're there, do you? No, of course not. Come on, and see if you think we're a very funny pair! I'll get a torch from Ann, and we'll go by the tunnel. You'd like to see it, wouldn't you?"

"A torch, please, Ann! Maidlin's coming to tea with me. You

might bring her nighty along after you've locked up. If she finds she can't stand us, of course she'll come back to you. I don't intend to kidnap her. But she's going to give us a trial. Thanks! Come on, kid!" and Joy returned to Maidlin, who had hung behind in the cloisters, leaving Ann breathless but delighted.

"Race me to the old door!" Joy commanded, and broke into a run and a laugh together, at thought of their flight with Madam across the garth and through the back window of the chapter-house. "Now go carefully down the steps! Don't fall over the edge! And now follow me. This is my private Underground Railway! All stations to Mansion House! Change for West Ham and Barking! First turning on the right for Abinger Hall and tea!"

CHAPTER XI

JEN'S "THINK"

"THIS," said Joy indignantly, "was *not* a part of the entertainment I had planned for you, Madalena! But I'll own I've always known it would happen some day. The beastly thing's bolted on the inside, and we're stuck."

They were still in the secret tunnel, but had climbed the steps and made their way along the passage which ran inside the wall of the big entrance-hall of the house, the door at the top of the inner stair having yielded at once to Joy's key. The panel-door was less obliging, however. She had unlocked it with the key which hung on a ring with the key of the abbey gate; but to her dismay the door still would not open. She pushed and shook, then gave it up.

"Thank goodness, we didn't try to bring Madam this way! How she'd have shrieked at me! She'd have 'nearly died,' as she says, if I'd found myself bolted out of my own house!" she muttered. "Just yell 'Help!' when I do, kid! We've got to make somebody hear us. Jen has evidently gone upstairs. Pity we had all the holes in the panelling blocked up! Are you laughing at me? Well, I don't blame you, really!"

Maidlin, grasping the fact that they could be released, and would not have to go all the way back to the abbey, was on the verge of a giggling fit. It had been an exciting afternoon for her; she had been forced, she hardly knew how, into doing the thing she had said she would never do; and not only that, but she had been forced into wanting to do it. This calamity to her conqueror was such an anti-climax; she did not know the word, but she knew she felt ready to giggle.

Joy knew it too. "You can laugh as much as you like, once we're inside. But just now it's your duty to yell, my dear kid!"

Maidlin got to business promptly, and they both shouted and hammered on the door to such good purpose that presently it was thrown open, and Jen stood eyeing them severely.

"Not at home to-day! By the other entrance, please! No hawkers, canvassers, or circulars allowed! Oh, Wild Cat, what a lunatic you are! You bolted it yourself! You know you did, because of the wedding presents!"

"I know. I haven't a word to say. I forgot," Joy said limply.

"When you remember anything, it will be more worth mentioning!" Jen said crushingly. "Isn't she awful, Maidlin? You'll need some time to get used to her!"

"I've told her I'm not a fit and proper person to be a guardian to anybody! I say, Jen, isn't it just as well we didn't bring The Duchess home that way?"

"She'd have loved it," Jen said, with conviction. "You'd never have heard the end of that either! I bet she'd soon have made somebody hear *her*!"

"She'd have loved teasing me afterwards, anyway! Come and wash, Madalena! If you're as dirty as I am, after thumping on that door for ten minutes, you'll be glad to."

Maidlin was very quiet during the hour that followed, but her dark eyes were very busy, taking in everything—the beautiful staircases and bathrooms, the glimpses of big rooms as she passed, the long corridors, the pretty bedroom, next to Jen's, which had been prepared for her that afternoon by the interested maids. She was still quiet, but still very busy, during the homely tea in a corner of the big lounge hall, when, with Joy and Jen and Mrs. Shirley, she sat by the blazing fire on the big open hearth, and had a little black wooden table all to herself for her cup and plate; a funny arrangement, she thought, and much more trouble than setting one big table for everybody, but very jolly, since it made it possible for all to sit close to the fire. She answered Mrs. Shirley's kind remarks shyly, was very careful not to drop crumbs, and listened in breathless interest and surprise to the stream of chaff and chatter between Joy and Jen.

Every detail of the visit to town was rehearsed for Mrs. Shirley's benefit. Jen told, with a reminiscent shout, of the greeting to "Shirley" and the reference to "Hobart," and of the way most of the girl-students addressed one another by their surnames only. "I suppose it's always done at college, but I never went to college. It sounded so funny!"

"Oh, that happened at the Christmas School!" Joy explained. "We found they all did it, so we did it too."

They told of the Pixie and her artist's flat—"She's about so high, Maidlin. You shall see her some day soon. She says she's nearly five feet, but she looks about three and a half!"—of Madam and her sword class—"She's the one who came here and got buried in the crypt. She won't let me forget it either!" Of Jacky-boy's struggles with "rappers," and her delight in them now that she was used to them.

Then the tea tray was carried away, the tables disappeared, Mrs. Shirley went upstairs again, and the three girls drew the curtains, made up the fire, and sat in its light to talk.

"I've a gorgeous plan for next week!" said Joy. "Maidlin ought to go and see her lawyer—it's all right, infant! Don't look so scared! I'll do the talking. But he ought to see you do really exist—and she'd like to do some shopping. If she's game for all the things I think she ought to do, she'll need more clothes than she's needed so far." Joy had said she was not tactful, but she did not hint that better clothes might also be advisable. "You'll have to choose them yourself, Madalena! But Jen and I won't mind giving you a little elder-sisterly advice. We'll go up in Eirene on Thursday, do business all day, and run along to Jack's after tea. You know how she begged and prayed this morning that we'd come for the party, so that we could take her home! Jacky-boy is Jen's chum and other half; her adopted husband, Maidlin; and she lives in town, and we spent last night with her, and she loved having us. But her dad and mother have to go away for a few days next week, and she's just dying to have us to keep her company. She wanted to borrow Jen, and I might have had to let her go, if I hadn't had this plan for all the lot of us in my mind. We'll *all* go to the party, Jenny-Wren! Maidlin will love to see it. How's that?"

"Oh!" Jen gave a little shriek of joy. "I've been dying to go to one for years! Months, anyway! Ever since I heard about them! But it was too far to come. Oh, Joy, that's tophole! I'll get some good out of being a member at last. Tell me who'll be there? You went once with Cicely and Joan!"

"Everybody, my dear! Everybody who counts for anything at all will be there; Madam, and her man, and all that lot, and, of course, the Prophet and his Little Page. And we'll dance country-dances for two hours; and the Director will play for us himself. And you know that's worth living for!"

"I can't wait till Thursday!" Jen sighed happily. "It will be just like Cheltenham!"

"And on Friday we'll see. Perhaps we could take the Pixie out to lunch, or go to call on Madam. I'll do some ringing up, and see what everybody's plans are. We'll show Maidlin a little of London, and see how she likes Eirene."

"But I can't go seeing all your friends!" Maidlin faltered, aghast.

"Why not? You're lucky to have the chance. They're topping

sort of friends to have! They really are a very jolly crowd, and quite harmless," Joy said solemnly. "You'll like Jacky-boy; she's just a kid, anyway. As for the party, nobody will take any notice of you! They'll all be far too busy enjoying themselves. You'll just sit in a corner and watch. It's really rather pretty, with all the colours and all the evening frocks, even if you aren't keen on the dances themselves."

"I'd like that," Maidlin admitted.

"Of course you will! You'll love it. There's nothing to be scared of in any one I'll take you to see, kid. They're all folk-dancers; and that means they're ordinary jolly natural people, who love to have a good time and who don't swank or put on side, and who aren't any of them a scrap affected, or they couldn't do those dances! Jenny-Wren, isn't it so?"

Jen had been staring into the fire in absorbed silence, but woke with a start. "Rather! That's part of the big think I had in the car this morning."

"And now you're going to tell us all about it!" Joy commanded. "I want to know what kept you so quiet for such ages! Most unnatural, it was!"

"I was thinking about last night—the whole of it. The sleet, and the wind, and the wet, cold streets, and that dark tunnel entry; then all the jolly crowd of girls inside, forgetting all about the weather and their work and worries, and just giving themselves up to the old music and those wonderful dances. And it seemed to me that people like Madam, and the Pixie with her men and girls down at Plaistow, and others, I suppose, in other places, aren't doing such a very little thing at all. They aren't merely holding dancing classes, and helping teachers to get extra certificates. To heaps of those girls, who work really hard all day, in one way or another, those evening classes once a week must be something to live for, something they'll count up the days for, a kind of oasis in a desert. Think of being in an office, and adding up figures all day—"

"I can't! Can't think it, I mean. I should die!" Joy murmured. "But I see what you mean. Go on, Jenny-Wren!"

"Well, suppose you had to! Wouldn't you live for your morris and country classes at night, and nearly die when they were over for another week? Wouldn't you think about swords all the time you were adding up? Wouldn't you do dances in your head, as you walked along the streets to the office or went out to lunch?"

"And get run over at every crossing! I should do more than think them. I should hum and whistle till I was arrested as a lunatic, or till my boss had to get rid of me."

"Some of them are in offices. The Writing Person told me; she knows a lot of them. She says she's been in that class for a year now, and having got there, she means to stay for the rest of her life, as she can't get any higher without passing exams, and she seems quite sure she could never do that! So she's had time to get to know a lot of the girls. One lives near Oxford Circus— a tomboy-looking girl with bobbed curly hair, and a dinky little frock instead of a tunic; made it herself, too! Goes camping in a real proper tent in August, and comes to the Summer Schools for dancing; prefers it to any other kind of holiday, though she doesn't get very long. She *lives* near Oxford Circus, and works in an office all day, and simply has to fly to get to the Friday classes; I do think some girls are plucky! Has to do all the work of looking after her room, and dressmaking, and so on, after she gets home at night. Well, don't you think the dancing means a good lot to a girl like that? I suppose girls who don't know of folk-dancing go to the pictures, or to theatres, or walk about the streets, or belong to clubs; think how much better it is for her to come and do morris and sword and country, and enjoy the music, and meet a jolly lot of friends, week after week!"

Jen paused for breath. Maidlin was listening in rapt interest, her wide eyes showing how new such talk was to her.

Joy said urgently, "Go on! No wonder you were wrapped in silence all morning! And don't forget to tell me your tomboy's name. She's the kind who could easily come out here for a weekend. But how did you find out so much about the girls, all in one evening? Oh, was it that Writing Person?"

"I asked her about them, in between dances. She calls the tomboy Topsy; I'm sure she'd love to come, and you'd like her too. Most of the girls are teachers, and want their certificates because they could get better posts if they had them. Well, fancy if you'd taught a class of sixty small infants every day for a week! Think how you'd feel by Friday night!"

"I can't!" Joy said again. "I'd be dead!"

"Some of them love it, of course, and feel it's the only work in the world worth doing. I don't see how anybody can be a teacher unless she does feel like that. It must be fearful if you don't. But even if you love it, you must get very tired. When they're just about done in, at the end of the week, they come along and do 'William and Nancy,' and 'London Pride,' and 'Queen's Delight,' and 'Haste to the Wedding,' and 'Beaux of London City'; and they're bullied themselves, instead of having to worry about bullying their infants; and don't you think it's a *rest*? Even if it nearly kills them with hard work, it's a rest! The Writing Person says they once did nine country dances in an hour, and she could hardly lie still in bed after it, because she was so sore! But her work went beautifully next day. She's another argument; she doesn't teach or do office work; she says either would kill her in a week. But she's writing all the time, and she says it's fearfully hard not to get stale, and I can quite believe it. And nothing she's ever found yet helps her to keep fresh so well as folk-dancing does. She says time after time she's worked all day, till she felt just empty, like a balloon without any air in it—writing, or typing, or correcting proofs; and then, when she's felt only ready for bed, but really too fagged to sleep, she's made herself go to dancing instead, and done an hour or two; and she's gone home far less tired than she went out. Then she's slept well, and done stacks of work next day. She always works best the day after classes. Isn't it funny?"

"I expect it stirs her all up, and so she gets new ideas," Joy said shrewdly. "Cicely always said anything to do with folk-dancing stirred her all up. And the music would help, I should think, and meeting people, if she's so much interested in them."

"She says it all helps, every bit of it. She loves every tune in any of the books, and if she wasn't allowed to dance, she says she'd go just the same, to look on, and to watch the teaching; for teaching like that is worth watching any day; I've always thought so, and she said so too! Well, Madam and all those people are helping her, just as they help the teachers and the office people! I think they're doing a big thing for girls who have to work, by giving them folk-dancing in the evenings, to keep them fresh and help them to carry on. And there are classes almost every night. If I were a business girl living in town, I'd go to them all, and have dancing every night of the week! I shall, too, if we have to live in town for a while. That's what my 'think' was, Joy; what a big thing those London classes are for London girls! Is there one before the party on Thursday? For if so, I'm going to watch, or to join in, if they'll let me!"

"Sword, morris, and country! We'll take Maidlin; she'll love it. I wonder who'll be teaching, though?"

"You can't have Madam all the time!" Jen laughed. "I don't mind who's teaching! Play us something, Joy! Maidlin ought to hear your piano."

"What do you want?" Joy went to open her treasure.

"Something of your own. Something about the woods in spring, or weddings, or dances; whatever's in your head at the moment! I heard you trying over something after lunch. Had you got a new idea?"

"'Tisn't nearly ready yet; it's only scrappy," but Joy began to play wandering chords, and then drifted into a swaying melody.

Maidlin, sitting on a stool by the hearth, watched her with spellbound eyes. The hall was dark, but for the firelight; she could only dimly see Joy, who needed no light for this kind of music.

Jen, leaning on the piano, listened critically. "There's dancing in that," she said, as Joy paused. "But not indoors; it's windy. It's not last night's classes, is it, Joy?" She was used to being challenged to say what she could hear in the scraps of music Joy produced continually.

Joy shook her head, and played the notes again. "There'll be more of it. You've asked for it too soon. It's what I said to the Pixie; I saw it as I spoke; the daffodils dancing in the orchard under bare apple trees, millions of little yellow faces, all with golden trumpets."

"I can hear the trumpets, now you've told me! Don't let it get too sentimental, though, Joy! Keep it brisk and March-windy! Daffodils always buck me up, like a tonic after the winter!"

Joy laughed, and wandered into another of her dreams, and from that to another, with now and then a glance at Maidlin's enthralled face in the firelight glow. Presently, however, she broke into a swinging chanty tune, and Maidlin jumped with surprise as Jen, laughing joyfully, took up the words,—

"I think I heard the old man say,
   O you Rio!
  I think I heard the old man say,
    We're bound for Rio Grande!"

"Oh, Joy! Cheltenham! Doesn't it bring it all back—just that tune? The Prophet looking so happy at the piano, and 'Joshua' singing the solo, and the Pixie sitting in the head master's throne in her little black tunic—she always does, you know—and all the lot of us in our gymmies, singing the chorus for all we're worth! Cicely, and Joan, and Newcastle, and Tazy, and Karen, and the Torment, and Madam, and everybody! Play another! See if they'll all do it. Play 'Shanadar'! But it almost makes me ill with longing for next August! It's such ages to wait! Just a minute, while I give Maidlin the book! You must learn them too, Madalena, and we'll have choruses!"

And while Maidlin listened in growing surprise and delight, Joy played on and on, and her voice and Jen's rang out and filled the room, in ballad, and carol, and chanty, but most of all in folk-songs of the countryside, songs from Somerset, from Gloucestershire, from Dorset, from the Midlands; all learned the summer before under the leadership of their "Prophet."

"She's fond of music!" Joy murmured once, as she turned the pages. "She's sure to have inherited a voice along with the fortune and the temper and the name! Goes with the black hair and eyes! We'll coax it out one of these days. She's probably shy; she would be with us, anyway. But she likes music, and that's a big thing."

"She'll love Thursday evening in town!" Jen said, with conviction.

CHAPTER XII

MAIDLIN, in a prettier bedroom than she had ever dreamed of, sat up in bed and listened to the laughter and chattering from the next room. Joy and Jen, declaring themselves tired out with the dancing of the night before, and the two days of motoring, following immediately on all the excitements of Joan's wedding, had gone to bed early, as soon, indeed, as they had seen their guest safely in her room. But "going to bed" did not mean settling down for the night, in Joy's house, it appeared. Maidlin had heard light footsteps pass her door, and now judged from the sounds she heard that Joy was sitting on Jen's bed, and that they were apparently talking over all their previous lives. She listened wistfully, and felt lonely.

It was nearly an hour before she heard Jen's door open and close again, very softly; and then her own was opened, almost without a sound, and Joy, in her dressing-gown and long heavy plait, crept up to see if she were asleep.

"Why, kiddy!" she whispered. "What's the matter? You aren't nervy or homesick, are you? Were we keeping you awake? I am sorry! We tried to whisper, but I'm afraid we kept forgetting. We always pow-wow at bedtime. Is there anything you'd like?"

Maidlin, shrouded in her black veil, had been sitting up waiting, but had crouched suddenly at her approach, her face hidden in her pillow. "I wanted you," the words were stifled. "I was waiting till you went back. I wanted to tell you something.

141

I don't feel honest. You don't understand. But I couldn't say it while anybody was there."

Once more Joy had that wild desire for Joan, that sense of unfitness for a crisis. "What's the row, kid?" she asked gently, sitting on the bed.

"You thought I didn't want to come!" Maidlin panted. "I was *dying* to come, all the time! I'd heard about you; aunty told me all the stories; and I'd watched for you in the abbey. And—and— you seemed somebody so wonderful, and—and beautiful, and— and nice; and so jolly and kind; and I loved to hear you laugh and talk with—with Jen!" with a little gasp; it was still a difficult lesson to learn. "I was watching you on the garth in the morning, before that lady came. I'd seen you dance there; and I'd heard you sing. I'd been looking at you as if you were a princess, or a fairy person, and—and miles away from me. It was enough just to look at you. I'd have done anything for you, but there wasn't anything I could do. You'd got everything. And then aunty said she'd *ask* you to have me, *ask* you to take me to *live* with you, in your beautiful house; and I knew you'd feel it was awful cheek, and you couldn't help hating me; and—and I nearly died. I nearly went mad, with thinking how awful it was. I didn't know what to do. I thought I'd run away, but you caught me. I hoped you'd say no; I thought if you said you'd have me, because you felt you'd got to, or because you were too kind to say no, it would be just too awful for words. I knew you couldn't *want* to have me. Then aunty said you couldn't think of it, but you'd find a nice place for me to go, and I felt better, though I knew I'd feel just sick when I had to go away and not see you any more. But even that was better than being shoved on to you when you didn't want me. It nearly killed me to know aunty had asked you; I'd rather have died! I felt better when you said no. And then you came suddenly, when I couldn't get away, and somehow you made me believe it was all right, and I could come, and you wouldn't mind having me. And the whole world seemed too wonderful to be true. But—but you know how it is at night! I thought it must be all a mistake. And I thought I'd tell you how I'd felt, and how I'd wanted to come more than anything I could think of. And—and I thought I'd ask you to send me home again. For you can't want me, really."

Joy's arms had been round her long ago. A queer thrill went through her as she felt the quivering little body, the shoulders shaken with breathless sobbing. Unconscious of it at the time, she knew afterwards that she had grown in that moment, that something new had been stirred in her for the first time. If responsibility had been wakened in her on the day when she believed Jen lay dying through her carelessness, the mother-instinct to protect and help woke when Maidlin lay sobbing in her arms. All her life Joy had been mothered, though motherless herself; Joan and her aunt had filled her mother's place so thoroughly that she had never missed her. But she had never felt the instinct to give as she had received; Maidlin's need called it out for the first time.

But it was very difficult to know what to say. Some might have been satisfied to say nothing, to cry a little in sympathy, and let kisses and a reassuring hug tell their own story. But Joy could hardly be content so. She was very practical; things were better properly settled!

"And is that all, kiddy?" she asked presently, holding the girl closely to her.

Maidlin quivered again. "What more can there be? You *can't* want me really!"

"I think there's something else, and you're fighting against it, because you won't quite let yourself believe it. If there isn't, I'm sorry, and I'll be a bit disappointed; for it will mean I haven't done everything I should. But you'll have to forgive me; I told you I wasn't clever. But is there anything else, Madalena? You've said a lot; but have you said it all?"

"To-night!" Maidlin whispered, gaining courage, "you were so jolly, and the other one too, as if you really did mean it. You— you made me feel as if I'd come home and you were glad to have me. But it couldn't be true!"

"Right-o!" Joy said happily. "Then all's well. If you've only got a fit of the nerves because it's nearly midnight, then I needn't worry! I thought for a few minutes I'd made you feel I didn't want you; and I was going to feel really *bad*! Silly!" her voice was caressing, in spite of its reproof. "Things are bound to feel queer the first night. That's why I came to see if you were all right. You might remember that I did care enough to come, next time you begin to get doubtful of me, will you? I thought I was going to be your guardian and big sister for a little while, but it seems to me it's more a mother you need! Silly kid, lying imagining things in the dark! I shall say things, dreadful things, to you if you do it again! Now tell me just once more! *Did* you feel at home to-night?"

"Yes! Oh, yes, I did! But it seemed too impossible!"

"Nothing nice is ever impossible!" Joy said largely. "You've only got to believe in it, and you'll find it's possible enough. Now have I disposed of that bogey for you? It was only a nightmare, silly kid! As for the rest, all that you started with—it was awfully nice of you to tell me. I'm fearfully bucked to know you felt like that. Of course it's all rot, and I'm not what you think. I'm not half good enough. But it was fearfully nice of you to think it, and I just hope you won't get disillusioned too soon! It was jolly honest of you to tell me, too. I'm glad you felt you'd rather start square. I want to know how you feel about things. The more of that sort of thing you'll tell me, the better

I'll be pleased. Now I just want you to remember that we're chums, and if you've any worries you're to come straight to me with them. I may not know how to help, but I'll do the best I can, and we'll see you through somehow. Now are you going to sleep, like a good kiddy, without worrying about anything more at all?"

"There isn't anything left to worry about," Maidlin whispered fervently. "I didn't know even you could be so kind!"

Joy laughed, but gently, and kissed her and laid her down. "Poor kid! You have had a day of it. Now do go to sleep, or I shall be worried about you in earnest."

She resisted the temptation to go and tell Jen all about it, and went to her own room. But Maidlin's outburst had roused so many new thoughts that now it was Joy who could not sleep; and half an hour later she crept into her ward's room to see if all were well, that new mother-instinct strong within her.

Maidlin was sleeping quietly, and Joy crept back to bed. "Poor infant!" she said pitifully. "It's been fearfully rough on her. I could kick that silly old Ann for making things so hard for us all! Why couldn't she have the sense to come to me and say nothing to the kid? But she has no more idea of decent behaviour than a bedpost! Maidlin has, though; she feels things, and inside her she knows what's what. I'm jolly glad of it. I'd rather have a scene now and then than have her like Ann, just a block! There's far more hope of making something of her. It's all there; it only needs bringing out—training. But—help! I'm not good enough to do it! Doesn't it make you feel your own shortcomings, having somebody look up to you like that! I wish I could be different!" and she sighed, with a real one-o'clock-in-the-morning despondency.

Things looked better in the Sunday sunshine, however. Before breakfast, in the bare apple orchard Joy found Jen

145

gathering wild daffodils for the house, well wrapped up in furs, but revelling in the sun which tempered the keen wind. The Hall and the abbey, lying at the foot of the hills, were sheltered from east winds, and as soon as the sun shone spring came back.

"Where's Maidlin? Haven't you brought her out? Isn't it just great, this morning? I knew, the moment I woke, that I'd got to pick daffodils!" Jen's voice rang out in greeting. "Joy, will you give me about a hundred to-morrow?"

"A thousand, Jenny-Wren! What for?"

"To pack in a box and send to the Pixie for her East End men and girls. Don't you think she'd be pleased?"

"She'll love it. But she'll give them all away. She always does. She shares everything."

"I know. That's why I want to send them; to give her something to give away. Where's Maidlin?"

"Maidlin's sleeping the sleep of the very-much-tired-out-infant. I peeped in to see. I knew you'd be out, as soon as I saw the sun; it always wakes me. I was going to bring her along. We mustn't leave her out of a single thing! But she was dead asleep. So I told them not to wake her, even for brekker. You see, Jenny-Wren, we had a bit of a pow-wow last night, after I'd said good-night to you," Joy said soberly.

"Oh?" Jen looked up quickly from her golden sheaf. "What, with Maidlin? At that time of night? *Joy!*"

"I know. Wasn't it awful? But the kid was sitting up waiting for me. She had to get it off her chest. I want to tell you about it," and as they went towards the house, Joy repeated the conversation, her face very serious.

"How nice of her!" was Jen's only comment, but she looked sober too. "I say, Joy, it's a big responsibility, to have a kiddy who feels things so deeply!"

"I know. I've been thinking a lot about her. I'm rather scared. But I'm glad too. It makes her so much more worth while."

"Yes," Jen gave her a quick, relieved look. "I'm glad you feel that way. She's got a lot in her. How are you going to start, 'Traveller's Joy'?"

"I want to talk it over with Aunty Pixie again! I feel as if we'd moved on several steps since we saw her. But, so far as I've gone all by myself, I've come to this—just to let Maidlin live with us and be one of the family and get used to our ways. In time, of course, she'll have to go to school, but her father may come home and arrange that. What she needs first of all seems to be to get used to living in quite a different way from anything she's ever known, so that she won't be frightened and awkward and shy. If you watch, you'll see how scared she feels just now, because it's all so strange. That will soon go off; she's only an infant; she'll soon adapt herself to the change. I want first of all to help her to feel at home with us. D'you think that's all right?"

"It sounds quite all right," Jen said thoughtfully. "She's not half so bad as she might be, you know, Joy. I thought you might have bother with her grammar, and her manners, and all that sort of thing. She's been well taught. There's nothing wrong with her."

"Only a touch of north-country accent, which, of course, you'd never notice! That Cumberland aunt has been a brick."

"I didn't notice it!" Jen laughed. "I thought she spoke very prettily! What I can't stand—don't tell the Pixie!—is a London accent."

"She's got none of that. I want to see the other aunt. She must have taught Maidlin very carefully, always remembering that her father might want her some day. No, she hasn't much to unlearn. She only has to get used to us, and that will soon come. She's been to good schools; I asked a few questions. The only thing I'd really like to start her on at once would be French conversation. For her, that really is important. But I can't talk French, and you can't talk French, so there we are! I'm beginning to wonder what there is I can do! Do mothers always feel what useless creatures they are?"

"Mothers!" Jen laughed. "Is she adopted, then? You were only her guardian yesterday!"

"I felt like her mother last night. You once adopted a family—a daughter, so you've been a mother too. Did you at once become conscious of all your feeblenesses?"

"Oh, I gave my family reams of good advice!" Jen laughed. "And it cried a lot, and promised to be a good girl! I say, Joy, what about the other girl—Miss Macey's kid?"

"What about her? She'll come after school to-morrow. You saw the letter from Mackums. I think I'll fetch her in Eirene."

"How much are you going to tell her about Maidlin? She'll know you hadn't any other girl living here. How are you going to account for her?"

"I've been thinking about that. There are only two ways; to tell her the whole thing, or just to say Maidlin's here on a visit."

"Yes. Well, wouldn't that be wiser? Suppose she's snobby, and isn't nice to her? Maidlin will know in a minute. She's evidently very quick at feeling things. It would upset her, wouldn't it?"

"Hideously! It would be easier to know what to do if I knew Rosamund even a little. Schoolgirls are so different! Of course, the school has always been very anti-snobbish, ever since the day Cicely started her crusade against the club subscriptions and became the one and only President of the Hamlet Club!" Joy laughed. "I've always wished I'd been there! But I've heard enough about it from Edna and Peggy and others. It must have been 'some' stunt, even for Cicely! I'm inclined to tell Rosamund the whole story and risk it, Jenny-Wren," they were standing by the sundial on the lawn. "I hate hiding things, and I'm not clever enough to do it successfully. If none of Maidlin's people were here, it would be easy enough. But with her aunt as caretaker of the abbey—no, I daren't risk it! It would be worse if we'd tried to make a secret of it. Then not only Rosamund would think we had felt there was something to hide, but Maidlin would feel it too; she'd think we were ashamed of her aunt. No, I can't risk that. I'd rather risk the other kid being a little snob. But I don't think it's likely. She's a Hamlet, isn't she? Didn't Mackums say so in her first letter?"

"Yes, said she was a keen member of the Hamlet Club."

"Well then! We'll hope she's got some sense. Probably she'll be thrilled with excitement at living with so romantic a heroine as an heiress to an Italian fortune! I know I should have been, at her age."

Jen laughed. "We'll hope so. I say, Joy, we'll have some dancing! There will be four of us. We'll teach Maidlin 'Hey, Boys' on the cloister garth, as Joan taught me. We could do all the squares for four. It would be awfully good for the kid! We'll see if she's fascinated by Thursday night!"

"I'm game. But I'm not game for secrets. I hate them. I shall have a talk with Rosamund, and tell her all about it. She can help Maidlin a lot, if she will."

"I do wonder what kind of kid she is!" Jen said thoughtfully, as they went towards the house. "It will make a lot of difference to everybody! Maidlin's going to shake down all right. I hope this new one won't upset her again!"

"I wish she wasn't coming," Joy said frankly. "One at a time would have been quite enough for me! It complicates matters to have a second so very soon after the first! I really would rather *not* have had twins!"

"It is a handful for you, you poor dear!" Jen laughed sympathetically. "I'll do anything I can to help!"

"I know you will, and I'm glad you're here. But when all's said and done, they're my twins, and I've got to see the job through," Joy said mournfully.

CHAPTER XIII

THE UNKNOWN QUANTITY

"You are lucky, Rosamund!" Barbara, the Queen of the previous May Day ceremony, paused enviously at the big gates, as she wheeled out her cycle, the gift of her married sister.

"I know. I wish you could all come too. No, I don't! The most priceless part of it is going alone," there was a flicker of suppressed excitement in Rosamund's blue eyes.

"Aren't you fearfully thrilled, kid?" and Molly Gilks and Nesta, seniors of seventeen, stopped also. "It's a gorgeous chance for you, to go and live at the Hall! Joy's a perfect sport to have you."

"I know," Rosamund said again. "It's awfully jolly of her. Thrilled! Yes, I'm simply dying to get there!"

"If Jen Robins is still there, give her my love," said Nesta. "I was one of the first girls she ever danced with. It was rotten when she had to leave, a year ago! And she was only sixteen! Tell her Moll and I haven't forgotten her."

"Is she nice? I've only seen her in the distance. She didn't come for Babs's crowning, last May!"

"Oh, awfully jolly, and always good fun! I wish we were all going with you! We did once, you know; the whole school, in the dip. time. And we lived in the Hall; it's a gorgeous old house!"

"I've never seen it, or the abbey. But I've heard heaps about them. And I've seen Joy at Club evenings. She looks awfully good fun, too," Rosamund's eyes were on the Risborough road. "She's fetching me in her car. Isn't it topping of her?"

Then with a warning toot, Eirene swept down on them from the other direction, making them all jump.

Joy, in her chauffeur's leather suit and cap, jumped out. "Which is Rosamund? Right-o, kid! Pitch your things in behind, and get up beside me. Don't squash my parcels, though; some of them are hats. I've been doing a little shopping. I'll just run in and speak to Miss Macey. Hallo, Babs! How are Mirry and the baby? You all right, Nesta? Give my love to Peg and Edna, Moll!"

Her eyes had cast a quick, anxious glance over her new "twin," but it was not easy to tell much from a mere look. Rosamund was tall for her age, and pale, and looked as if life in town had not suited her. But her eyes were very bright and her face eager, and she did not look shy. She wore the school hat and regulation blue tunic and green girdle, under a warm blue coat, and her hair hung to her waist in two yellow plaits.

She was in the car, with all her belongings, by the time Joy came striding out, and the envious friends, reinforced by several more, were waiting to see her off. They shouted their farewells as Eirene crept away; then the car gathered speed and raced along the High Street, and the girls turned regretfully to go on their own much less exciting homeward ways.

"Lucky little bounder!" sighed Molly Gilks. "Fancy living with Joy at the Hall!"

"I should be shy, I think," one ventured.

"Shy! There's nothing to be shy of. She won't be shy of Joy Shirley for five minutes!"

"She won't be shy at all, being Rosamund. She never is," said Queen Babs. "She never needed any looking after, even when she was quite new."

Rosamund turned to Joy, before they had rounded the first corner. "It's awfully decent of you to have me!" she said warmly.

"I do hope it's not too much fag. I will try not to be a trouble to you. But—I must say it! It is simply gorgeous to think of living with you at the abbey!"

Joy laughed. "You may not think it's so gorgeous when you have all this ride on very hot days, or in pouring rain! Where's your bike?"

"Miss Macey said I'd better come by train to-morrow and ride home, as you wouldn't want to take the bike in the car."

"I'd have squeezed it in. Mind you're up early, then, or you won't catch the train. You won't want to do that often; it's too roundabout. You have to change at Risborough, you know; an awful fag. Look here! I've something to tell you," Joy said abruptly, as they left the town behind and began to climb the road to the hills.

"I wasn't ragging when I said I'd been buying hats and things. I've been all over the town, seeing if I could pick up anything decent for a girl. She's dropped in among us suddenly, and some of her things aren't—well, quite nice enough. We're going shopping in London on Thursday, but I wanted to get her something to go in. I want to tell you about her."

Rosamund was looking at her curiously. "A girl? At the Hall? Another girl?"

"Yes. It's a weird story; do you revel in stories? But don't tell this one at school; not at present, anyway. We'll see later. Just say you found I had another friend staying with me, besides Jen. But it will be jollier for you to know all about it."

Joy's voice was as steady as the strong hands that gripped the steering-wheel. She showed no sign of the anxiety she felt as to how her confidence would be received, though she knew how much must depend on Rosamund's attitude to the story she was now to hear.

But Rosamund's face was alight with interest as she waited

eagerly. "I love stories! The girls say the abbey is full of them, and that they're always happening to *you*!"

Joy laughed. "We've had our share. But this one simply came to us. We aren't responsible for it in any way. For Joan couldn't possibly have known, when she engaged Ann Watson as caretaker to the abbey, that in six years Ann would produce a niece who was heiress to an Italian fortune!"

"Help!" said Rosamund. "More heiresses? Weren't you one, Miss Shirley?"

"I was. That's really why I felt I must give this one a leg-up. Now listen very carefully!" and Joy began on the story she had told to Madam in the crypt, with its later developments, leaving out nothing but the fact that Maidlin's coming to the Hall had been suggested by her aunt.

"Now you understand the situation! You're going to drop into the middle of it, and I'm counting on you to be sporting enough to give Jen and me some help, and not make things harder for us," Joy said frankly. "You can help, or you can hinder. I'd really rather have had you and Maidlin separately; it's not too convenient all happening at once like this. I'm perfectly willing to have you, but I'd have been glad if it hadn't been just now. I'm being quite straight with you, you see! I feel it might have been easier to get Maidlin into our ways if you hadn't complicated matters by turning up at the same moment. But I can see quite a chance that you may be able to help, and to make things easier all round. On the other hand, you may make them much harder. Now you will be sporting, and help us out, won't you?"

Rosamund had been looking grave. But now her face lit up. "I'd simply love to help! I'm sorry I'm not very convenient, but I'm sure Miss Macey didn't know. I could go back, you know; I don't suppose a few weeks would make much difference. But if

I could help you, Miss Shirley!—Oh, do tell me how! I'd simply love to help! You've been so awfully decent about having me. What is there I can do? How old is the heiress? What do you call her?"

"Maidlin—Madalena. Fourteen. She's not uneducated, or anything like that. But she's shy and awkward, and feels everything fearfully strange. If she thought you were going to laugh at her, she'd die."

"I never would! It is awfully hard on the kid, not to have a mother or anything! Well!" as Joy laughed. "I'm a year older, and a year means a lot, when it's been a year at school!"

"Rather!" Joy assented gravely. "Maidlin has been to school too, though, but not to live. Presently, of course, she'll have to go. Perhaps she'll go to France. She'll need to speak French well; and she hasn't begun yet. I want you to be nice to her, that's all, and to behave as if it were the most natural thing in the world for girls to come into Italian fortunes! Maidlin's shy, as I've said; she doesn't feel any too much at home with us yet. Now you aren't shy! I saw that in two secs. You'll shake down and be at home in no time, long before she will, if she's left to herself. I thought perhaps you could take her along with you! Kind of tow her into harbour, you know. But you mustn't for the life of you patronise her; she'd know, and resent it fearfully. And if you let her feel you're looking at her as a curiosity, because such a weirdly romantic thing has happened to her, she'll hate it and feel queer and frightened. I didn't tell you to make you feel that; but I do want you to sympathise with her! Can't you just be jolly with her, as you would be with any other girl who happened to be visiting in the same house? If you'll do that, you'll really help me and Jen, and we'll be glad you're there."

Rosamund's eyes were alight. Joy had done wisely in appealing to her for help. "I'll do any mortal thing I can! I'll be fearfully bucked if I can really help. How does Maidlin feel about my coming?"

"Feel? I don't know. I just told her. How do you mean?" It had not occurred to Joy that there could be any difficulty here.

"I thought she might feel I was a nuisance, coming butting in. She might want you all to herself."

"Oh, that would be too silly! I'd be mad with her if I thought that. 'Tisn't any business of hers whom I choose to ask."

But Rosamund was nearer Maidlin's age, and in some ways more able to understand her point of view. "I hope she won't loathe me, that's all—Oh!" as they came to the edge of the hills and saw all the view of the vale of Aylesbury spread below them. "Oh! How perfectly gorgeous! Do we go down there?"

Joy laughed. "That's something like what Jen said when she got to this very spot for the first time. She was on the step of my bike. Yes, we go down," and they took the winding road carefully.

"It is ripping of you to let me come here!" Rosamund breathed, when she saw the Hall. "Oh, what a topping house!"

"That's why!" Joy said bluntly. "Why I let you come; and Maidlin. I'd be a pig if I kept it all to myself. I have tried to share it with other people. Yes, I thought that would bring Jen out!" as in answer to the blast of the horn Jen appeared in the big doorway. "Where's Maidlin, Jenny-Wren? This is Rosamund!"

There was only, after all, two years in age between Jen and the Schoolgirl. Their eyes met steadily for a first questioning look. Then each smiled in frank friendliness, finding a kindred spirit.

"Glad to see you!" Jen said hospitably. "How's everybody down at school? Seen any of my crowd lately? Nesta or Molly, or any of that lot?"

"They saw me off. They all sent their love, and said, when are you coming to see them? They say they haven't seen you since the Hamlet dance at Christmas, except in the distance at weddings," Rosamund laughed.

"Sounds as if I spent all my time attending weddings!"

"Well, you do, rather!" Joy jeered. "You only come to see us when we provide a wedding for you and let you be a bridesmaid! You'll have to take the chief part in the next, though. I'm never going to have one. So perhaps we'll get a rest from weddings. Where's Maidlin?"

"She ran away when she heard the horn." Jen looked troubled. "I suppose she's upstairs. She's been awfully queer all afternoon, Joy. I think she's been missing you. She's hardly had a word to say about anything. She helped me pick and pack the daffodils and take them to the post, as you suggested; but she wasn't a bit jolly about it. I don't know what was making her so grumpy."

"Me, I expect," Rosamund said grimly. "I rather thought she wouldn't be frightfully pleased to hear I was coming. What do we do now?" and the eyes of all three girls met in dismay.

"Smack her!" Joy burst out explosively. "Gracious me! I'll talk to her, silly infant!"

Jen caught her arm. "No, Joy, don't! Don't be a donkey. You'll make fearful trouble; you'll ruin everything! Don't you understand? I say, come inside. If she's in her room, she'll hear us talking, and that won't help. Joy, remember Saturday night! You said you were glad Maidlin felt things a lot; that it made her more worth while, and that you didn't mind having a scene now and then; that it was better than having her stodgy, like Ann!"

"Yes, but she has no business to fly off in a temper at things I do in my own house! Why should she expect to be the only one? D'you suppose she's in her room?"

"Wait a minute, Joy! Don't you *see*? It's because she's so crazy about you. She can't bear to think of sharing you with anybody. Don't you see how she feels? She's been through a lot these last few days. She adores and worships you; funny to think of, of course! But it's a way kids have; and Ann would make her worse, by the way she'd talk about you, and turn you into a heroine of all kinds of stories! Maidlin said she'd watched you in the abbey; and you can just imagine it! Then she hears she's to come and live here, and you go and make her feel she's not a stranger or visitor, but that you've adopted her, for the time being; you know you did, Joy! You were awfully nice to her. And the poor kid can hardly believe it, and feels as if she'd got to Heaven, or as if she were living in a dream, or a fairy tale, or something. Didn't you see the unbelieving look on her face all yesterday, especially when she looked at you? Her eyes just followed you round; but she obviously hardly believed she was really wide awake. Then to-day, before she's had time to get used to it, and— and find her balance, so to speak—you coolly inform her there's another girl coming! Now, I ask you, could you expect a kid who feels things deeply to take it calmly?"

Joy, standing before the fire, was pulling off her big gloves, her head bent. "Yes, I think so!" she said defiantly at last. "I see what you mean, Jen, and how you think she felt. I won't fly at her in a rage, if you really think you're right about her feelings. But I do think she's to blame. I still don't see that she had any right to expect to monopolise the house and—and me! I must ask whom I like. She's got to see she's wrong, and she's got to be nice to Rosamund."

"I'm awfully sorry about it!" Rosamund began, but Jen interrupted.

"I don't say Maidlin's right. I know she isn't. But I do understand how she feels. Joy, it's small and petty and ungenerous of her, perhaps, not to be willing to share; though I'm not so sure that any of us are willing to share the friends we care most about! I know at school I used to be furious if any one talked too long to

Joan! And only last summer I've heard the President say quite indignantly, 'Like her cheek!'—if a girl got Madam in a corner and kept her there talking, when Cicely wanted her herself, though the poor girl may only have been asking her advice about the exam! But Cicely liked to be the one who talked to Madam, and she used to glower at anybody else who dared to go near her. Joy, what right have you to expect Maidlin to be perfect at fourteen?"

"I don't. But jealousy's a horrid, catty thing. Oh!" Joy sighed. "Why did I ever take on this job? To let the kid live here was all right, but to bring her up properly is quite another thing!"

"How could she have big ideas, after the way she's been brought up?" Jen insisted. "You said yourself her aunt had done awfully well for her; but she couldn't do everything. You have to give her the big ideas, Joy; the Pixie said so. Or rather, she said you had them, and you'd put them into Maidlin."

"The Pixie always sees the best in people, and sometimes she sees good that isn't there! I don't feel at all fit to turn a jealous baby into a generous girl! What am I to do now, then, Jen?" Joy spoke wearily, with a worried look.

"Wouldn't it be better to take no notice, if we can? If you go and row her, she'll cry quarts, and she'll hate Rosamund. She'll feel it's Rosamund's fault that you're mad with her. Tea's ready; shan't I go up and tell her, and pretend there's nothing wrong?"

"Well, if you think it will work," Joy tossed her cap on to the settle. "I'm sure Rosamund's dying for her tea. I say, I'm most awfully sorry about all this!" and she turned impulsively to the schoolgirl. "I hadn't the faintest notion the silly kid would get the wind up in this way. It's horribly rough on you!"

"I'm just awfully sorry I've upset her," Rosamund said anxiously. "I feel as if you ought to send me back to school."

"Not for half a second! I wouldn't give in to her for the world!

She'll have to learn, and the sooner the better. Would you like to go upstairs? What's up, Jen? Isn't she there?"

Jen had come flying down again. "She isn't in her room, nor with Mrs. Shirley. Where can she have gone, Joy? Out into the garden?"

"Tea is once more postponed!" Joy said dramatically. "With an explosive article like an Italian heiress, you never know where you are. She may have run away again; or she may be hiding; or she may have gone to do some desperate deed! Search-parties will be sent out immediately! Rosamund, if you're faint and famished, take a bun to keep you alive. We must find this priceless infant. I foresee that life will not be dull again till we've got rid of Madalena! You go and help Jen to search the garden. Take a torch; it's almost dark. You'd be no good in the house till you know your way about. I'll search the attics, and come downwards gradually. Oh, help! How trying it is to be a mother! Especially to such an unknown quantity as an Italian temper!" she sighed, as the search-parties scattered in various directions.

CHAPTER XIV

"She couldn't have thought of the tunnel, surely!" Joy murmured, her search of the attics having proved fruitless. She sped downstairs, and found the panel door unbolted, as she had half expected. "The monkey! She must have noticed I'd never locked it after coming home by Underground on Saturday! Here, Jen! Rosamund! You haven't found her? No; well, I believe she's gone down the secret passage. Where's that torch we had on Saturday?"

"Oh, may I come?" Rosamund pleaded. "I'm dying to see the passage! I've heard about it, of course!"

"I guess you have! Come on, then, and we'll see where this silly infant has got to."

"It's awfully decent of her to give me a chance of seeing it so soon!" Rosamund said joyfully, as, full of excitement, she followed Joy by the light of the torch.

"There is that way to look at it, of course! I thought you'd be mad with her because she's done you out of your tea."

"Oh, what's tea, compared with secret passages?" Rosamund laughed delightedly. "I say! Fancy living in a house with walls so thick that we can walk inside them! Aren't you afraid of burglars?"

"The door's bolted on our side, just in case any one got into the abbey, though I don't see how they could do it," Joy was holding the torch low and searching every corner. "The little monkey can't have gone far without a light, and she had no time to get one."

"Don't fall over her, then," Jen was just behind them.

"Well, Madalena, I do think you're unkind!" Joy had stopped suddenly at the door at the end of the passage. Beyond it were the steps leading down into the real tunnel. Maidlin, in a miserable heap, was crouched against the door. "I'd locked this door, had I?" Joy said, with satisfaction. "I'm glad I remembered to do one thing properly, anyway! Well, infant, what kind of game do you call this to play with us? Spoiling our tea and nearly starving us to death! Hide and seek's a very good game, but you're awfully inconsiderate in the time you choose for it! But we've won, for we've found you. Now would you really rather stay here, or are you coming back to tea? For I can't wait another minute for mine."

"Oh, couldn't we explore the passage?" Rosamund begged. "We've only just started!"

"No, my child, you could not! You shall, of course; but not to-night. Maidlin can take you through, all the way to the abbey, some day, and tell you all about it. But at this moment there's tea, tea, and nothing but tea. And then I suppose you've homework. Or things have changed since my day. Madalena, you can stay here in the dark, if you'd really rather, but I think you'll find it lonely. Now that we know where you are, we shan't worry. There's no way out but through the Hall. But you'll probably catch cold, and then you won't be able to go to town with me on Thursday. I'll have to take Rosamund to see the party instead. Come on, you two! My inner man is demanding hot scones and cakes."

Maidlin, breathless and half-sobbing still, saw them go, saw the light grow fainter. In desperation she started up and ran after them; the dark and the silence had been terrifying before; she had been glad to hear the voices, as she crouched there, too frightened to try to find her way back, once her passion was gone.

Jen was bringing up the rear. She felt a shy touch on her arm, and, without turning, she drew the trembling hand into hers, making no comment. Maidlin, subdued enough now, went in bewildered silence, sure only of one thing, that she did not understand these strange new people. She had not been scolded; she had not been stormed at, nor reproached. They did not seem to understand how she had felt, nor why she had gone. Joy had spoken as if it had been only a game. Jen had taken her hand gently, almost kindly. The new girl was talking all the time, to Joy and Jen alike, and had not seemed to notice that she had been crying. Maidlin, utterly bewildered, began to wonder if she had been silly.

When they reached the big hall, Joy's only comment was, "Tea will be poured out in three minutes, but only those who have washed their hands *and faces* will get any. Jenny-Wren, you're all smutty! Go and wash! Now scoot, everybody, or aunty will think we're a troop of morris dancers come to perform. They used to wear smuts on their faces. Maidlin, you might show Rosamund the bathroom. Miss Robins, you and I, being no longer children, will retire to our own rooms to attend to our toilet!"

A shout of derisive laughter from Rosamund greeted this remark. Maidlin, in increasing bewilderment, stared from one to the other.

"Oh, that was a *very* feeble joke!" Joy said crushingly. "I can do *much* better than that! Glad to have amused you, all the same, children. Come on, Miss Robins, *do*!"

"Where is the bathroom? I'm dying for some tea!" Rosamund turned to staring Maidlin. "Is Miss Shirley always like that? The girls said she was frightful sport," she remarked, as they washed. She had taken her cue from Joy, and no one could have guessed from her casual tone that any awkward feeling lay between them.

"I don't understand her, half the time," Maidlin's tone was dangerously shaky.

"Oh, well! You just laugh, when she's rotting. I guess she and Jen Robins go on like that most of the time, don't they? It will be awful sport, if they do."

"But how do you know?"

"When she's pulling your leg? Oh, you just know, you know!"

"I don't. I don't know what she means, half the time. My aunty never talked like that."

"No, I don't suppose she did!" Rosamund said to herself. To Maidlin she said lightly, "I'll wink at you when it's all utter rot they're talking, and then you'll know. Think I ought to do my hair again? Oh, I guess I'll make it do! Why don't you plait yours? What stacks of it you've got! Can you sit on it? But it must get in the way. I'll plait it for you to-morrow, shall I? I love doing people's hair. Have you ever tried putting yours up, to see how you'll look? Let's do it one day, both of us, and go down and give them a shock, shall we?"

"I perceive," said Joy solemnly, from the doorway, "that we have taken a Chatterbox into the bosom of the family! Are you stunned, Maidlin? You look a bit dazed! Do you go on like this all the time, Rosamunda?"

"I'm afraid I do! Do you mind?" Rosamund laughed, but looked apologetic and a trifle anxious.

"I like it!" Joy assured her seriously. "You see, I do it myself, and so does Jenny-Wren. So do all the rest of our crowd, so you won't be any shock to us. There were seven of us, last August, all sleeping in one room, and we *all* talked! Till past midnight sometimes, and Jen and I had to crawl down in the dark and raid the larder for provisions because we were all starving. However much you talk, I don't think you'll out-talk *me*! I'll race you to the tea-pot!"

Rosamund gave chase, and flew down the big staircase after her. Maidlin, bewildered and lonely, was standing staring after

THE WISDOM OF JENNY-WREN

them, a tremulous quiver about her lips, when Jen came out of her room, and put her arm round her and led her gently down.

"Didn't Joy break it to you that she hadn't really grown up yet? You'll have to get used to that. Sometimes she's just a big baby; but a baby that everybody loves."

"But that first night she seemed—she was so—so nice!" Maidlin faltered. "She seemed to understand. To-day she doesn't seem the same."

"Perhaps she understands well enough!" Jen said warningly. "Don't be too sure she doesn't understand! But Joy's two people, you know, Maidlin; lots of us are. You've got to love both sides of her. You will, too, as soon as you get used to her."

That was not yet, however. During tea, Maidlin sat in her corner, silent, puzzled, suspicious, listening in stunned, incredulous amazement to the chatter of the other three. Was it possible that Rosamund had not been in the house an hour? She was teasing and being teased, chaffing Jen, talking nonsense with Joy, as if she were an old friend. Yet that morning Joy had been wondering "what kind of a kid she would be!" Maidlin watched and listened, and formed her own conclusions. She did not utter them, but the results were soon apparent. She withdrew into a shell of silence and shyness, sat in a corner with a book while Rosamund, calming down, worked steadily at the big table for two hours; was as silent during supper as the rest were lively, and cried herself to sleep that night.

"Well, Wild Cat? Good hunting?" Jen inquired, when Joy came to brush her hair and talk. "Satisfied with your new family?"

"No, I'm just sick about it!" Joy said vehemently. "I've done my best, and here's the result! Rosamund, who's only supposed to be staying here for the good of her health, is as chummy and as much at home in half an hour as if she'd been here always. Maidlin, whom I'm supposed to be bringing up nicely, is in the sulks, and hasn't a word to say! And it *isn't* my fault!"

"No, it's the difference between them. They couldn't be much less alike. But so far as I've thought it out, Joy, the difference is a good thing, and, of the two, I'd rather have Maidlin. I mean, I think she's got more in her. There's more chance of making something of her. Rosamund's all right, of course. I like her; she's a jolly kid, and easy to get on with, a regular ordinary sporting sort, and good fun and ready for anything. She's quite the easiest kind of girl for you to have to take in! But at present she's all on the surface. I don't say she's shallow; not for a second. We haven't had time to know yet; we may find out her deeper side later. Or she may grow a deeper side as she grows up. But she's got a very attractive surface-side, and probably— *probably!*—she's content with that at present, and just has a jolly time and gets along easily and makes friends quickly, and doesn't trouble much about anything or let things upset her very much. But Maidlin's another matter altogether."

Joy had stopped brushing her bronze mane and was staring at her. "Go on! Now describe Maidlin's character to me! You're right, of course. But how you can sit there, half undressed, with your baby curls, and look about nine, and pour out all that wisdom, is more than I can understand! *Am* I four years your senior? Instruct me some more, please! I'm humbly drinking in every word!"

Jen, sitting on the edge of her bed, very much undressed, laughed as she took the slide out of her hair and let the short locks fall about her face. "If you said, 'looking like a Skye terrier,' you'd be nearer the truth! Look at the length of me! I *would* be tall for nine!" she jeered. "I'm not pouring out wisdom. I'm only telling you what I think."

"But such thoughts!" Joy mocked. "Such dark, deep wisdom, in one so young and fair—untidy, I mean! No, shaggy; that's the word! In one so young and shaggy! Go on! Tell me all about Maidlin? Am I to be glad she's sulking, did you say?"

Jen threw a pillow at her, and dodged its swift return. "Don't wake the children! She's not sulking. She's frightfully unhappy and lonely, and feels left out of everything. I should have thought even you could see that!"

"Who's leaving her out of anything? I've done my best. She sulks, and won't join in."

"She doesn't know how. She doesn't understand us. She said, when you'd been rotting one time, that her aunt never talked like that. I can quite believe it."

"I can, too," Joy admitted. "I'm sure Ann never talked nonsense in her life."

"And probably the farmer-lady was far too busy and practical and north-country to have time for it. So Maidlin is quite stunned by the way you go on. She's never seen anything like you before," Jen explained politely.

"Well, I like that! You do your share!" Joy said indignantly. "Rosamund played up too. It wasn't only me!"

"That's the worst of it. Maidlin sees this other girl come butting in, knowing just how to fool about with you, and she feels more awkward and more out of it every minute. I shouldn't wonder if she's been crying in bed to-night. She worships you, but she doesn't know how to talk to you, so she sits in a corner and feels bad, while this other kid, who only thinks you're a jolly good sort and great fun, fools about and plays up to you and gets on with you far better than she does. It's been a gloomy evening for poor Maidlin! In time she'll thaw, of course; but in the meantime you simply mustn't go thinking she's sulky, when she's feeling so sick she can't speak!"

Joy whistled under her breath. "Mustn't wake my twins! I see your point. It's a good thing you're here to keep me straight,

Jenny-Wren! But how can I help the kid? You make me feel bad about her!"

"Be nice to her, and wait!" It was Jen's way of pleading for patience and gentleness. "She is worth it, Joy! The very fact that she feels it all so deeply shows she has a lot in her. When she gets used to us, it will begin to come out. Of course, having Rosamund here has done the trick; made the difficulty, I mean. Rosamund has made Maidlin feel her own shyness and awkwardness in a way she hadn't done before; quite unconsciously, of course. She means to be awfully kind to the kid. But she can't help being just exactly what Maidlin would like to be; our kind, you know. And so far Maidlin knows she's not."

"It is rough on her," Joy agreed slowly. "But I couldn't help Rosamund turning up. I knew it would complicate matters. Somehow I never thought of the difficulty being on Maidlin's side, though! Will the few days in town help, Jenny-Wren? She'll be alone with us then."

"Yes, I think it will. She'll see you're as chummy with everybody—Jack, and the dancing lot, and all that crowd—as you are with me and Rosamund, and that there's no sense in being jealous; that it's just your way. And she'll get to know us better. Why don't you have her to sleep with you, at Jack's? You know Jacky-boy said she'd get a bed ready for the heiress! You could tell her not to, and Maidlin could go in with you, and I'd tuck in with my husband. You know she always wants me to!"

Joy made a face. "I like my little bed all to myself! *Must* I?" she wailed.

"I think you'd better do something to make Maidlin feel she's on a different level from Rosamund! That Rosamund's just a visitor, but she's one of the family. It may be kiddy, but I believe it would mean a lot to her!"

"Oh, if it would be a comfort to the poor infant!" and Joy

resolved on the spot to sacrifice her own ease for a night or two in the good cause. "If you think she wants to be cuddled by mummy at midnight, I'll ring up Jacky-boy, and tell her one pair of sheets can be saved! And, of course, Rosamunda will be away at school most of the time; Maidlin can have her innings then. It's a good thing she has to go with us to town; we'd have had to take her, in any case. For we couldn't have left her here!"

"Help, no! Not in the present state of things! Wouldn't it have been fearful for her and Rosamund alone?"

"Well," said Joy, "I'll go to my own little bed. Thank you for your kind advice, Mrs. Wren! Why you should know so much about people's inner feelings and hidden thoughts, is more than I can tell! At your age, too! But then you always did see farther than most, even in the days when you were all long legs and long pigtails and a very short tunic, when you discovered the story of the Lady Jehane, and so helped us to find the jewels and the buried church! Oh, you've been quite useful in your little way, Jenny-Wren! Now I," mournfully, "I never see anything till it hits me on the nose."

"Oh, go to bed, silly!" Jen laughed, and switched off the light, and left her to find her way to the door in the dark.

CHAPTER XV

THE PIXIE AND THE CLUB

"I HAVE to break it to you, Rosamunda, that you will be alone with aunty for two nights," Joy said weightily on Wednesday morning. "Be nice to her, won't you? Make up to her for our absence. See if you can't be as nice as Jen and Maidlin and me all rolled into one! Don't overstrain yourself trying to be as noisy, though. She won't mind having a few days' rest. She puts up with us very kindly, and of course I've brought her up to be used to *me*, but I dare say it's a bit of a strain at times. If she were perfectly honest, I shouldn't wonder if she'd say she's quite glad we're all going up to town for two days. But being so polite and kind, I dare say she'll say she expects to be lonely without us."

"I always miss you when you're away," Mrs. Shirley laughed promptly.

Joy sighed. "Yes, but how? Sure it's not with a pleasant sense of relief?"

"I shall miss you all fearfully!" Rosamund wailed. "Bother your old party! Why must you go to parties in town?"

"To wear our ultra-swish frocks, my child! You must see the point in that, after last night!"—for the party frocks had been turned out, at her special request, put forth the instant she heard of the dance in town.

"Oh, *do* let's see what you're going to wear!" she had begged, and she and Maidlin, the one excited, the other all interested eyes but few words, had sat on Jen's bed while the frocks were tried on for their benefit. Rosamund's delight in Jen's blue dress and Joy's white one had been ecstatic and excited; Maidlin's appreciation had shown chiefly, as usual, in her eager, wondering eyes, as she looked from one to the other, and looked last and longest at Joy.

"Some day," Joy had said, seeing her look, "I'm going to take to black, and black only, for evening frocks. I keep on meaning to, but aunty persuades me not to every time. And Joan says I'm to let her do it first, since she's married and wants to look dignified."

"You'll look lovely when you do, with your gorgeous hair!" said Rosamund fervently. "But you can wear almost any colour. Green or blue would be topping!"

"But not pink!" Joy said grimly. "It's always so awkward at school, because in the May Day procession I have to follow Marguerite, and she will wear strawberry-pink," she said to Maidlin. "The girls try to separate us and get our bridesmaids in between us, or something, because we clash so."

Rosamund went off to school on Wednesday morning lamenting her coming loneliness, and after lunch the three girls, with a considerable amount of luggage, packed themselves into Eirene, and sped away across the hills to town.

"It does look a lot for three days!" Jen acknowledged. "But then look at the changes we need! Party frocks for the dance, tunics and gym things for the classes first, and underneathies to match both; for we're not likely to lose the chance of a class just because it means changing in between, when we're in town so seldom! And we can't wear either gymmies or evening frocks at Jack's in the morning, or for shopping during the day."

"The wisdom of Jenny-Wren is really amazing!" Joy turned politely to Maidlin, squeezed between them on the front seat. "How does she do it, do you think? We can't wear gymmies or

171

evening frocks in the morning or for shopping! Now fancy that! Neither we can! Who'd have thought it? It hadn't occurred to me, I confess. Had you thought of it?"

Maidlin's startled look gave way to a ghost of a smile. "But you do sometimes, in the mornings; in the abbey, you know. Not evening frocks, but the drill dress."

Jen chuckled. "You've got her there, Madalena! Doesn't she look a sight in it too? You'll see lots more of them to-morrow night."

"I think it looks nice, only not—not grown-up enough."

"Undignified, I suppose!" Joy sighed. "Wait till you've seen my morris! 'Miss Shirley, your galleys are atrocious! And it's disgraceful that you can't do kick-jumps yet! As for your R.T.B's, they're hopeless!' That's what will happen if Madam chooses to turn on 'Bledington.' I hope it *will* be Madam! I do love her classes!"

"You had all Friday night with her! It would be much better for you to have somebody else for a change!" Jen retorted.

The decision to go to town on Wednesday had been made after Joy had spent Tuesday morning ringing up people and making arrangements.

"Come and have tea with me on Wednesday!" the Pixie had said. "I'll show you my room, and the club, and if you can wait you shall see my men. They come to me for morris, and they're frightfully keen." So Eirene sped hooting through the West End, on past St. Paul's and the Bank and the Monument and London Bridge and the Tower, and dived into the unknown crowded whirl of Aldgate.

Even Joy, though born a Londoner, knew nothing of this end of the City. She asked her way of policemen occasionally, but for the most part found it by means of a certain sense of direction which rarely failed her. She knew she had to go east, and east she went, and had no difficulties till Whitechapel lay behind her and she was heading for the river and the docks.

"I've a bump, you know; a bump of locality. I always had," she said briefly, as Jen commented admiringly on her unhesitating decision when they came to a choice of roads. "I could always find my way in the woods, as a kiddy, even in the dark. I used to spend days exploring, when I ought to have been doing useful things at home. I always know which is east and west; and I don't often lose my bearings."

She pointed out the well-known places they passed, for Jen's benefit as well as Maidlin's, but explained frankly that she only knew the outside of places like St. Paul's, and that only from picture post cards.

"You can't mistake it, of course. But I've never been inside, so far as I know; nor in the Tower. Yes, it is awful, isn't it? When you come and live in town, Jen, I'll bring Maidlin up and we'll do the sights of London. There! That's the Tower, of course. I haven't an idea what it's like inside; all bloodstains, I believe. I don't think London people do go to the Tower! Country cousins and Americans do that. Londoners go to the Boat Race, or to see the opening of Parliament. Of course, they *all* go whenever there's a procession! Now we must be getting near the club. Is this the kind of place the Pixie's teaching folk-dancing in?"

And they looked at the crowded streets, and the unemployed men standing at the corners, the squalid houses, the mud and dirt and bustle, with startled eyes.

"Is this the place we sent the daffodils to?" Jen murmured. "I wish I'd sent more! How little we know, away there in the abbey, of the places some people live in, 'Traveller's Joy'!"

Joy was frowning, though not over difficulties of the road. "We ought to know more," she said shortly. "I feel a pig. Did you see those children? Think of our orchard; and those daffodils!

Think of our lawns and fields! I don't suppose these kids have ever picked a primrose. I'm going to run that hostel. But that's such a little thing. I'd like to take them all away out of this; all the girls and children, and those tired mothers in that doorway; did you see? It doesn't seem right! But there must be thousands of them. I shall ask the Pixie. We ought to help; she'll tell me how."

Maidlin glanced at her in wonder. This was the other Joy, the one who had come to her in the refectory, who had won her over, who had held her in her arms that first night; not the lighthearted, laughter-loving, mocking Joy she did not understand. This was the Joy she loved best; though the other, happy and full of jokes and fun, was a bright and beautiful person to be worshipped from afar, in awe tinged with bewilderment. She began to be curious about this other person, this "Pixie," who was so full of wisdom. It was difficult to think of Joy looking up to anybody, but her tone said that she looked up to this Pixie and waited for her advice.

"Will I be afraid of her?" she asked doubtfully.

Joy's lips twitched. "I don't *think* so!" she said gravely. "Will she, Jen?"

"If she is, she ought to have first prize for being a nervous, silly little object," Jen said severely. "Maidlin, you really mustn't go about expecting to be afraid of people! Afraid of the Pixie! Silly kid!"

"Well, I don't know her!" Maidlin was roused to defend herself. "And if she's so clever—"

"She knows everything!" Joy said solemnly. "Every mortal thing you can think of! I'd take her advice about anything. And if you knew all the things she did in the war!"

"Joy, don't tease the kid. You'll love the Pixie, Maidlin. I say! Doesn't it strike you two that a country-dance club for men and girls down here, in the middle of all this, is rather a fine idea?"

"Been having another 'think'?" Joy queried. "But I agree; an awfully fine idea. For a moment it seems out of place—country-dancing in these slums, among all the factories and offices and works. But it's just what's needed."

"Yes, to give the people something different; new ideas, and something to freshen them up. It must be as big a thing for the Pixie's girls as it is for all those teachers and people at headquarters every week; something in the background, behind their everyday lives, to think about and look forward to. How they must love it! I'd like to see a party down here. But think of 'Gathering Peascods,' and 'Sellenger's Round,' and 'Jenny Pluck Pears,' and—and 'Spring Garden'! The very names don't fit in with the streets, and the smoke, and the public-houses at every corner!"

"It's just like the Pixie," Joy said soberly. "Country dancing didn't fit in with the war! What could be more unsuitable for camps and convalescent depots? But you know what she made of it out there. Ordinary teaching, of comfortable, nicely-dressed classes, wouldn't be enough for her, I believe. She must be where she's really needed, where there's more to be done than just teach dancing. She wants"—Joy laughed—"to mend their shirts and darn their socks, the dears! Didn't she say so?"

"Well, it's like her. I love the thought of dancing clubs down here. Oh, what's that big white place?"

"I shouldn't wonder if it's the club we're going to, considering the picture she showed us last week."

"Why, it's a palace! How—how gorgeous for the people living round about! Can any one go? Or have you got to be something to do with the Y.M.C.A.?" and Jen stepped out of Eirene and stood gazing up at the great white building in delight.

Maidlin followed her in an amazed dream. She had never imagined a "club" of this size, even in fashionable London, let alone in the slums; her only experience had been of a village club-room and small parish hall. In a whirl of incredulity she followed Joy and Jen up the big steps, and stood with them at the top of the first staircase to read the marble tablet proclaiming the beautiful building a memorial to the men of the district who had fallen in the war.

"Now that's a war memorial worth putting up! Far more sensible than some of them!" Jen said, with approval. "Jolly decent of the people who thought of it! Doing something big for those who are left!"

"It's tophole," Joy said gravely, and they all looked wonderingly about them, at the wide double staircase, the entrance to the cinema close beside them, the glimpses of big lounge and billiard-rooms through open doors.

"It's a gorgeous place! I wonder if she'll take us over it? She said, turn to the left, and we'd find her in the restaurant at four-thirty. Oh, here it is!" and Joy pushed open a swing-door and led them in.

Maidlin gazed eagerly round the big hall, with its high windows, little tables, brown woodwork, and waiting-girls in brown with hanging veils to their caps. Then she looked anxiously, and still a trifle nervously, for the great person in whose wisdom Joy had such faith, the Pixie.

"Here she is!" "Here you are!" the greetings rang out together, and the Pixie ran to meet them.

"So you've found me all right! Did you have any difficulty? *Good!* It is nice to see you here! Isn't it a beautiful place? You must see it all presently. But first we'll have tea. What will you have? You can have anything here, you know. Toast and cakes? Sandwiches? Eggs? Oh, you've had lunch! All right; tea, toast, and bread and butter and cakes for four, please, Beatrice. And is this your new abbey girl? Just tell me her name again, Jenny-Wren! Don't tell her I've forgotten it, or she'll never forgive me! But I know all about you, you know," to staring Maidlin.

Maidlin was staring, indeed. She had vaguely expected some one imposing and awe-inspiring, though she could not have said why. This little person was no taller than herself, though she had enough to say for two. Maidlin's first relieved impression was that there was no need to be frightened; others came later.

"And how are you getting on at the abbey? Oh, I say, thank you so much for the flowers! My classes simply loved them yesterday. Did you help to pick them for me? I know you did!" to Maidlin, who suddenly felt glad that she had helped. "It was beautiful of you all to think of it. Everybody had some; every single person I saw yesterday."

"And you never kept any for yourself. I know you! But it was Jen's idea. She and Maidlin did it all."

"Didn't you keep *any* for your own room, Pixie?" Jen asked severely.

"I still have those you gave me last week; they're lovely! My men did love them so when they saw them! And has your other girl arrived? What's she like—the schoolgirl? Don't you get on well with her?" the lightning question took Maidlin's breath away.

"How did you know?" she gasped. "I never said—"

"But you don't know her yet. She hasn't been there long enough. You mustn't judge too soon, you know. She'll be all right; girls are all dears! You should see some of mine. You'll be great friends in no time!"

At sight of Maidlin's confusion, Jen chuckled, and Joy gave a shout of laughter.

"Oh, Aunty Pixie! You can't dispose of our problems as easily as all that! It's jolly nice of you to try, but Maidlin just thinks you don't know anything about it. And you don't!"

"Only what you told me over the 'phone," the Pixie, not at all abashed, looked up at her with a twinkle. "You said it wasn't all plain sailing yet, and Maidlin didn't quite understand the new girl, but you thought things would soon be all right. Didn't you now? Didn't you say that?"

And Joy, who knew very well she had never added the last hopeful sentence, and had put Maidlin's attitude very much more strongly, accepted this tactful amendment with a grin.

"I've come to ask advice, as usual, Pixie," she changed the subject hastily, however, to give Maidlin time to recover.

"What's the trouble now?—Good-afternoon, Jack! All right again?"

"Yes, thanks, aunty!" and a big man paused on his way to the door, and looked down at his tiny friend.

"Now you take care and don't get another chill. Have something hot next time you get home soaked; but it needn't be whisky! Tea's just as good; and much cheaper in the end. Much better for you too."

"Yes, aunty!" and he grinned and passed on.

"How's the foot, Bob?" to another, who had just come in. "Think you'll be able to dance to-night? These friends have come a *long* way just to see you dance!"

Bob grinned sheepishly. "Aw, miss! I'm going to dance, though."

"Of course you are. See you aren't late, and bring the rest up with you."

"I'll fetch 'em all up, miss," and he too passed on.

"I'm *sure* you darn their socks, aunty!" Jen sighed. "Are you mothering the whole establishment?"

"I don't know what they'd do without you!" Joy had been helpless with suppressed amusement.

"They're dears, all of them. I love them. And I think they like me too. What's the worry, Joy?"—the keen eyes had seen that Joy was in earnest.

"What ought people like us to do for people who live in those streets we just came through?" Joy asked bluntly. "I feel a perfect pig to go back to the Hall and have that huge place all to myself. I feel as if I ought to chuck everything and come here and work with you. You're doing a big thing for the people who live here; any one can see that. But I couldn't teach! But it seems so hateful and—and callous to do nothing!"

The Pixie looked at her thoughtfully. "The last thing in the world you have to do is to 'chuck everything.' That's not what the money was given to you for. You can do far more by using it properly. By living at home, and asking some of our people there to share it with you, you'll do far more than by living here. Don't you feel that?"

"I suppose so. I shouldn't be any use here, of course. But it feels so mean!"

"You could be of use here. Your music alone could give pleasure to hundreds. You could play to them, and you could teach them to sing! But—"

"Didn't we say she always saw the best of everybody?" Joy interrupted. "Here she is, remembering the one little thing I *can* do!"

"It's not such a little thing. But I think there are others. You're going to use your house and money for other people. I don't say you can't do something here, too. You can do a lot; and if you'll come and see us often, and join in what we're doing, and be friendly and one of us, it will be a big thing. You've no idea the kind of things that are wanted down here! I heard of one lady who had been speaking to our girls, and some of them said to her, 'Oh, miss! if you'd only come and teach us to talk like you do!'—and they've had a class for English conversation all the winter; yes, really! You must come along sometime to the university settlement round the corner, where I sleep when I don't go back to the flat, and see all the friends there are doing; wonderful work! And a very real bit of help you could give would be to bring Eirene down now and then, and take some of our cripple children out for a ride. Think how they'd love it!"

"Yes, I'd like to do that! Shall I come once a week?"

"Aunty Pixie, how wise you are!" Jen said softly. "You don't ask Joy to do difficult or impossible things, but just little ordinary ones that she can do quite well. And yet they're such *real* things!"

"But they're the things that are wanted. Besides," and the Pixie gave her a quick, straight look, "Joy's difficulty won't be in doing them once or twice, but in keeping on with them regularly and not getting tired. Some people have to do big things; others do little ones, but keep on doing them. And that's harder!"

"I guess you understand me pretty well!" Joy said grimly. "But I won't slack off, Pixie. Those streets were a shock to me, and I'd like to do something to help. We'll plan it out. I could come up to town regularly, one morning a week, and give your kiddies rides all day."

"And stay the night with me, when we're settled in our flat, and go to classes at night!" Jen said joyfully. "Oh, Joy! What a topping plan! You must come on Fridays, for those are the jolliest classes! Except when there's a party; then you'll come on Thursday!"

"I wasn't thinking about classes, or any fun for myself!" Joy said indignantly.

"No, of course you weren't," the Pixie said soothingly. "But there's no reason you shouldn't have it," she added practically. "May as well get the good of your fare to town!"

"My petrol, you mean!" Joy laughed. "You are an unromantic little person, you know, Pixie!"

The Pixie's eyes twinkled. "Oh, I believe in getting the most you can out of everything. Now will anybody have more tea? Then come and see the club!"

CHAPTER XVI

A MORRIS PIPE AND A PIXIE

"I'VE no words left!" Jen said weakly. "I've used them all, three times over! It's the most gorgeous club I ever saw!"

"And for people *here*! Living in those houses we saw!" Joy added. "Pixie, it's very wonderful!" she said gravely. "Isn't it rather ripping to feel you're part of such a big thing?"

"Oh, rather! I love it. I'm fearfully bucked at being here. And such *nice* people to work with!"

"Oh, but you'd say that about anybody!"

"Oh, no, I shouldn't. There are people I can't work with. But they're all dears here."

She had led the girls to the beautiful gymnasium—"We dance here, on party nights. I play for them, up there!" pointing to the piano on its platform under the roof. "I go up the ladder. I'm always lifted down very tenderly off the last three steps by some of my men. It does amuse me so!"—to the billiard-rooms, with their big green tables and low, shaded lights—"Any one can have a game here by paying a little. It's not only for club-members. Much better than going to the public-house for your game, you know!"—to the big lounge and reading-room, the boys' club-room and the girls' club-room, with their huge red-brick open hearths, restful brown wooden furniture, big red leather easy-chairs and settees, tables with papers and magazines, and cosy corners arranged for discussions;—to the cinema-theatre; and last of all to the big swimming-pool, used during the day by the schools of the neighbourhood, and at night open to members of the clubs. It was this last, and the well-fitted gym, that reduced Jen to a limp state of joyful wonder. Maidlin was dumb with surprise, though her bright, eager eyes showed how much she was taking in of new ideas and impressions. Joy, though not too stunned to speak, was graver than usual in her appreciation of it all, with the constant picture of the streets outside before her eyes.

"Cheers for the Y.M.C.A., *I* say!" said Jen, as they came to rest at last in the Pixie's upstairs office.

"Or for the great men who gave it to the Y.M.C.A. It was a splendid gift, you know. Yes, isn't it a wonderful thing for the people down here? And they love it so. All our clubs are full. We could do with another place as big, and still take in more. Now I've got to change; it looks more business-like. You can fold up my things when I fling them off!" and she hurled her garments at them, and in five minutes had changed from her silk jumper to a smooth little black tunic and cream blouse, and was once more the Pixie of the Cheltenham School.

"It takes me right back to Naunton Park!" Jen laughed. "I think we ought to walk the 'Ilmington Hey,' Joy; 'walk it just once, for luck!' Oh, Pixie, dear, you were a treat to us that day!"

The Pixie's eyes were dancing. "Joy was a horrible shock to *me*! *Two* of them in my class! And that man turned up, and threw you all off your balance. I couldn't think what was the matter with you, for I could see you knew 'Shepherd's Hey'! And have you buried anybody lately?" wickedly, to Joy.

"Only myself and Maidlin. What do you do for music up here, aunty? You said your men came here for morris. But you've no piano!"

"That's my old bus under the table," and the Pixie pointed to her little gramophone. "We do 'Blue-Eyed Stranger' and 'Rigs' to her. For 'Rodney'—they love 'Rodney' and 'Lads a

Bunchun'—I play for them myself. I have my pipe, you know," and she took up a tin whistle.

"Oh, play to us! Do play to us! We didn't know you could!" Jen cried delightedly, and Maidlin's eyes kindled.

The Pixie, in her tunic, perched on the edge of the office table, and began to pipe; and Jen, in the midst of her enjoyment, treasured this new picture for her letter to Joan. Tune followed tune, in clear, sweet notes and such perfect rhythm that the girls' feet were tapping in sympathy, while they strove wildly to identify the airs—"Chelsea Reach," the "Helston Furry," "Nonesuch," "Oranges and Lemons," "Ladies' Pleasure," the "Tideswell Processional."

"I always remember an old lady where I once lodged," and the Pixie paused. "I was playing 'Chelsea,' and she came in and said, 'Miss, I do like the way you *turn the tune*!' My men would rather have the whistle than the piano, you know. They say they can dance to it better; they can hear it better."

"That's because you dance as you play it; I mean, you play it as a dancer. An ordinary pianist can never do that," Jen remarked.

"I suppose it's that. Here they come! You'll have to tuck yourselves into corners, if they all turn up. Maidlin, you can sit on Jen's knee in the big chair," her eyes had danced with amusement at Maidlin's amazed look when she donned her tiny tunic, but she had made no comment.

"We ought to go. We'll be late for Jacky-boy's dinner. And Maidlin was to go to bed early to-night, to make up for to-morrow," said Joy maternally. "We're going to the party, you know. Will you be there?"

"No, I have classes all evening. Just wait and see us do 'Rodney' and 'Blue-Eyed'! We really are getting some rhythm into it."

"If you're going to sit on the table and pipe for 'Rodney,' like a cupid or cherub, I simply won't go!" Jen laughed. "Joy can take Maidlin out to the West End and come back for me. Or I'll go by bus or train. I must see your men dance to your piping! It's a simply priceless idea!"

Deeply interested, she and Maidlin sat in the big leather chair and Joy perched on the arm, while half-a-dozen lads came in, overcome with shyness and amusement at sight of three girl visitors at first, till the Pixie's welcoming chatter made them forget themselves and the strangers. Conscious that they had faded into the background, the girls watched in absorbed silence as the six crowded round the table on which their tiny mentor sat enthroned, explaining the absence of others, making rough jokes, exclaiming at sight of the flowers, curious as to the budding almond, which was evidently a mystery.

"Those were given to me last week. Aren't they lasting well? They came right from the country. That's almond blossom, just coming out. Isn't it pretty?"

"Coo! Will there be almonds on *that*?" jeered one unbeliever, who evidently had only met almonds in shops.

"Now get your bells on. Fetch them out, Bob. Get the sticks, Peters. Take your places, and listen to the tune. Be careful of your cross-back-step, Andrews. D'you remember the tapping, Tom? Right! Let's see it, then!"

The lads were only beginners. They forgot their Foot-up, and with shouts of embarrassed laughter had to begin again. They got lost completely in their hey, went too far in Cross-over, muddled the tapping and forgot to repeat it, bumped into one another in Back-to-back, and roared with laughter at each new mistake. The jingle of the bells and the clatter of the sticks could not drown the thunder of their boots, for several had forgotten their shoes. But their enjoyment was overwhelming; they fairly radiated delight and good humour. Every keen criticism from the little autocrat on the table was received with laughter; every boy who failed or forgot was admonished by the other five as smartly as by her. They wanted no rests; as soon as "Rodney" had been practised, as a whole and in bits, with the familiar command, "Do it once more, for luck!" which drew Jen's eyes to Joy's in reminiscent laughter, they crowded round the table, begging for "Blue-Eyed Stranger," picked up and fixed the gramophone, found the record, and produced huge, wonderful handkerchiefs of varied hues. Their circles were wild in the extreme, but here again was the abounding enjoyment, and the shout at the end was a real triumphant "All-in."

"How they love it!" Jen whispered. "Isn't it topping to see them? This is the real thing, Maidlin; real men's morris, even if they are just beginners! It's got life in it; it's tremendously real. And one or two of them are jolly good!"

"Yes, that leader's rhythm is wonderful," Joy too had been watching enthralled. "And others are getting hold of the idea. I wonder how long they've been at it?"

"Only a few weeks," said the Pixie, swamped in a crowd of boys, but overhearing the question. "Some of them have only had two lessons; haven't you, Andrews?"

"Then they are really wonderful. You'll have to give a demonstration!"

"I'd rather give a party! But we shall give a show some day. They danced 'Rigs' to the girls at our party last week," and the boys grinned awkwardly, and then shouted with laughter at the remembrance.

"I'm sure the party loved it. But we really must go," and Joy rose resolutely. "I could sit here and watch all night, of course, but we simply mustn't. Be strong-minded, Jenny-Wren! Maidlin, haul her out of that big chair! You'll have to show us the way down," to the Pixie. "I'm hopelessly lost in this mansion!"

"I'll take you into the girls' lounge, and any one will show you the way down. I must hurry back to my men, though."

The boys were eyeing Joy's leather suit. One, a true Londoner, quite untroubled by shyness, asked in a tone of respect, "Drive a car, miss?"

Joy gave him a swift, radiant smile. "Yes, just a little one. But she goes very well. But I'm not much good at cleaning her or crawling about underneath, so I don't really do the thing properly, do I?" and did not explain that the car was her own.

There was a laugh from the crowd, as one awkwardly but readily offered to help her into her big coat. "'Tain't no job for a girl, messing about with engines," said one.

"Now, men, I'll be back in two minutes. You practise the tapping of 'Rigs.' Come along, girls!"

"But why, oh, why, did you call them 'men'?" Jen burst out, before the door was fairly closed. "They are dears, as you said; I'd love to see them again! But when you said men, I supposed you meant men! They're only boys of sixteen!"

"The wily flattery of the very tiny but very wise!" Joy began.

The Pixie interrupted her sharply. "Every one of them is over eighteen. They belong to the men's section. We have a boys' section as well; that's why. You have to be careful."

"Pixie! Eighteen! Why, they aren't—aren't tall enough, for one thing! Only one of them was a decent size! They only looked like boys!"

"That's Plaistow!" the Pixie said grimly. "They're old enough for eighteen! Of course, eighteen is only a boy, until you compare him with fifteen, though he likes to be counted a man! But that's the size and build you are at eighteen, if you've lived always in overcrowded homes, perhaps one room or two, and been underfed all your life. Those are eighteen-year-old boys of these parts; not the big fellows you meet in West End classes, I'll admit! There's only one in my little lot who's really well grown. And the girls are just the same; active and full of life, but small and stunted; cheated of something."

"And pasty!" Jen said, in a low voice. "I noticed the queer pale colour, no matter how much they laughed or how jolly they looked. Oh, Pixie, it—*it isn't right!*" she said helplessly.

"And yet they can take as much and as deep delight in a purely artistic thing like folk-dancing as any of your West Enders. You saw how they loved it; and the girls are the same in their country-dancing. You should see the joy, and life, and energy in our Saturday night parties! I never saw heartier dancing. They'd tire you out in one evening. And yet they're City people; shows 'country' dancing isn't really the best name. It's because it's folk, of course; folk-dancing. It appeals to everybody; that's folk. It's sincere and natural, and they all respond to it, just as the Tommies did in France. My lot here simply love it. They have modern dancing too, but they like our parties best; they've told me so. And they love it in the best way; their dancing is as artistic, and as musical, and as full of rhythm and beautiful movement, and of delight in it all, as any you'd find anywhere, even at your Vacation Schools or big town classes. But you've seen the streets they come from; only the big streets, of course! You don't know anything about their homes, really; but you've seen enough for a beginning; and you've seen the results in them. Those are our 'men'; those little slips of lads, with no height or growth to speak of; that's Plaistow! I love them, and I love being here. And they like me, you know! Now I must run back to them, or something will be getting smashed. They are dears; but talk about high spirits!—Molly!" they had entered the big lighted girls' lounge. "Show these friends of mine the way down, will you? They're afraid they'll get lost. Thank you, awfully! *Good*-bye! I'll ask you to a party some day!"

Maidlin sprang to hold open the swing door for her. The Pixie, catching the look in her eyes, as of one who had seen and heard so many new and bewildering things that her brain was in a whirl and quite beyond speech, paused to say a word of thanks. "You'll come again, won't you? If you learn a few dances, you shall come to a party too. And see you're nice to that other girl. Remember you were one of the family before she came. You have to do your share in making her feel at home. She can't be quite happy unless all three of you welcome her. You have to work together, and all help Joy. Now, good-bye, everybody!" and she ran down the steps to her own room, a tiny, eager figure in fawn knitted coat over smooth black tunic, black band round smooth fair hair.

"Darling!" murmured Jen, as Molly led them across the lounge, where girls were sitting at tables or in corners, standing round the piano, or practising a one-step in preparation for the next "modern dance."

"That's all very well!" said Joy sombrely, when—after curious glances into the many lighted rooms, all busy now with club-members; games, music, cinema, restaurant, all in full swing—they were racing in Eirene through the crowded brilliant streets back to the City and so to the West. "But I want to say more than 'Darling'! Think of what she's doing, just by being there, just by existing, just by meeting those people every day! It would be worth their while to pay her to stay there, even if she never taught a class. Just to have somebody about, thinking and talking as she does, is a big thing. And then think what she's taking those East End people, in our music and dancing. Talk about your 'something in the background'! It must change all their lives!"

"Yes!" said Jen thoughtfully. "If we, with all we've got, can imagine looking forward all week to our dance-evening, what must it be to girls living here and working in factories and shops, or living at home in those dreadfully crowded places! Think of coming even once a week and dancing country-dances in that beautiful gym!"

"With the Pixie in command, bullying them all in her own jolly, happy way, and making fun out of everything! I should simply live for it, I know. It sounds silly and sentimental, but that dancing once a week must be like a trip into gorgeous sunny country, it seems to me. They'll be fresher, and have new ideas, and—and be bigger in every way, because they've danced with the Pixie for an evening. She's doing a big thing," Joy said fervently. "I'm just sorry there's only one of her. She ought to be multiplied by umpteen thousands. There ought to be one of her in every street!"

"Oh, Joy!" Jen laughed. "But I do agree! I beg most heartily to endorse every statement the last speaker has made, Mr. Chairman! Them's my sentiments entirely! But all the same, I say again, *Darling!* Oh, that morris pipe, and her perched on the table! I'm dying to tell Joan!"

CHAPTER XVII

EDUCATING MAIDLIN

"She's a bit stodgy, isn't she?" Jack said doubtfully.

She had been "nice" to the heiress, though privately intensely curious about her. She had watched her all through the riotous supper, when Rosamund's place in the chatter had been ably filled by Jack herself, and Maidlin, shy and overcome as usual, had been wide-eyed but quiet and dumb. Now "the child" had been peremptorily ordered off to bed by "mother," with the remark, "I'm coming myself in half a sec."; and the three friends were sitting round the drawing-room fire for the indispensable confidences which were the happiest moments of these occasional meetings.

Jen looked expectantly at Joy, and Joy did not disappoint her. "No, she's not a scrap stodgy!" she said shortly. "It's only that she doesn't understand us, and hasn't learnt how to fool about yet. She's never been with people who turned into noisy lunatics every now and then. Stodgy! You should see her in a temper! Stodgy's the last word you'd use. She simply blazes up! She's got to get used to you, especially when you and Jen are together, which multiplies you both by X. Well, what's the matter with *you*?" as Jen gave a shout of laughter.

"Joy, you are funny! But you are a dear, as the Pixie would say! You won't have a word said against your infant by anybody else, will you? So you're giving Jacky-boy the benefit of all *my* arguments, that I used to you two nights ago! You are priceless, really! None of that's original, husband, except the bit about me multiplying you by X, which is true, and quite good! But none of the rest is, so don't look at her too respectfully! *She* said Maidlin was sulky, and I had to stand up for the kid! But if you say she's stodgy, you get all my words of wisdom fired back at you from Joy! 'Traveller's Joy,' it's really awfully sweet of you to speak up for Maidlin like that, when you know you don't understand her yourself!"

Joy's first wrath at this betrayal gave way to a merely indignant laugh. It was difficult, for her, at any rate, to be really angry with Jen. "Jenny-Wren, you're a little beast! Why do you need to go and give me away like that? Besides, you're not fair. You made me see how the kiddy felt, and I know now you were right. I spoke quite honestly, meaning every word; I forgot you'd said it all first. You make it sound as if I'd just said it for argument, to crush Jack."

"Oh, but I never thought that! I know you meant all you said. And I do think it's nice of you to stand up for her. She is hard to understand!"

"I'm trying to get to see her point of view," Joy rose and stood before the fire, still in her chauffeur's suit, for they had been so late for dinner that Jack had begged them not to change, as she was all alone. "It's a new stunt for me. I've always been content only to see my own; nobody else's even existed. Seems to me it's where I've gone wrong. Some people know by instinct what other folks are feeling and what to do to help them. You do fairly well, Jenny-Wren! I suppose you can't help it! And the Pixie, now; you feel all the time you're with her that she knows all about everybody, and loves them all, even their faults and failings and sillinesses. I love to watch her with people, bossing a crowd, and saying the right thing to every one. Big people are like that, I suppose. I never have been, but I'm going to try—"

"*Big* people? The Pixie, Joy?" Jack laughed.

"Oh, don't be a perfect infant, husband!" Jen said indignantly. "That's too obvious! Give us a rest! Joy's right; Newcastle said it when we first met the Pixie, and so did Cicely—'There's a lot more of her than you can see!' She's one of the all-round biggest people you're likely to get the chance of meeting. Now dry up, and don't make any more obvious jokes at this time of night! Joy, I feel just the same when I've been with her," as Jack retired into crushed silence for a few seconds.

"Of course; everybody does. That's why I took Maidlin along. I'm curious to know if she'll have anything to say about her. I had a word with the Pixie while you two were saying 'Oh! Oo-er!' over the swimming pool; I told her how difficult Maidlin was, and she said, 'Try to get to see her point of view.' I'm going to try. And to give the kid a chance I'm going to bed now, in case she wants to unburden herself when it's dark and there's nobody there but me! Mustn't keep her awake too late! She's been watching everything all day, with such huge round eyes, that she may have to unload some remarks about it all before she goes to sleep! You children can sit up and babble and yatter as long as you like! You'll only keep one another from going to sleep. I'm going to bed with my infant. Good-night!"

"Joy's an awfully good sort," Jack said tentatively, at risk of another snubbing. "She never used to be like that, did she, Jen?"

"She's one of the best, and she's getting jollier every day, without any idea she's doing it," Jen said warmly. "I think the Pixie thinks so too. I saw her look at Joy now and then, in her quick, bird-like way, as if she were finding her really *very* interesting! And of course, Joy looks down at *her* as if the Pixie were some kind of priceless little treasure! It's rather great to watch them both! Let's go upstairs, anyway, Jacky-boy! We can talk in bed. I don't say we'll go to sleep, but we might begin getting undressed!"

Joy said nothing when she went into her room, but only switched on one light, as far from the bed as possible, and undressed quietly. But when she was slipping into bed, Maidlin turned towards her at once, and Joy, with her new sensitiveness, which had begun to come as soon as she "began to try to understand," and was growing with every effort she made, knew the child had something to say.

"D'you mind sleeping with me, kid?" she whispered. "You aren't shy still, are you? Not with me? I thought you'd be such a scrap in a big room all alone in a strange house, in the middle of London!" But she knew the answer already; Maidlin's radiant face, when the suggestion had been made casually to her before they left home, had shown how she felt.

"I'm glad. I'm not shy!" the whisper came vehemently, and Maidlin crept into her arms. "Joy, will you listen? I've been dying to tell you!"

It was then that Joy began to reap the reward of her efforts at patience and understanding. Feeling that it had been well worth it, she put her arms round the child, and found her quivering with eagerness. "Tell me, kiddy! I've been dying to know. I know you think we're all very queer; but you will get used to us, you know."

"*You* think *I'm* queer!" Maidlin burst out, and Joy wished Jack could have been there to take back that "stodgy." "I know; I've seen! I've seen you look at Jen, when I sat in a corner and couldn't think what to say, and Rosamund could talk and laugh and play about, as you did. I'm a bother to you, and I'm sorry. I'd be different if I knew how. I—I'm two people, like Jen said you were; and—and neither of them's your kind!"

"Oh, Jen said that, did she?" Joy laughed. "I'll ask her what she meant by it! Jen's two people herself, Maidlin; or more than two! Jen's a tomboy, and great fun; she's grown up with big brothers at home, and lots of girls at boarding-school, and she's used to being one of a crowd, and jolly and noisy and happy. And yet she's understanding, and artistic in all her thoughts, and musical; and she's done a lot for the children in the frightfully lonely village on the moors where she lives. She teaches them folk-songs and dances, and she's making them love music and colour and pretty things, and they simply worship their 'Miss Jen,' and she never says a word about it to anybody down here. She's a different person when she's teaching her village kiddies; and she loves them no end."

"Oh! I didn't know! I hadn't heard about all that. But she is nice! She—she tries to understand."

"She understands better than I do, ever so much. You get her to tell you about her children! But tell me about being two people yourself? I suppose we all are. There's one bit of you that's very quiet, isn't there?"

"I *can't* say things! They're all shut up inside me!" Maidlin panted, expressing herself with difficulty even now. "I don't know why. I feel things, and think things, but I can't get them out. You all say such a lot, and it sounds so easy! I don't know how; I can't say anything, and the more I want to say, the worse it gets!" She knew no other way to describe the self-contained, repressed nature of her north-country ancestry and training. "Aunty was like that, and uncle," she was feeling after the explanation, and coming near it. "We never talked a lot, or laughed much, or made jokes, as you do. We never said things we didn't mean; you do it all the time!"

"Just talking nonsense," Joy amended. "I'm afraid we do. Aunty would have said we were dreadful fibbers, wouldn't she?"

"She'd have thought you were very funny!" Maidlin tried to put it politely.

"In the sense of queer, or odd. Not humorous!" Joy's lips were twitching, but fortunately it was dark.

195

"She'd have said you were awfully good and kind!" Maidlin spoke fervently, and with unmistakable sincerity; it was no mere phrase to gloss over her first criticism. "But she'd have said you were different from us, and she didn't know how to take you, many a time."

Joy laughed at this quaint expression, which rang so true. "You poor kid! It has been hard on you to be plunged in among us so suddenly! But you will get used to us, kiddy! And the other part of you is the Italian side, I suppose? The side that flares up like gunpowder, and makes you do and say things you'd never thought of before?"

"I can't help it!" Maidlin whispered, quivering again. "I don't know when it's going to happen. I don't know what I'm doing sometimes; something seems to take hold of me from somewhere. It is just like being two people, Joy!"

"Of course it is! And one's your daddy, and one's your English mother, and they've each made a bit of you. What you have to do, kid, is to find the best bits of both; calm down your daddy's temper—I don't say he has it himself, but it was in his family, and he's passed it on to you; and soften your stern, dour, silent side, that's come to you from generations of north-country farming people; awfully good people, and honest, and hard-working, and people you could trust to the limit—Jen knows heaps of them!— but narrow, you know, and unable to enjoy life and see its beauty; and unable to say what they felt, if they did see it. You've got the feeling for it all right; your daddy gave you that. You love music; and you're going to love dancing—which your aunt probably thought was wrong! Didn't she, now?"

"Yes, she said it was bad," Maidlin whispered what she realised must be heresy to Joy.

"And you've always believed it. But did you think it was bad to-night, when you saw those Plaistow boys—*men!*—all so jolly and happy, after working hard in business all day? Did you feel you were watching something wicked?"

"Oh, no, no! Not that kind of dancing! It was good for them, and—and they did love it so much! And—and *she*—she's lovely!"

"The Pixie? How did you like her? She's a dancing teacher, you know; she teaches it because she feels it's good, and a help to people, and will make them better and happier and more friendly."

"I loved her! I couldn't say it, but I'd—I'd like to help her, like you said you'd try to do."

"We'll help her together," Joy promised seriously. "You shall talk to the lame children when I take them out driving."

"I couldn't. I wouldn't know what to say."

"Oh, yes, you will! We'll make up a list of jolly things to say, for the first time! You'll soon get into the way of it!" Joy said helpfully. "Must feel funny not to know what to say! It's never troubled me!—I say, though, kid! You've not only got to learn to get things out, but to keep them in too! You can't think how awful I felt when you flew off in a temper because I'd brought Rosamund home! It was fearfully unkind to *me*, you know! I'd brought her to my house, and you made it awfully awkward for me, and difficult for me to welcome her properly. You simply mustn't go doing things like that!"

She had felt Maidlin's jump of surprise, and had talked on purposely to give her a moment for recovery.

When she paused, a shamed whisper came at once. "I am sorry! I didn't think of it that way. I've been sorry all the time, but I—I couldn't say it. I don't know what made me do it. She's—she's very nice!" bravely. "And she's heaps cleverer than I am."

"Poor infant!" Joy thought pitifully. But she only said gravely, "I don't know about that. Rosamund's just a jolly usual kind of girl. But she wants to be friends with everybody, and she doesn't understand you yet. It may comfort you to know that *I* once had a beast of a temper, and used to go off like gunpowder, as you do. Things happened once or twice, at school!"

"You! Oh, you couldn't!"

"Oh, yes, I could, and I did! My grandfather gave it to me, as well as giving me the Hall. But it keeps more in its proper place now. Just occasionally it pops its little head up and worries me still. You've got to learn to keep yours under too; and at the same time you've got to help other things to come out. You want to learn to fool about, as Jen and Jack do; weren't they idiots at dinner? To say nothing of myself! I say, would you like to start at once? It would be frightfully mad, and an awfully improper thing to teach you; but it would be frightfully good for you!"

The light over the bed switched on under the pressure of her fingers, and she sat up, shaking back her long red plait and looking down at dazzled Maidlin with laughing eyes.

"How? What? What do you mean?"

"You're wide awake! It can't do you any harm. Listen, then! I owe Jenny-Wren something for telling you I was two people at once; and you owe Jacky-boy something for saying you were so—quiet! Yes, she did; when you'd come up to bed. Don't you want to pay her out, and show her you're not? She thinks you're rather a shy little mouse; let's give her a shock, and show her you've some spunk in you!" Joy tempted wickedly. "They won't be asleep; not if I know them! They'll talk till midnight easily, and it's not that yet. I heard them come up, but they'll have reams to say. They haven't seen one another for four whole days! Bring your pillow, and any cushions you can collect, and we'll bombard them. I'll take the bolster," and Joy found her slippers, and staggered to the door, the unwieldy bolster in her arms.

Maidlin gave her one amazed, incredulous look. Then she gathered up pillows and cushions and followed, breathless with excitement, to see what would happen.

"It's this room. I guess I know my way about Jacky-boy's house by now! Yes, they're babbling; listen! Bad children!" at a low laugh from within the room. "The light's out, of course; they have got that much sense! Now the bed's to the left. When I open the door, you fling those pillows one after another, as fast as ever you can. Don't make a sound. Just shy them straight and hard. Oh, good for you!" as Maidlin gave an uncontrollable giggle.

The corridor was in darkness. Joy flung wide the door, and two startled voices demanded sharply, "Who's that?" The light flashed on; but as it did so, pillows and cushions hurtled through the air, and a stifled yell from Jack—"You brutes!"—told that one had got home.

Then Joy, invisible behind the bolster, pinned Jen down on the bed. "Jenny-Wren, I'm two people, am I? *That's* from the stern avenging one! *And that's* from the spoilt baby! I'm sure you said I was a baby!" with a vigorous punch from each. "Come on, Maidlin! Stifle them both! I owe them one since last August, when they nearly battered the breath out of me at Cheltenham! This is R-r-r-revenge! Seven months I've waited for my revenge!" she hissed. "Vengeance is sweet! Are you enjoying it, you two?"

"Oh, don't!" gasped Jen, weak with laughter, holding her sides. "Joy, get away! I'm going to die! I thought you—you said— you'd never kill me again!"

"It's a simply beastly way to behave in another person's house!" Jack spluttered, writhing under the pillows. "As for Maidlin, it's disgusting! She's hardly been introduced yet!"

"I'm introducing her, as hard as I can. Shut the door, out of consideration for the maids, kid. Now you may laugh, all you want to! Put that on first, though," and she threw Jack's dressing-gown at Maidlin's head.

"It was well worth spoiling your night's rest, to see the kid laugh like that, instead of staring like an owl!" Joy said, when she apologised next morning. For Maidlin had collapsed in a heap on the floor, helpless with hysterical laughter.

"It's simply priceless!" Jen sobbed into her pillow. "Joy talks like a mother about not keeping Maidlin awake late, and then—then this! Joy, you aren't fit to be a mother to anybody! Your solemn face when you went up to bed!—and look at you now! Oh, you are an idiot! It's as good as Cheltenham!"

"Have you got any jam-tarts, Jacky-boy?" Joy asked gravely.

Jack darted out of the room, a silent barefoot shadow in pale pink pyjamas and tousled black curls. Jen stifled another shriek of laughter.

"Joy, why did you? We don't want them! We've only just had dinner! Maidlin thinks you're mad!"

"I like being mad!" a gurgle came from Maidlin on the floor. "It's—it's jolly nice!"

"Tarts I crave and tarts I must have; they are a necessary part of the entertainment. I hope Jacky-boy can rise to the occasion. If she can't find any, she'll have to make some. What a picture! Jack, in her pyjams, making tarts in a silent kitchen at midnight.— It's part of the cure," she mumbled in Jen's ear, rolling her over on the bed. "It's working, too. We've broken the ice, I do believe. Don't you see, you ass? We *never* did this with Rosamund!"

"Oh!" Jen came to attention. "'Traveller's Joy,' how deep and wily you are!" she whispered. "Is it all part of a Deep-Laid Scheme? A Plot? A—a Ruse?"

"Part of her education. She can't be scared of us after this. Oh, cheers! Here's the Bold Adventurer come back! What has she brought?"

"Cream buns. You'll have to wash again; you'll be sticky all over; I didn't bring forks. I thought of these as soon as you said 'tarts,'" Jack explained importantly. "I bought them; they're mine. I meant them for to-morrow night, after the party; but we'll get some more. You know we always have to stodge after dancing. Come on and make pigs of yourselves! Isn't it a good thing mother's away?"

"If mother hadn't been away, I should have thought twice before allowing Maidlin to amuse herself in this fashion," Joy said maternally. "She was most anxious to give you the shock of your lives."

"Oh, *Joy*!" gasped Maidlin, and Jen and Jack giggled.

The plate, heaped with cream buns, was placed impressively, but rather unsteadily, in the middle of the very dishevelled bed. Jen lay back, limp and exhausted, with all the pillows she could reach thrust behind her back, and held out her hand wearily for a bun.

"I'm weak! But it has been rather nice! Awfully sporting of you, Maidlin and Joy!"

"Stand by with a sponge!" Joy said anxiously. "Oh, she's not going to faint!"—callously. "But she's far too shaky to eat cream buns safely. We'll have to mop her up. Come along, infant! Now have you *ever*, in all your life, done such a thing before?"

"Such a mad thing!" Jack supplemented. "Don't you wonder Joy ever gets invited out by anybody? I don't believe she does, as a matter of fact. She invites herself. I hesitated a long time before I said I'd have her. I didn't think it was quite safe; especially with Jen!"

"Oh, but it wasn't me this time!" Jen said happily. "It was Maidlin!"

Maidlin curled herself up beside Joy in a corner, and tucked her feet under a spare pillow. "I've never had a chance to do mad things before. But I like them. I think perhaps I'll do this *often* now!" said she.

"You jolly well won't! I'll see to that!" Joy assured her warmly.

Then the cuckoo on the mantelpiece came out to tell them it was midnight, and the eyes of all four met in conscience-stricken amusement. Joy grabbed a bun in each hand, and rose with dignity. "Thank you for your kind hospitality, Jacqueline! Kindly precede us bearing our pillows, bolsters, and cushions! Our hands are— er—otherwise occupied. Grab two of those buns quickly, kid, or Jen will have taken them all, and then she'll be jolly sick. Lead the way, Jacqueline!"

"I wouldn't do it, Jacky-boy!" Jen vowed.

"Oh, it's worth it, to get rid of them! I want to get to bed. You have to humour lunatics! Shall I sing a farewell dirge?" and Jack gathered up the pillows.

"Do the 'Helston Furry'!" Jen began to laugh again.

"You'll have hysterics!" Jack said warningly. "Do come away, you two! It's awfully bad for her! There!" and she dumped the pillows on their bed. "Now clean yourselves up and make your room decent! And do stop in it this time! I call it simply a disgraceful way to behave, in a respectable house! Respectable when it isn't sheltering lunatics, at least!"

"You'll have to apologise to the maids in the morning, I'm afraid, Jacky-boy," Joy said seriously. "I'm sure they must have heard us!"

"I'm sure too! But I shan't. They know what to expect when you and Jen come!" and with that parting shot Jack fled back to bed.

CHAPTER XVIII

"CUCKOO'S NEST"

"IT was *fun*!" Maidlin whispered, as she snuggled down into Joy's arms again.

"Rather! Wouldn't Rosamund have loved it? If you're sporting, you'll tell her all about it. She's missed it all."

There was silence for a moment. Then Maidlin whispered, "I will be sporting, Joy. Because—because you are."

"Nice kid!" But Joy was touched. "Now go to sleep, baby! By-bye!"

When Maidlin met Jen and Jack at breakfast next morning, the vision of pillows, pyjamas, and cream buns that rose before her eyes was irresistible. She broke into an infectious giggle, and Jen laughed.

"And I meant to look so severe! It was simply disgraceful of Joy! Didn't I tell you she was a baby?"

"I liked it!" Maidlin said stoutly. "I like her like that!"

"Oh, you do, do you?" Joy retorted. "I rather thought you didn't! Don't you look at me any more as if you thought I was an escaped lunatic, then, Madalena!"

"I never did!" Maidlin protested indignantly.

"Oh, yes, you did! We'll see if cream buns at midnight have cured you! Now hustle, infant! We've got a busy day before us."

The day was something of an ordeal to Maidlin, still struggling as she was to get her footing in these unexpectedly deep places. Joy had plunged her far beyond her depth into the new life, and her silent awkwardness during these first few days had only been in self-defence, while she strove desperately to get her breath and readjust her ideas.

She was quiet again as they interviewed her father's lawyer by appointment; but Joy was at ease in business of this kind, and the visit did not take long. The great man was interested and very kind. He listened respectfully to the plans proposed by Maidlin's aunt for her immediate future, and to Joy's suggestions for carrying them out; and approved warmly of all she had done, thanking her in a way Maidlin echoed in her heart, but could not have put into words.

"All the same, the poor old chap doesn't begin to see through my ideas for you, Madalena!" Joy said solemnly, when they were in the car again and driving towards the West End shops. "Perhaps I'll tell you what I mean to-morrow! And perhaps I won't. Perhaps you'll feel it for yourself. But it's quite beyond *him*! Now for your trousseau! Jenny-Wren, you've got to help here. No skulking outside in Eirene when there's work to be done!"

Jen had politely stayed out in Eirene during the visit to the lawyer's, but came joyfully into every one of the big shops Joy patronised, and gave her advice without hesitation. Joy, fresh from trousseau-hunting with Joan, knew where to go; she knew also what she wanted, and what she meant Maidlin to have. But she had arranged with Jen privately that for her own sake Maidlin must be encouraged to choose for herself, and that it would be interesting to see what her choice would be.

"We can guide her tactfully to the right things at the last moment, and she'll never know. We'll easily make her think she chose them herself!" she had said, and on those diplomatic lines they proceeded.

Maidlin's double personality soon showed itself in the matter of choice. Inherited tendency clashed at once with all the ideas of her upbringing. At first she turned towards sober, good garments, which would wear well—"That would be useful!" she said shyly. And in the next breath, much more shyly, "Of course, this is lovely! But you couldn't wear it, could you?"

"Why not?" Joy asked bluntly.

Maidlin gave her a startled look. "Why, the—the colour! It's so bright!"

"It would suit the young lady excellently," said the shop-girl, with interest.

"With your hair, and your clear skin, it would be tophole," Jen said decidedly. "You niggery people always look gorgeous in vivid things."

"D'you like bright colours, Maidlin?" Joy asked carelessly, a length of flame-coloured silk in one hand, and one of soft gray in the other.

"Oh, I love them!—to look at! But—I never wore colours like that."

"Missy would look well in any of these," and the girl heaped pinks and reds and yellows and vivid greens and blues before them, till Maidlin gasped.

"Wait till you go home! To Italy, you know!" Joy remarked. "Don't be so terrified of colours, kid! You're born to them; you've inherited them. Now get over the shock, and tell us just which you like best. Not that gray! That's the colour Miriam and Joan used to wear for dancing; lovely for them, but not for you. Wear some of those glorious reds, and be thankful, child! I've been wanting them all my life!" and the attendant smiled.

Maidlin's choice, when it was freed at last, was all for colour and richness; for neutral or pale tints she had no use. "That's your daddy," Joy said grimly. "Fortunately, he gave you the looks to go with them! Your mother—by whom I mean her whole family, you know; all your aunts, and everybody—know nothing whatever about colour; it simply doesn't exist for Ann, for instance! But you know, inside you, what a big thing it is and what a difference it makes."

"I'm trying to rub that fact into my kiddies at home!" Jen laughed. "You should see their jumpers! We've brightened up our gray little hamlet a trifle, between us. Oh, I *am* enjoying myself to-day! I love shopping! Maidlin, do you realise what a boon you are to Joy and me? It's priceless to have the chance of dressing a girl right through, top to bottom, and one who knows pretty things when she sees them!"

"She means it! Don't look so unbelieving, kid. We're both having a gorgeous time. Don't you make any mistake about that!" Joy said exuberantly.

After that, Maidlin settled down to enjoy herself also, and went home at last, having ordered a number of frocks to be made, and the possessor of an incredible quantity, as it seemed to her, of dainty underclothing, whose fineness awed and delighted her. There was a pretty coat and hat for immediate wear, also a red dress for home use, and a silk frock of deep rose pink which she was ordered to put on for the party that same evening.

The guidance of the elder girls had been needed occasionally, and had been given very gently, but quite firmly, generally in the matter of blending colours.

"Yes, it's lovely!" Jen would say warmly. "But not with that hat you've just chosen, Maidlin! You couldn't, you know." Or again, "I like them both, but of course, not together!" And gradually Maidlin began to understand that while bright colours were not as sinful as she had supposed—apparently because her hair and eyes were black—yet discretion must be used in mixing them. She was quick to grasp and remember, and did not realise that her education was going forward by leaps and bounds.

"Get into the pink frock while we change!" Joy commanded after tea. "We're going to a morris class, which implies tunics, as

I think you know by this time; but you're only going to sit in a corner, so you may as well be ready. We'll have a fearful rush to get changed."

So Maidlin arrayed herself—no lesser word would do justice to her feelings at the moment—in the new dress, and went in shyly to show herself, bright spots of excitement on her cheeks.

The three girls, in business-like blue tunics with green girdles, which they still wore for their old school's sake, were getting into big coats and picking up their dancing shoes; hats could be dispensed with on a fine night, when the hall was just round the corner.

"Some swank!" Jack stared at Maidlin frankly. "Swish! I love pink frocks!"

"It suits you, Madalena," Joy's tone was carefully offhand. "Don't say too much!" she had warned the others. "It isn't good for the young to be admired! She'll look a dream! But don't dream of telling her so!"

"Jolly nice!" Jen looked her over with approval. "You've put it on nicely too, Maidlin. Have you got the foreigner's knack? Be thankful if you have. I don't suppose you've had a chance to find out yet, but we'll soon know."

Much of this Maidlin did not understand. But she knew they were satisfied, and her happiness and excitement grew.

Joy's anxiety as to who would be teaching that night had been increasing all day, and Maidlin had heard so much about her hopes that she almost understood. It might be some one referred to as "Madam," or "The Duchess," and in that case Joy was going to be blissfully happy; or it might be one of several others, and any one else would be a severe disappointment, it appeared. She followed the three across Great Portland Street to the big hall, pausing only to satisfy Jack's craving for a long look at the lights of Portland Place and to show Maidlin that side of London life

"Maidlin went in shyly to show herself."

for the first time; and fell behind diffidently as they ran up the steps.

By Jen's laugh and Joy's groan, she knew the teacher on the platform was not the beloved "Madam," of whom she had heard so much. Jen went forward to ask permission to join in the class.

"Do you mind? We couldn't resist the thought of some morris. If your sets aren't all made up, may we go in a corner somewhere? We've done a little 'Field Town,' so we'll try not to be too much of a bother to you;" she had heard the music as they crossed the hall.

"Have you come up for the party? We didn't quite kill you the other night, then?" the teacher smiled.

"No, but I was stiff! I suppose it was 'Argeers.'"

"You'll be stiffer to-morrow, if you've done no morris since the summer! All right! Go into that back set. But we shall make you work, you know."

Jen laughed and nodded, and ran to fetch sticks. "It's 'Bobby and Joan,' isn't it?"

"You squeeze into a corner, and watch," said Joy to Maidlin, and her eyes followed the teacher, whom she had often seen at Cheltenham, as she led a girl out into the middle of the floor and gave her a demonstration of the hop-back step, showed how she had been doing it and just where she had been wrong, and how she could correct the fault. The girl, laughing a little because she knew all eyes were on her, pluckily tried to understand and copy the movement, and with a smile of approval and a word of encouragement, their mentor left her at last to practise, but only when she was satisfied the explanation had been understood.

"Doesn't she take a lot of trouble, just over one person?" Joy marvelled, in an undertone. "I don't know if I'd like to be hauled out and put through it before the crowd like that!"

"You would, if you were keen enough," Jen said wisely. "She

knows who are the keen ones, I bet! Doesn't she?" and she looked
with a smile at the Writing Person, who had just come in, in big
coat and hat and carrying shoes. "Aren't you dancing to-night?"

"I've come for the party. Two hours of party, after an hour of
morris, would do me in. I just crawl home as it is. But I love to
watch the classes first. Some people do two hours and a half of
classes, then a quick change, and dance for two hours at the party.
I'm keen, but I couldn't do that. I should be dead. Besides, there's
to-morrow night! I can't afford to kill myself outright on a
Thursday. May I ask you something?" to Joy.

"If I may ask something too!" Joy said promptly. "We've
brought a kiddy with us; over there, in the corner, with the big
eyes! She's been reading one of your books. May I bring her to
speak to you? She'll be too shy to say a word, but she'll love to
see you. Jen bought the book for her last week, after meeting you
on Friday night."

"How awfully nice of you!" the Writing Person laughed to
Jen. "I hope she wasn't disappointed in it! I'll go and talk to her
while you're dancing. Where are the rest of your crowd? There
were a lot of you at Cheltenham. Do tell me if there have been
any weddings? I was sure there was one coming, and perhaps
two."

Joy laughed. "We've been bridesmaids twice since Christmas.
Joan and Cicely are both abroad now."

"I am glad! Thank you so much! It's tremendously satisfying
to know the end of the story. I couldn't help wondering, of course.
You had no men when you first turned up, but before the end of
the month there seemed no doubt of their intentions."

"Are you going to put them in a book?" Jen asked. "You'd
better come and see Joan's abbey; it's full of stories. Things simply
will happen there!"

"Make up sets for 'Cuckoo's Nest,'" said the teacher on the

platform, and the other four with whom Joy and Jen had danced made frantic signs to them to come and take their places.

"Good luck to you!" said the Writing Person. "I've been hauled out into the middle of hall for this! The capers, you know; she came and worked my arms to show me what she wanted, and criticised my capers at the same time. As I'm still only able to control one part of me at a time, I didn't manage to satisfy her. I nearly died when she stood over me."

"Of rage?" Joy asked sympathetically.

"No, of amusement. Oh, you don't have to mind that kind of thing! I'm keen enough on morris to want to get it right. I dare say it was awfully funny for the rest, but I hadn't time to think about that. It was jolly decent of her to think I was worth taking trouble over. I hardly think I am, myself," and she walked down the room to Maidlin's corner.

The girls saw her say something—apparently, "I hear you've been reading something of mine. Which book was it?"—for Maidlin's face lit up in incredulous interest, and they were soon deep in talk.

The class, failing to give satisfaction in its shuffles, found its sets ignominiously broken up and everybody set to practise up and down the room in long lines. Forward for two bars, then shuffling backwards for two, they went time after time, till they thought they must know every mark on the floor, for all had their eyes on their feet. Their teacher walked up and down between the lines, watching critically, making comments and suggestions, and very occasionally giving a sparing word of praise. Jen's eyes met Joy's, bright with suppressed amusement, but they kept their feelings to themselves, till after ten minutes of steady shuffling they were allowed to rest a moment.

"Don't you feel an infant in arms?" Jen laughed, as she dropped into a chair near Maidlin. "But it's just what I needed! I knew the less said about my shuffles the better. And of course, she saw!"

"I never knew what was wrong with mine before. I knew they were bad! But she spotted it as soon as she looked at my feet; did you see her stand over me till I got them the right width apart? It's a different thing altogether when you're made to see it."

"She's been telling me about people!" Maidlin whispered to Joy, when the morris class was over, and in the interval the Writing Person had gone to speak to others. "There! That one she's talking to now! She's a Wise Brown Owl; doesn't it sound funny? It means she's the leader of a lot of little children, called Brownies, who aren't old enough to be Guides yet; and she teaches them singing-games, and plays with them, and does Nature-study with them, all in the middle of London somewhere. The Writing Lady says the Brown Owl once gave up a whole evening's dancing to go out with her into the country, to a wood where there were all kinds of birds' nests and baby birds, because she wanted to tell her Brownies about them afterwards."

"She's the tomboy-girl from Oxford Circus, Joy," said Jen, glancing at the round-faced girl with wavy, bobbed dark hair, who was chatting eagerly with their new friend.

"And that one she's going to now!" as the Writing Person turned to another friend. "She told me about her too," Maidlin said eagerly. "She's the drill and games mistress in a big school, with four hundred girls, and she teaches them all country-dancing, and they dance beautifully. She doesn't look nearly old enough, does she? But then none of them do. I suppose it's the drill dresses, isn't it?"

"And the bobbed hair; you see how many of them have it! I suppose you know everybody?" Joy challenged the writer of books, when she returned from her chat with the jolly, happy-looking gym mistress.

"I wish I did! But I've been coming to classes for some time now, and the same people keep turning up."

"Tell us about some of them!" Jen urged. "We aren't going to dance in this. We're going to race home to change for the party in a moment."

"I'm going out for coffee. I can't go round asking questions of them all, though I'd love to. Everybody has some story behind, but it's only by chance you hear about them. If I asked questions, they'd think I was after copy! As if I had time to think about my work, once I get here! I'm far too busy enjoying myself. I believe some of them suspect me of coming to find things I can make use of afterwards; if they only knew, it takes me all my time to keep up with people like Madam, who expect you to be frightfully quick at picking up things. I never think about work from the moment I get here till I'm safely away again; haven't a second to spare for it. That's why the classes are such a rest, such a thorough change. As for thinking, 'I could use that in a story,' and at the same time paying decent attention to all those thousands of tiny points you have to remember in morris, or the figures in country, it simply can't be done. I'm far too rattled to think about anything but the business of the moment."

"But you have used the dancing in books, haven't you?"

"Oh, yes! But I've never consciously come to classes or schools to look for material. What does happen, of course, is that when I've enjoyed a thing enough, it has to come out later; generally after some months. Things lie for a while, and then they work up into stories. But not at the time! And I never go about asking questions from that point of view. But I am always interested in the stories lying behind people, of course, and sometimes things come out in talk. One thing that always surprises me is the girls, just bits of girls, who answer to 'Mrs.' when the register's called. I suppose it's a result of the war. That one, first woman in this set, the very pretty dancer; do you see?"

"Yes? She's not married, surely?"

"Got two children, a boy of three, and a girl of five. Well, she says so!" in answer to their incredulous protest. "I've only seen a photo of them. We asked if she'd been married at eleven, but she was nineteen, and it was in 1914. She's a war widow; oh, yes! The husband's dead. There are other stories I could tell you; just now and then I hear about some one. I had a little partner once, with straight, bobbed hair; looked about seventeen. But if you'd heard that kid talk about geology and botany! She was taking her B.Sc. at Chelsea Polytechnic, and giving up all her holidays to specimen hunting. She got it, too; and also got engaged to a boy who was the same way inclined. You'd never have thought she was brainy, to look at her!"

"Tell us some more!" Jen begged eagerly. Joy was listening in deep interest.

"Oh, I can't go on telling life-histories! But there is one very interesting thing about nearly all these people! If you talk to them long, you find they have 'girls' in the background. You hear about 'my girls' or 'my children.' Sometimes it's the children in their day-school classes; most of them are teachers, of course. But very often it's big girls, Guides, or a club, or Guildry, girls to whom they're teaching folk-dancing in the evenings, mostly just for the love of it. They nearly all do it."

"And have you girls in the background, too?" Joy asked curiously. "Real ones, I mean? Or are the book ones enough? You don't teach, do you?"

"Not regularly; I wouldn't have the patience! But I have girls too. I doubt if one could go on having the book ones otherwise. I mean, you want to be with real girls sometimes; don't you think so? Mine are a Camp Fire; I've been their Guardian for six years."

"A Camp Fire? What's that?"

"Oh, there really isn't time to tell you that!" she laughed. "But see my Guardian's pin; isn't it neat? You'll never see me without that! And there's the ring; our sign of membership," and she took a silver ring from the little finger of her left hand, and told the meaning of its symbols. "We're very keen on sword and country dancing. The girls would like morris too, but they can't give the time to practise that I think it needs. My respect for morris is too high, and my opinion of my own is too low. I'd hate to have it badly done. So we stick to swords and country. I remember the excitement the first time I suggested country-dancing!"

"Did you begin it so that you could teach the girls? Jolly decent of you!"

"No, I'm afraid I didn't. That idea came later. I began because I loved the music, and wanted to know what dances fitted the tunes. But the girls were keen from the first. I remember our first night with 'Earsdon,' too," she laughed. "We couldn't untie our Nut. And I'd thought I understood it! When I told Madam, next week, she stared at me for a moment, and then just shouted."

"'Earsdon!' Help! Fancy teaching rappers!"

"The girls love them; but then they're a fairly brainy lot; I only taught one team, you know, not the whole crowd. We tried it in our dining-room first, and nearly smashed the electric light."

"I should think so!" Jack, leaning on Jen's shoulder, was listening round-eyed. "Couldn't *untie* your Nut? Don't you mean you couldn't tie it?"

"We tied it beautifully," the Writing Person assured her gravely. "But we couldn't undo the wretched thing again; short of flinging it on the floor and kicking it to pieces, of course. There was always that as a last resort. We didn't know which handles to take when it was lowered; that was the trouble. I'd learned it as Four, and, without realising it, I'd been content to take the last hilt and point, the one everybody else had left for me; and it had always come right. I'd had the feeling all along that it had just happened by chance, but that I didn't know why. When the girls tried to untie, their hands came all crossed, and we were tied up in the most awful knot."

Jack giggled. "Did you 'phone for Madam to come and undo you?"

"I thought we'd have to. The girls all looked at me most accusingly, and I felt desperate. We pulled the thing to pieces on the floor, and tied it again, very carefully, and then we all stood and looked at it for a long, long time, and talked about it, till we knew just which hands had to be on top, and how many hilts and points there must be between each. I even suggested tying coloured threads on our own handles, to be sure we'd get the right ones again, but the girls wouldn't hear of it; they wanted to understand, and, of course, they were right. We've never had any trouble with our Nut since. We had a frightful experience a few weeks ago!" she said pensively. "We'd worked up 'Sleights' and 'Earsdon,' and were going to show them for the first time, and all the parents and heaps of friends were invited; and the night before the show, Number One in 'Sleights' and Three in 'Earsdon' began with measles!"

"Help! The night before? What did you do?"

"Put in a reserve who knew her Single Guard and Nut, but not her figures, and did double work myself taking care of her and telling her how to turn, and at the same time keeping up my own end as Five. And went into 'Sleights' as One myself. I was in 'Earsdon' already, because the girls wouldn't face it without me to whisper the names of the figures. Unfortunately, they have fancy names for them, and I don't always remember. 'Prince of Wales' is known as 'Kitty's arm exercises,' or 'Where you swish round'; 'Fixy' is 'Putting on Kitty's braces'! It needs presence of mind to think where you're doing it."

"Yes," Jack laughed. "If you come out with those names in class, Madam will stare! How did it go, after all those troubles?"

"Fairly correct, but very slow and careful. No life in it, but nobody in the audience knew that. They'd never seen rappers before, and they were properly thrilled. But we all knew that our stop-gap had a doubtful elbow, that might give way at any moment; and that she'd just put her knee out. And there she was doing 'Prince of Wales' and step-and-jump over the swords! We were all in terror of what might happen any second."

"Frightfully plucky of her to see you through!" Jen remarked.

"Yes, it was jolly decent. But she didn't give way anywhere, and the situation was saved. But I thought my hair would be white before the end of that evening."

The girls laughed. "But if you've taught 'Earsdon,' why do you keep on coming to the class every Friday?" Jack asked curiously.

"For the fun of doing it. I love it, now that I've stopped being terrified"—Jack laughed sympathetically—"Besides, I don't say I could do any place! I've got it all written down, and I've taught my own team, and I could teach it again; but I never know how they're all going to turn in 'Fixy'! I leave that to them; they all know their own places. If I had to be anything but Five at a moment's notice, you'd see me feverishly reading it up. I always think you need to learn 'Earsdon' at least five times. I say!" she hinted, "hadn't you better—did you say you were going to change?"

Jack gave one glance at the clock, and fled. Joy paused to say to Maidlin, "We shan't have time for any dinner. You wait here for us, kiddy, and I'll bring you in a bun. You can hold out, can't you? It isn't worth while coming with us. We shall simply fling off our tunics and jump into frocks and come tearing back."

"She'll come with me, and have buns in the shop at the corner,"

217

said the Writing Person. "I always go there for coffee before the party begins; there's such a crowd in here, and it's such a waste of time to have it when you might be dancing! You'll come, won't you, Maidlin?"

Maidlin looked up at her with shy interest. "Will you tell me more funny things about your Camp Fire?"

"Funny! That concert wasn't funny! It was a fearful occasion—at the time! But I'll talk Camp Fire, if you like—Indian names, and gowns, and symbols. You know all about it, of course!"

"It was in the book. I've never heard of it before. I'd like to go camping! Did you ever have a cat just like that one?"

"Grey Edward? We've got him still. He's supposed to be *very* proud because he's been put in a book and everybody's heard about him. He says it doesn't happen to *many* pussies!"

Maidlin laughed. "Does he talk as much as he did in the book?"

"Well, my sister says he does. She translates; he's her cat. We have to take her word for it. Slip out quietly; don't let the door bang. It's a fearful crime. The noise when it bangs nearly reduces Madam to tears," she laughed, to Joy and Jen, who had changed their shoes and were hurrying out. "It gets on her nerves till she nearly weeps, and wants to swear, and her husband does it for her. I saw her sit down and cover her ears and shudder once; so he expressed her feelings for her, quite forcibly, and then said soothingly, 'It's all right, dear! I've said it for you! You can go on now!' See you later, then! Come along, Maidlin!"

CHAPTER XIX

ONE JOLLY EVENING

IT had been another day of new experiences for Maidlin, but not the least of them came in the last two hours. Hoisted up on to a wide window-sill by Joy, she sat enthralled as the big square hall filled with girls and men, till all the wide floor-space was a mass of moving colour. The dances had no meaning for her yet; she had never seen a country-dance except in that evening's class. She saw that sometimes the dancers were in rings, flying round with linked hands, sometimes in long double lines stretching the whole length of the hall, sometimes in square sets of eight people, sometimes in short lines of six or eight, and sometimes, in little squares of four. Sometimes suddenly they were all in lines hand in hand across the hall, running up towards the platform; she did not know how it had happened, but it had come about quite easily and naturally, with no bustle or confusion; one moment they were facing one another in the double lines, the next, all were facing up hand in hand, without any sign or word of command. Maidlin wondered greatly how they all knew what to do at the right moment, as she saw it happen so easily, time after time.

She saw, too, that they were never in couples, going round and round the hall, as in all the dances she had hitherto seen, but were much more "mixed up all together," as she vaguely phrased the more sociable character of the country-dances. She saw that the dancers sometimes clapped their own hands, or their partners', and that they skipped and ran, in steps children might have used in their games, but that there was never a difficult step, or one which she could not understand, used during the whole party; nothing in any way like the morris she had watched with wondering eyes. She noted a great many who were not "dressed up" at all, but wore light summer frocks or coloured silk jumpers, though there were more, like Joy and Jen, in pretty evening dresses and "ultra-swish" frocks of vivid colours; the blending and interweaving of the colours was wonderful. And she saw, without a shadow of doubt, that the dancers were all enjoying themselves immensely; the talk and laughter, and the eagerness for places in sets, testified to that.

She saw the teacher of the previous morris class dancing all through the evening, as if she had not taught for two hours and a half, with only an apple to keep her alive. She saw Joy and Jen dash to welcome another, a brown-haired, happy-looking fair girl in a black evening frock with touches of vivid blue, and bare neck and arms, and heard their greeting, and the jolly, infectious laugh with which she gave them answer.

"Duchess! You've got a new frock! And you *do* look regal in it! Is that because you've got married?"

"No wonder you weren't here to take us in morris, if you were getting into that! We came early on purpose to have a class with you!"

"Have you buried anybody lately?" Madam retorted. "Or do you only do that on Thursdays?"

"Only on Thursdays. So Jen brought me up to town yesterday, for safety's sake. Are you going to dance 'Butterfly' with *him*? For if it's going to be as wild as that 'Haste to the Wedding' on our lawn, I'm going into another set. You two will do some damage indoors."

"We'll be very careful when we come near you and Jen," Madam promised kindly, and went with her husband to a place in the line, and presently danced down the room and up again like a schoolgirl.

"You'll kill somebody, you two!" Joy warned her, when they met, and steered Jen out of the way. "You want the whole hall to yourselves!"

"We're only enjoying ourselves," and the husband quite obviously tried to take his partner off her feet, and failed ignominiously, in spite of the challenge of her dancing eyes.

Maidlin saw other greetings, too; heard a plump, jolly girl greet Joy with a shout of, "Hallo, Shirley! You've turned up again! Good news from Hobart? Where's Joan got to now?"—and recognised her as the heroine of one of Jen's stories; saw Jen rush up to a black-haired girl of her own age, and, after demanding a dance, begin to talk eagerly about Cicely and Dick, and end with a question, "Have you burgled anybody lately?" That was evidently another story, by the laugh it raised; and the two went off arm in arm to find places in a longways set, Jen declaring, "I've never done it! I don't know a step of it. Can you shove me through? Is it fair, or shall I put everybody out?"

"Oh, I'll haul you through. It's as easy as easy," said Avvy Everett, Cicely's new sister-in-law. "It's only 'corners back-to-back, skipping ring of four once and a half round, and change with your partner back to places,'" and this, cryptic as it sounded to Maidlin, seemed to reassure Jen.

"Sure that's all? Oh, I won't funk that!" she laughed, as the piano and violin struck up "The 29th of May."

"What a topping little dance! I love those skipping rings!" and Jen came to rest, breathless and exhausted, on the chairs below Maidlin's perch, where Joy had already collapsed, to pant and fan herself. "Joy, how the Hamlets would love that! We must give it to them soon! How have we missed it so long?"

"Didn't know it ourselves. Yes, they'd love it. We'll have a

221

party and teach it to them, Jenny-Wren. The Club must have a good thing like that."

"I'll fetch lemonade," said Jen. "This is where it would be useful to have a man. Avvy, can't you find a man to scrounge lemonade for us? We're dying! Haven't you any more brothers?"

"Madam dances every dance with a different man, and sends 'em all in turn to fetch lemonade," Joy said enviously. "I'm sure that's the fifth or sixth. She'll be ill!"

"Useful, sometimes, to have all the men buzzing round!" Jen commented, and went to take her turn in the crowd round the table.

"The jolliest party I ever was at, except perhaps an out-of-doors one at Cheltenham, was down at Plaistow, with the Pixie's girls and men," the Writing Person had danced with Jack, and now sat down by Joy to rest.

"Oh, have you been? We're to go to one sometime. What is it like?" Joy asked eagerly.

"Priceless. They all dance fearfully hard, and the Pixie, in a white frock, stands up on the high platform under the roof and acts as M.C., and shouts orders in a voice that every one can hear; and if there's too much noise she uses a whistle. When she wants to come down, she clings to the rope and runs down the ladder, and some big man, or two or three men, lift her off and deposit her tenderly on the floor. Then she runs round and arranges the sets, and hustles everybody into the places *she* thinks would be best for them, and breaks up the little cliques, if they're beginning to form, and nobody minds; they'll all do anything for her. She simply won't stand cliques. If you go to her parties, you've got to be ready to dance with anybody and go just where she thinks you'll be most help to those who don't know the dances well. You really haven't any choice in the matter. But then you don't want it. You feel, as they do, that you'll do any mortal thing she wants, if only it will help her. And you've only got to look at any of those men and girls to see how much they think of her."

"Do you often go to see her?" Joy asked soberly. "I'm going. I haven't been often yet, but I'm going oftener."

"I like to go when I can. I feel better for going. When I went last," and the Writing Person laughed, "I was very busy on a new story, and I hadn't had a minute to get to it all day. I had an hour in the train, to reach Plaistow, with no changes; so I took the story with me, settled down in a corner seat, and took no more notice of anybody. Fortunately, I woke up at West Ham, or I might have gone on to Barking. I told the Pixie I'd had a very happy journey, as I'd written a thousand words since I'd left home. She looked at me in astonishment, though I don't know why she should! It's no funnier to write in the train than to do lovely crochet, as she does! Then she said warmly, 'Well, you've made your fare, anyway!' How I laughed! I'd never thought of it like that. I just knew I'd cleared a worrying chapter out of the way, and now I could go ahead. And I did a big bit more on the way home."

"I wonder you could write in the train?"

"Oh, I forgot all the rest of the world! The other people in the carriage simply didn't exist. I was a long way away."

"Where were you?" Joy asked curiously; but the Writing Person only laughed.

"When are you coming to see me?" Madam flung the question at Joy and Jen, as they met her coming down the line in "The Whim."

"When may we? We'd love to. But you're always out. We must go home to-morrow;" they were passing her in the changes of the hey.

"Early afternoon? I'll give you tea! I have that sword class at six, remember."

"We'll love it!" and then they went up the line and she went down.

"If you wait till I write and ask you, you'll wait for ever," Madam called, when presently they met again going in the other direction; for the dancers had refused to stop when the music did, and had clapped till the Prophet at the piano, with a kindly laugh of pleasure in their enjoyment, struck up the air again and gave them a little more. "I never touch a pen till I'm absolutely obliged," she said, as she did back-to-back with Joy. "Is that the child who fell out of the pulpit on to us? The Italian heiress? Bring her, too. What have you done to her? I said she was pretty!" as they changed places in the hey.

"Put her into a pink frock. Joy's adopted her, and we're bringing her up and broadening her mind," Jen explained. "Oh, last time!" regretfully, as she bowed and Joy curtseyed. "What a dear little dance! The Club must have that one too. We didn't know it; that's two new ones to-night!" exultantly, to Madam. "It is topping to feel there are still new dances to learn!"

"Oh, you don't know a hundred and twenty-five yet!" Madam retorted.

"Can I get you some lemonade?" Joy asked politely.

Madam missed the mischief in her eyes, and answered innocently, "I think my partner's getting me some. Thanks, all the same."

"Every single partner does! And you were ill last autumn! Do you think it's safe?" Jen teased.

"Oh, I'm quite all right now. And it's *not* as bad as all that!" indignantly. "Have you rotters been keeping count?"

"I think we'll retire," Jen laughed, as the partner and the lemonade arrived. "See you to-morrow! Thanks awfully!"

"Do they often have parties like that?" Maidlin whispered, as she crept into Joy's arms that night.

The final closing dance, in a huge ring that filled the whole big hall; and other smaller rings inside, till five circles were swinging round at once; the hearty, laughing farewells; the run through the quiet streets; and the hasty but much-needed supper, had all seemed dream-like to her, for after the exciting day she was very tired. But it had been a very happy dream, and the music and laughter were ringing in her ears, and the vivid moving mass of colour still danced before her eyes—that wonderful "wave" moment of arms-up to the centre—the five widening rings swinging round and back again—as she crept into bed, less tired in her limbs than Joy and Jen and Jack, who had crawled home "in the last stages of exhaustion and starvation," they declared, but more weary in mind because to her it had all been so new and surprising.

"About nine in the year, in London; three in each term; but they have them at holiday schools as well. They have lectures and singing-evenings and dance-shows as well. Now don't ask me to talk to-night, kiddy! I'm simply dead; and to-morrow we'll all be stiffer than stiff! Wait till you hear our groans when we try to go downstairs! Are you wondering why we do it? Because we can't help it; that's all I know. Madam says it's mania; but she's got it quite badly herself. You saw her?—the big, jolly, pretty one, with heaps of friends, who danced *all* the time, and in a way nobody else does, quite. Cicely and Joan say so, anyway. She's asked us to tea to-morrow. Cheers! I want to see where she lives. Now go to sleep, infant. I'm too dead to talk!"

CHAPTER XX

MADAM AT HOME

ENTHRALLED and amazed, Joy and Jen and Maidlin stood and looked at the wonderful hand-wrought book, an old French love-poem, which the artist-husband of their loved Madam laid before them. It represented years of patient, careful work, incredible almost in the amount of labour and skill and knowledge given to its minutest detail, and could only have been created by one who was a great craftsman as well as an artist, and who loved to do beautiful work for its own sake, with no thought of gain in the doing of it.

Joy had exhausted every adjective she knew. Jen, gazing in rapt delight at the tiny miniatures, the larger pictures, the lettering with its beautifully coloured initials, the designs and symbols in the margins, was dumb for a while. Then she looked up at the artist—a very different person from the one who danced so wildly at parties—and said gravely, "It's like the work of the old monks, who lived in cells and cloisters, and had no time for outside, but only lived to make beautiful things. I didn't know anybody could live nowadays and do work like this; and love it like this. It's as beautiful as any of the books at Grace-Dieu, and we thought they were as wonderful as any in existence. When it's finished it ought to be in a museum, alongside the most precious ancient missal that can be found, to show it can be done nowadays, and to prove we're as good as the fourteenth century. But I'd never have believed it if I hadn't seen this glorious book."

Madam had been standing watching their delight with satisfied eyes, that had more than a hint of pride in them. As they left the studio and went into the cosy sitting-room, Jen added, to her, "He may fool about and make us laugh, as he loves to do, as much as he likes! But no one who has seen that beautiful work could ever forget. Whenever I see him, I shall think of that wonderful book; and the pictures; and the colour. He's a different person altogether when he's talking about his work."

"Oh, quite!" Madam assented, with a laugh. "But when he comes to my Saturday class for singing games, he joins in and plays like a two-year-old, and everybody bucks up and begins to play harder than they've played all term."

"I can quite believe that! They would! He does make things hum, wherever he goes!" Joy remarked.

"And I suppose these are *his* pictures; and those are *his* sketches; and you say *he* painted this screen; and—what else did he do?"

"Oh, a few other little odd jobs!" Madam laughed.

"It must be gorgeous to have your house full of your own husband's work!" Jen was wandering round looking at everything, and showing things to Maidlin. "So nice to feel things are all different from other people's! Not just things you could buy in any shop! I call it a most original flat!"

"If you come back in the summer, you shall go up on the roof and see our garden. We're going to grow hops and have a sunscreen," Madam came in with a big tea-tray.

"Oh, have you got a roof-garden? How glorious! Do you grow things in tubs?"

"We plant things in tubs. They don't always grow," the part-owner of the flat came flying in, in a long, white painting-coat, for some tool he had missed, and disappeared again as breathlessly as he had come.

"He won't want any tea. Where will you have it? At the

table, or round the fire?" Madam demanded.

"Oh, what pretty china! Gorgeous cups!" Jen exulted, standing by the black shining table, bare of cloth, but spread with coloured plates and dishes.

"We like the cups because they're all different. We can't stand things all alike! Well, where are you going to sit?"

With one accord, the girls looked at the table and then at the cosy corner by the open fire, with huge cushioned couch, small black tables, and big golden screen drawn round to shut out draughts, and a faint glow from a just-lit lamp in a flame-coloured shade.

"Oh, may we have it by the fire? How that lovely screen reflects the light! May we sit on those cushions? We'll fetch things from the table! The plates can stand on the mantelpiece!"

"I don't suppose I'll ever be strong-minded enough to get out of this corner!" Joy sank down on the huge divan. "You'll have to haul me out, or I shall never move again. You take that stool at my feet, Maidlin. Jen shall wait on us!"

"I'll *never* set that table for visitors again!" Madam said indignantly, as Jen flopped in the other corner and also refused to move.

"It's a beautiful table!" they assured her hastily. "It couldn't be more so. But this fire and these cushions are one shade more beautiful still. We simply can't resist them. Nobody could!"

"Besides, we aren't visitors. You've made us feel far too much at home," Jen added. "It's the homiest home I ever saw. I feel as if I'd been coming here always, for years and years, instead of about forty minutes. How do you manage it? You're a beautiful hostess, Duchess! Has anybody ever told you so?"

"It hasn't a bit the feeling of a newly-married flat," Joy remarked. "And yet you've only been here a few months. How do you do it?"

"It's because we didn't get new things. We both had some, and they were all old. And we picked up other old things, or had them given to us. It is cosy! I'm afraid it's not very tidy, but we both work here, you see."

"It only looks lived-in, not spick and span," Jen looked round in approval at the books and papers, knitting and unfinished needlework, painting materials and tools, laid down where they had been last used.

"Tidy?" the husband had whirled in from his studio in search of something else. "Have you seen my knife, dear? Tidy? It's beautifully tidy! There's nothing lying about! Nothing but scraps of paper!"

"Oh, well!" Jen laughed. "Aren't those the very worst?"

"It's absolutely tidy! There's nothing anywhere! There's nothing under the beds!"—that evidently being the highest boast he could think of. "Have you asked Miss Shirley if she's buried anybody since last night, dear? Or doesn't she do it in town? Do you think it's quite safe for me to leave you with her?"

"Oh, I asked her as soon as I saw her," Madam assured him gravely.

"Some people ought to be buried!" Joy said scathingly, as he made a grimace at her and departed at lightning speed to his own domain.

"Do you like housework?" Jen asked curiously of Madam. "We can't quite get used to the idea! Morris jigs and country-dances seem more in your line!"

"I don't do much. I've a very good woman who comes in and does everything. I do a little dusting—sometimes!" Madam added honestly, with a twinkle. "And I'm getting *very* good at cooking," she added proudly, as the girls laughed. "I'm really frightfully domesticated. I cooked a chicken *beautifully* the other day. It was just perfect!"

"And had hot plates and gravy and everything, all ready at the right minute?" Joy teased.

"*All* ready, at the *right* minute!" Madam assured her haughtily.

Jen had been gazing again round the home-like living-room, with its original characteristic touches—the vivid blue curtains at the window; the circular panel-paintings on the dull green walls, with their rich blues and yellows and greens, and mediæval figures reminiscent of old Florentine masterpieces; the golden screen reflecting the firelight; the glow of the lamp in its orange shade; the dull red lattice-work all round the walls, at the top of the quaint green dado, with its roses; Madam herself, in a black velvet gown and string of big yellow beads, playing her part as hostess with the dignity which had made Cicely dub her "Duchess," moving about before the fire to bring fresh cakes or pour out tea, with the easy perfection of movement which was all her own—a very different person from the Madam of class-rooms and schools they had hitherto known. And as they said good-bye presently, remembering her classes at night, the thought in Jen's mind forced itself to utterance.

"It was simply awfully good of you to let us come! We hadn't any decent background for you before—only class-rooms and school halls, and we like you far too well for that. They're cold and empty and dead. I know now why the President is so glad she's been to see you. We'll always think of you now in these gorgeous, warm, artist surroundings, with all the lovely colours! It's a proper setting for you at last; those dull, cold school-rooms weren't good enough. I think," Jen added pensively, "I think *I'll* find an artist husband, and live in a bandbox flat, all squeezed close together, at the top of a high flight of stairs, in a quiet West End street, and have a roof-garden looking over half of London! And he shall decorate every corner of it for me, with lovely colours, and have nothing ordinary, and nothing that matches anything else; and then I shall feel picturesque and unusual too! Joy, your big old Hall will feel like a barn after this cosy little place! This is like a nest at the top of a high elm tree!"

"All right! Go and look for your artist!" Joy retorted. "Have we seen it all, Duchess?"

"Not the cupboards. Nobody sees the cupboards!" Madam confessed. "We have one each, and everything goes in there out of sight. I'm afraid they're not presentable."

"Oh, that's how you manage to keep it decent, is it?" Joy mocked. "What a topping idea! But I do echo every word of Jenny-Wren's poetical remarks! Thank you just awfully for letting us come!"

"It's just perfect for two!" said Jen, as they set out in Eirene for their long drive homewards through the dark. "But there isn't an inch to spare. If it should ever be a case of three—!"

"Jenny-Wren! You are in a hurry!"

"Well, when you're married, it often does get to be three in time!" Jen argued. "They simply wouldn't have room for another one; even a little one!"

"Oh, I don't know! You can do a lot by squeezing, when you want to. There are always the cupboards, you know!"

"Poor little Number Three!" Jen laughed.

"Maidlin, my infant, you're very quiet! Anything wrong?" Joy demanded. "Didn't your tea agree with you? Don't pretend it's shyness with Jen and me, after the cream-buns-and-pillows incident! Didn't you like Madam?"

"Yes, I liked her. She's kind. She was nice to me," and then Maidlin lapsed into silence again.

Over her head, the elder girls looked at one another with raised brows. "Overtired with last night?" telegraphed Jen.

"Got a bad attack of Rosamund?" Joy's eyes asked anxiously.

An unexpected question from the unconscious Maidlin startled them both. "Joy, why did you bring me to town with you?"

Again Joy looked at Jen, and Jen at Joy. Joy pursed her lips in astonishment; Jen shook her head helplessly.

Joy, to help matters on a little, said lightly, "To buy you some frocks, and to see that man yesterday."

"Was it only that?" persisted Maidlin doggedly.

"I couldn't think what the child was getting at!" Joy confessed that night, alone with Jen. "But I thought I'd better risk it and give her a straight answer. With some kids I'd have teased and laughed it off. But Maidlin thinks over things so; it's a good sign, of course; I hope she'll always do it. But I felt if she had really guessed I'd had a bigger reason, it would be wiser to ease her mind. She might have imagined all sorts of things! But fancy the infant finding me out! She has got something in her, you know; and it's something more than a jolly sharp little brain. That wasn't a brain-wave; it was instinct made her ask! Something told her there was more in it than shopping and business. She is worth while, and no mistake about it!"

She answered Maidlin quietly, definitely, and as simply as she could. "I took you because I wanted you to begin meeting people, and I wanted to be sure it was a certain kind of person you met. You'll need to learn a lot before you'll be all that your daddy will want you to be; you know that. Some of it you'll get at school. But there are other things; what you are matters more than what you know. There's a big, wide new life in front of you. If you're to be really fit for it, you want to grow up to be big and generous and open-minded, not small and mean and narrow. I don't mean that you are any of those, but I do think you can grow into one or the other, and I want to help you to grow along big lines, in every way. Now those people I took you to meet are all big, happy, hearty people, loving music and art and beauty for their own sakes, and giving up their lives to teaching and spreading them. Do you suppose Madam could settle down in her tiny flat, beautiful as it is, and enjoy it, after teaching folk-dancing all these years? She's too full of the love of it; she must go on teaching, and making new people love it too, and go about giving it to fresh people. I wanted you to see how big things, like music and beauty, could make people happy. Then that lovely work her husband does, just because he loves to make beautiful things; he isn't doing it for anything he'll ever get for it, but just because he must, because he has the love of it inside him. Then the dance last night; there was the love of beautiful music and movement again; you saw how everybody enjoyed it! As for the Pixie, you couldn't help feeling how great she was in every way; I knew that. I thought surely it would be good for anybody to meet her! That's all, Maidlin. I hadn't any other ideas, honestly; don't go imagining I'm deep and crafty, and playing games with you! I just thought we had some very jolly friends, whose lives are full of music and the love of beauty, and who are all very jolly and happy; and that it would be nice for you to see them. I hoped you'd like them. Did you?"

"Oh, yes, awfully! They're all nice and kind. But I—I thought perhaps there was something else."

Joy looked at her quickly. "Now what are you getting at? Did I show you anything else, besides what I've said? I mean, did you find anything else for yourself in town? You may have seen more than I did; it was all new to you. I know when people do their level best they sometimes find they've done more than they thought. If I did more than I knew when I took you up to town, you might just tell me! You've made me awfully curious!"

But Maidlin had lapsed into shyness again. "I—perhaps I'm silly. I'll tell you later, if I can. I'd like to think about it some more first."

Joy looked across at Jen again in amused agonised curiosity.

Jen plunged to the rescue. "I knew quite well the kid wanted to get rid of me!" she said afterwards. "She'll only whisper her deepest thoughts to you!"

"Joy, when are we going to give those two new dances to the Hamlets?"

Maidlin, finding herself ignored, breathed more freely, and listened with interest.

"Jenny-Wren, you are touching a sore spot; a secret sorrow!" Joy said gloomily.

"Oh? I beg pardon!" Jen laughed. "What's the trouble?"

"My conscience pricketh me sorely, that's all! I've been a slacker as regards the Club. I felt it acutely when that Writing Person talked about teaching her girls, and about the others all teaching their girls! The Hamlets look to me for help now and then. The older Queens, and Joan, are all married and gone; Mirry and Marguerite have each a kiddy, and Cicely and Joan are abroad. I'm the oldest Queen left who can be any use to the Club, in the way of giving them parties, teaching new dances, and all that; and I haven't been doing it, woe is me! Of course, for the girls who are still at school, the reigning Queen can do a lot, and Babs Honor does very well. But there are all the old members, those who were at school with me, and before, and since, and she can't do things for them. And I haven't been taking an ounce of trouble over the Hamlet Club!"

"Oh, but you've been fearfully busy with Joan's wedding, 'Traveller's Joy'!"

"I know; they understood that. But now that's safely over, they will expect me to do something. I feel I ought to, anyway. I'm the only one in the Club, except you, and you don't count, who is in touch with folk-dance people; I'm the only one who can really criticise the girls' dancing and keep them up to the mark, and give them new dances. It came on me last night—in the middle of 'Newcastle,' as a matter of fact—what a pig I was to come up to town and enjoy myself to the very limit, as I was doing, and forget all about the Club down in the country!—What did you say, Madalena?" at a curious sound, a choke, or a chuckle, or a subdued cheer, from the silent person between them.

"Nothing. I—I coughed," Maidlin explained hurriedly.

Over her head, Joy looked again at Jen. Then she went on, "I shall call a meeting for next Saturday afternoon, and give them all tea. If it's fine enough, we'll dance on the lawn; if not, we'll clear the big hall. We'll give the girls the two new dances, and *they* shall all have as good a time as *we* had last night!"

"Topping!" Jen said warmly. "They'll love it! Couldn't we teach Maidlin some dances, so that she could join in? We've a whole week! We'll tear Rosamund from her homework some evenings, and have dances on our own!"

"You won't have to tear very hard, if I know Rosamunda at all!" Joy laughed. "Will you learn morris and country-dances, Madalena?"

"Oh, could I? I would like it. It didn't look hard; only a lot to remember!" Maidlin said doubtfully.

"Oh, you soon get used to that! The music helps, you know. It tells you when to do things!"

"Oh, was that how they knew? I kept wondering! They all did things at the same minute."

"Of course!" Joy laughed. "The music told them. And, of course, you can learn. Right-o! You shall! And we'll show you what *we* can do in the way of folk-dance parties!"

"Cheers! I'm all out for parties!" Jen laughed happily.

CHAPTER XXI

MAIDLIN THINKS FOR HERSELF

"It has been a topping two days!" Jen sighed, as Eirene crept carefully down the winding road to the Hall. "Joy, hasn't it been jolly and—and refreshing? Don't you feel bucked up by meeting all those folks?"

"I feel I've got new ideas, and I want to work them out! And I've had a ripping time, and I want to do something worth while, to—to earn it, in a way! Give other people a ripping time too; and all that kind of thing, you know."

"It's like what the Writing Lady said," Maidlin ventured. "She said she always felt ready to begin again."

"Yes, I asked her last night if parties did it too, and she said yes, but not more than classes, and that if she ever had to choose between a Thursday party and a Friday night of classes, she saved up for the Friday, because she was keenest on that. I feel almost as if *I* could write a story after these three days! But I shouldn't have the foggiest notion how to begin!"

"Ask her to come and start it for you!" Jen laughed. "Here's a peaceful domestic picture for you, 'Traveller's Joy'! Aren't you glad to come home, after all? I apologise! It isn't a bit like a barn. It's a dear old house, and I love every stone of it!"

"And a barn's a very jolly place, as the Hamlet Club knows," Joy looked over her shoulder, as she peeped in at the window, where the curtains had not yet been drawn.

Eirene had been pulled up quietly before the big door, and no raucous hooting had as yet disturbed those inside. Mrs. Shirley sat in the corner by the big open hearth, busy with delicate white netting, her white hair framed by the black oak of the settle. Rosamund bent over her books at the round table, the light touching her yellow plaits with gold.

"Yes, it does look homey," Joy said quietly. "I wonder why *I* should have had so much? Think of the Plaistow boys and girls living in one room, or two! I must tell aunty. She'll think of ways to help. She's great at helping people. We've stacks of stuff to tell! I'm afraid Rosamunda won't get much more work done to-night. I suppose," and her voice dropped, "we'll have the same kind of uncomfortable time we had before! I don't suppose Maidlin will rise to anything better all at once. Nothing's happened to change her."

"But you never know what's going on inside Maidlin!" Jen murmured. "Look how silent she's been for the last hour!"

"Getting scared of Rosamund again—I say! She's gone! She can't have got the wind up and raced off as she did before, surely?" Joy cried in dismay, finding Eirene empty.

Jen, with quicker intuition, caught her arm and drew her to the big door, which stood open, for their arrival had been expected. Maidlin was just slipping through the inner door into the big warm entrance-hall. Unseen by her, the elder girls caught the door as it swung back, and followed.

To Maidlin's sensitive, shy Italian soul an ordeal lay before her; but to her sturdy, honest north-country nature there was only one thing to be done, and she had the courage to do it. She had been thinking about it and facing it steadily for the last hour, asking no help even from Joy, but she had never hesitated as to its necessity, and she did not falter now. There was no harm in getting it over as quickly as possible, however! While Joy and Jen were peering through the window, she disentangled herself from the rugs and slipped through the doorway.

"Rosamund, I was just horrid when you came. I was a pig, and I'm sorry. I didn't see how hateful I was. Will you forget all about it, and let me be nice now? You were jolly to me all along."

Rosamund looked up from her French verbs in blank amazement. "Oh, how you made me jump! Oh, but you weren't, Maidlin! You were only shy!"

"I wasn't shy," Maidlin said bluntly. "I was angry, because you could play and talk with Joy and Jen, and I couldn't, and I felt bad because I was left out. I wasn't shy. That's not shy!"

"I'm awfully sorry you felt bad," Rosamund said eagerly. "Have you had a good time in town? Where are the others? Did you like the party? Wasn't it fearfully scrumptious? I nearly died of envy last night! Tell us all about it, won't you? Every single thing! Oh, I say! You've got a new coat! And a red frock! Have you bought up the whole of London? How tophole! Let's see it!" and she unbuttoned the big coat with eager fingers.

Maidlin gave a little laugh of relief that the ordeal was over and friendly relations were established. It was not so difficult to behave properly, after all. And she knew she had felt very uncomfortable before.

"I've got heaps of new frocks!" she said, her tone one of shy importance. "I wore a pink silk one for the party. Oh, Rosamund, it was a lovely party! I do wish you'd been there!"

"I'm weak and limp with astonishment!" and Joy tottered to a chair. "Madalena, you do—you do take the biscuit! You do give me shocks, my infant! I can't keep up with you at all! I hadn't realised this was a dramatic and important moment! Why didn't you give me warning?"

Maidlin looked at her doubtfully. Then she turned to Rosamund again. "One night, when the cuckoo struck twelve, we were all eating cream buns on Jack's bed. Joy and I had been pillow-fighting her and Jen. And last night it was striking twelve again as Joy got into bed. We've had a gorgeous time!"

Jen went off into a peal of laughter at sight of Mrs. Shirley's horrified face. "Maidlin, *dear*! You'll get yourself sent to bed early for a week, to make up for it!"

"I'm green and blue with envy!" Rosamund wailed. "You'll have to tell me every single thing, to make up for missing it all, Maidlin. And I've gone to bed at nine each night!"

"We saw the Tower, and the Pixie, and men doing morris-dancing—but they were boys really—and her Club, and her flat, and Madam's flat, and The Book!" Maidlin's tone of awe was eloquent of the deep impression made upon her, though at the moment of seeing "The Book" she had been so quiet and dumb as to seem unresponsive. "And Joy and Jen were in a class and learned jigs and things. And—oh, Rosamund! The lady who wrote that Camp Fire book was there at the party, and I talked to her, and it's all true about the gray cat, and she's got a Camp of her own; she told me about her girls, and all about her gown! And she took me out and gave me supper! We had buns and coffee in a shop, and she gave me squishy cakes, but she would only have one herself, because she said she meant to dance the whole evening!"

The book referred to had been lying at Rosamund's elbow, ready for the glorious moment when her French could safely be left till the morrow. It had been handed to her on Wednesday, to console her for being left alone. She gave a wail of indignant envy, then poured out a stream of questions about the Writing Person. What was she like? What had she worn? What had she said? Maidlin must repeat every word, and miss nothing!

Joy sprang up from the chair into which she had pretended to fall, and went to kiss Mrs. Shirley. "I very nearly swooned! But those children will be all right now, thank goodness! Everything gone well, aunty, dear? Oh, a letter from Joan! Cheers! Jenny-Wren, come and hear all the news!"

"How have you managed to bring about this happier state of affairs?" Mrs. Shirley asked in a tactful undertone, glancing at the two girls talking hard beside the table.

"Aunty, dear, I haven't the foggiest notion! You saw how astonished I was. I nearly died of surprise. We hadn't the slightest warning."

"But Maidlin will tell you later," Jen threw off her fur coat and cap, and sat down at Joy's feet to hear the letter. "She'd evidently thought it all out very carefully. I believe I know how Joy did it, Mrs. Shirley, if she doesn't know herself. But Maidlin may not be able to explain. I shouldn't wonder if she just says it was 'because of that time in town,' or 'because of meeting all those jolly people.' That may be as far as she can get at present. Read up, 'Traveller's Joy'! They'll be quite happy for hours, now that Maidlin has found out how to talk!"

"Rosamunda never had any difficulty about talking!" Joy laughed.

In spite of Mrs. Shirley's wishes and advice, that was another late night for all the girls. There was so much to be told, so much to be shown. Joy had to glance at the letters which had arrived during her absence, though they could not be answered till the morrow. Rosamund's endless questions had to be satisfied, and there was a thrilling and extremely noisy half-hour after supper, when all four girls gathered in Maidlin's room, and the parcels were unpacked and their contents spread on the bed. Rosamund's shriek of rapture over the pink silk frock brought Mrs. Shirley in to look also, and the other purchases still to come were described in detail by Jen, while Rosamund listened enviously.

"I wish some one would die and leave me a fortune!" she sighed.

"There's one thing we haven't thought of," Joy remarked, as they turned over the white dainty undergarments. "But it's better it shouldn't come from a shop, after all. We'll get the stuff in Wycombe, and Maidlin shall help to make it herself. A country-dance frock, you know. What colour will you have, kiddy? She's going to learn folk-dancing, Rosamunda; you're going to help to teach her. Aunty, do you remember when we made my first one; the apple green? In those poky little rooms at the abbey, and you and Joan did most of it, but I helped, because I was so frightfully keen. What a little pig I was! Do you remember how I babbled on and on about school, and the dancing, till I made Joan cry? And never thought how rotten it was for her to have to stay at home; and she'd given me the chance! I was a little beast, and no mistake!"

"I'm sure you never were!" Rosamund cried indignantly.

"You couldn't be," Maidlin said, with firm conviction.

"No, only rather thoughtless," Mrs. Shirley amended quietly.

"Oh, I know very well what I was like! What colour will you have, Madalena? Now!"—sternly. "Say what you'd really like, remember! We've told you what colours you can wear!"

"Pink again, like the Pixie's almond-blossom, Maidlin?" Jen queried.

"No, my best frock's pink!" the practical temperament found utterance. "I'd like yellow," Maidlin said sturdily, "the goldy colour of a daffodil's trumpet."

"Good for you! Golden it shall be. We'll run down to town on Belinda and choose it on Monday. Rosamund, my child, is there any hockey match or other event at school to-morrow week?"

"Not so far as I know. Babs was speaking of a Club meeting to vote for the new Queen. It's time we chose her."

"Cheers! Couldn't be better. We'll ask them here. We'd decided to have a party that day, unless it clashed with anything at school. Who will be the new Queen?"

"I haven't an idea. I don't think anybody has."

"Not the Maid of Honour? I don't know her, but she's a great chum of Babs Honor's."

"No, she's leaving, so she can't. I don't know who it will be; there doesn't seem anybody *quite* good enough! Not any one better than all the rest, you know. I shall vote for dear old Meg; she's in our form, and she's a jolly good sort. But she's quiet, and some of the girls don't know her. I don't believe she'll get it, but I'd like her to know somebody wanted her, anyway."

"Nice of you!" was Joy's only comment. "We'll send a message to Babs on Monday, then, and notices to the old members. And then we'll have our work cut out for us, between making Maidlin's daffodil frock and teaching her enough dances to get on with!"

"Going to miss me to-night, baby?" she asked, as she kissed Maidlin at bedtime.

"I shall! Joy, couldn't I—oh, but you wouldn't want me all the time!"

Joy laughed. "You shall come sometimes! I like the feeling of having you there; feels like having a big baby to cuddle! But not all the time; only when you're invited! I don't approve of it, on principle. A girl ought to have a room that's all her own, that nobody will go into without being asked. Even if they can't, in places like Plaistow, yet they ought to!"

"But I like you to come into my room. I—I want to say something to-night, Joy!"

Joy had been waiting and hoping for this. "I'll come when you're in bed, then. No, I'll come and do your hair for you. You can't possibly brush it properly yourself every night. I'll come and give it a good hard brushing! And you shall get rid of whatever it is that's on your mind. I want to hear all about it, very badly!"

"Is it about you and Rosamund?" she asked curiously, half an hour later, as she brushed out the thick black mane, her own hair shaken loose and hanging down, for she and Jen confessed to being ready for bed after their two late nights, and it was no longer early.

"That's only part of it. It's what—what I thought you had taken me to town for."

Joy's interest deepened. "Yes? Tell me, kiddy!" she said, very gently.

"I thought you wanted me to see how—well, how everybody who felt they'd got something very nice tried to share it with other people! Like passing on that dancing, you know; those teaching people all do it; and the girls in the classes go away and teach other girls; and the Pixie, giving it to those men. They all give it to somebody, because they like it so much. You and Jen do it too!" Maidlin was warming to her subject and spoke vehemently, without noticing Joy's curious intentness of look. "You had a ripping time last night, and the first thing you both thought of was, how could you give the Hamlet Club a good time too? You thought of it while you were dancing, you said so; in the middle of the dance you call 'Newcastle.' I nearly laughed when you told Jen, in the car this evening; you didn't seem to see that you were doing just as all the other people do! And when Jen learned those new dances last night, the first thing she said was, 'When can we teach them to the Club?' And your Duchess-lady, going on teaching after she's married, because she likes the dancing so much that she can't stop, she has to pass it on. The Writing Lady does it too."

Joy had forgotten to brush, and was staring down at her. Maidlin looked up anxiously, "Do you mind? Mind me thinking about it, and about all your friends, I mean? It is true, isn't it, Joy?"

"Yes, it's true," Joy said slowly. "I'm only wondering that it should strike you so plainly. I never took you up to town to teach you to share your good things. But you are right! It's one of those times when somebody tells you something you've known all along, but never realised. Have you gone any further, Maidlin? For it doesn't stop with music and dancing and beauty, though those are good things to be able to pass on."

"Oh, of course, there's more!" Maidlin said eagerly, overjoyed to find herself understood. It had not been easy to speak out, but she had been sure of Joy's sympathy, if only she could express what she wanted to say. "It's everything! You sharing your flowers with those London people! And letting me come here! Wasn't that why you let me come, Joy?"

"Because I had so much myself that I felt I'd be a rotter if I didn't share it, and there were you, needing exactly what I could give. Yes, Madalena, that's why you came here—in the first place. But I'm jolly glad you did now, for your own sake. Rosamund too, of course. I felt I could take her and so I ought to, though at first I didn't want her a scrap. I'd rather have had only you. But now I think it's going to be jolly fine having the two of you!"

"And so I thought you were trying to show me, right at the beginning, what people who have lots of money or lots of nice things ought to do. I thought you meant that I was to share the things I'm getting, and—and so—don't you see? I'd had all that jolly time in town, and poor old Ros hadn't had any of it, and so I simply had to be decent and tell her all about it when we got back."

Joy began to brush again, very gently, with a little laugh at that unexpected "Poor old Ros," to hide how deeply she was touched. At last she said quietly,—

"Maidlin, my child, thank you for all you've said. I'd known it all, of course, but quite unconsciously. I'd never thought it out clearly and logically before. I knew I felt a slacker if I didn't go shares, and I've been feeling it more and more strongly since that visit to Plaistow. I'm sure the Pixie would echo every word you've said; she lives it all, every day! The rest teach the dancing because they want everybody to have it because they love it so much for itself; but *she* teaches it because she loves the men and girls in her classes so much that she must give them the best she knows. She teaches for love of the girls and men—particularly the men! The rest teach for love of their subject. I think it's jolly fine of you to have thought so much about it and to have seen all that it means, for yourself particularly; and I think it's *fearfully* decent of you to have acted on it so quickly, and in a way that can't have been easy, when you were so nice to poor old Ros! That was sharing in earnest, and you're a jolly good old sport to have seen it and done it! I'm glad I took you up to town, as it seems I was doing a much bigger thing than I thought. And I'm glad you told me; it's rather jolly to feel that you haven't been here a week yet, but you're willing to tell me things like that. Now, good-night, kiddy, and thank you again! Remember I'm really grateful to you, both for telling me all about it, and for making things so much happier here at home. Nobody could do it but you, you know."

She kissed her very warmly, and went away, deeply touched and very thoughtful, and did not even go to Jen's room for a chat that night. And Maidlin crept into bed happier than she had been since the news of her fortune arrived; happier than she had thought she could possibly be.

CHAPTER XXII

JOY lay long that night, thinking of Maidlin, with new and growing respect for the clear-sighted little brain, the logical powers she showed, and the courage and decision with which she had uttered and acted on her conclusions.

She woke next morning to brilliant sunshine, which in the sheltered grounds of the abbey and the Hall meant warmth and freedom from wind. Sure that Jen would be up and out, and that Maidlin would still be sleeping, Joy dressed quietly, and, glancing into Jen's room, found her guess correct. She slipped on a coat and ran out bare-headed to find her.

The garden, the abbey, or the orchard? Joy would have turned at once to the abbey, since it was of Jen she was in search, but for the remembrance of that other morning in the orchard, and the thought that came unbidden of the squalor and smoke and crowded streets of Plaistow. She knew Jen would have thought of those streets too, and of the Pixie's men and girls, and she thought she knew what she would find her doing.

But as she crossed the orchard, where the plum blossom was just beginning to show, she stopped and laughed. For Jen, in a jumper and a very short skirt, was dancing a morris jig under an apple-tree, a daffodil in each hand instead of a handkerchief. It was "Old Molly Oxford," which they had practised at Thursday night's class; she was whistling the air and dancing for sheer joy of life, right hand raised to her left side, then left swung up to her right, then "a *beautiful* galley," as Joy had said in the dark crypt, with hands wide apart, and a triumphant swing upwards at the end.

"Stop, you lunatic!" Joy cried laughing, and going forward to her among the daffodils. "Has the sun gone to your head? Or is it the country air, after your long stay in London?"

"It's everything!" Jen came to a breathless pause. "Just being alive, on a morning like this! I'm sure that's how morris began; nothing but a morris jig could have expressed my feelings! Oh, I'm so glad I don't have to live in Plaistow! I came out to gather daffies for the Pixie's girls, but I've remembered it's Saturday and we can't send them. We'll send her lots on Monday."

"I thought I'd send some regularly, if she says she'd like it," Joy said thoughtfully. "There's usually something we could send, that would be a novelty down there, even in winter. I'll tell you another thing you can do for her—for herself! You'll do it better than I should. Write her a long letter about the party, and tell her what everybody wore. You know how she loves to hear what people wore!"

"I'll do it!" Jen laughed. "And I'll tell her about Madam's flat, and The Book! I say, 'Traveller's Joy'! Is the Club going to choose our Rosamund for the next Queen?"

"I don't know!" Joy was swinging on a low branch, her hair glowing red in the early sunlight. "If she often has as jolly ideas as that one about voting for 'dear old Meg,' because it would be nice for Meg to know somebody had wanted her, then I shouldn't wonder at all if they did choose her. I should say they couldn't do better! I'd no idea 'our Rosamund,' as you call her, had got it in her. I say! They're quite a decent pair of kiddies we've adopted, aren't they?"

"Rosamund hasn't any idea of it. One could see that. But I thought you looked as if you had."

"Oh, they always try to keep it dark from the one they mean

to choose! It's meant to be a surprise! If they meant Rosamund to be the Queen, every one of them would tell her they hadn't the foggiest notion who would be chosen. I shouldn't wonder a scrap. She's good company and bound to be popular; she's pretty and attractive, and doesn't know what it is to be shy. If she really has jolly ideas for other people, as well as all that, the Club couldn't do better. Rather nice to have another Queen from the abbey—what?" Joy spoke casually, but her gratified tone showed how the suggestion had pleased her.

Then she turned from Rosamund. "I say, Jenny-Wren! That Maidlin! She took my breath away again last night!"

"Oh! Did she explain? Could she? I was sure there was something behind, but I didn't know if she'd be able to get it out. Tell me, then, 'Traveller's Joy'!" Jen came to sit on the branch also, and gazed contemplatively at her damp shoes.

Joy's eyes followed hers. "You silly kid! Go and change them! Of course the grass was wet! Get up and walk them dry, then; or dance some more! Your fairy-like weight will bring this poor old branch down with a crash. Come and see how the peaches are getting on," and she sprang from the bough, which had bent under tall Jen. "When the apple's a little further on, I'm going to leave some branches on Madam's doorstep, on my way to Plaistow some day. Did you hear her say she wanted apple-blossom and may? She shall have them—'Bless her!' as the Pixie would say. Oh, of course I'm going back to Plaistow! There are things to do there, real things. I'm going to help."

"I knew you would. But tell me about Maidlin, Joy!"

They walked up and down the sunny path by the old south wall, where the peach blossom was beginning to show touches of red, Joy's arm round Jen's waist as she told of Maidlin's vehement explanation the night before, and a little laugh as she repeated the astonishing reference to "Poor old Ros."

"I thought it was something like that," Jen said quietly. "I'm awfully glad she felt it. She is a good kid, you know, Joy; and she is worth while."

"Jolly well worth while! She's right, of course. It's just what you did, when you had to leave school a year ago, and be buried in your lonely moors. You thought how much you'd loved the dancing, and then you began giving it to everybody you could find."

"My poor kiddies will be missing it dreadfully. And they were getting really good," Jen said regretfully. "But it simply can't be helped at present. I say, 'Traveller's Joy'! Suppose you hadn't let Maidlin come here!"

"She'd have gone somewhere else, I suppose. And it might have been better for her."

"It couldn't, because she's so devoted to you. If only you don't disappoint her, nothing could be quite so good for her as being with you," Jen said wisely. "She'll look up to you and copy you, and try to come within miles of being as good as you—"

"Jen, dear, *don't* be an idiot!"

"I'm expressing Maidlin's feelings. I know it sounds idiotic," Jen said, frankly if not politely. "But it's how Maidlin feels. And Rosamund's nearly as bad. She thinks you're the decentest sort she's ever met. She said so."

"It's rather an awful feeling," Joy came to a stand beside the old swing. "I know kiddies are like that, and I was afraid these two were beginning. I told the Pixie, when we were going over the Club; she and I got behind you others, and I told her how fearful it was to have them looking up to me like that."

"I knew you'd asked her advice about something," Jen sat on the swing, and made room for Joy at her side. "She's always sensible! What did she say?"

"Only—'You'll rise to it, of course. You can't disappoint them.

They'd feel you'd let them down so horribly. You could never do that.' But while she said it, I felt I'd really have to. You know how encouraging she is, and how she makes you feel you can do anything! Now I'm frightened when I think about it. I'm not as good as they think."

"I should go to town often and talk to her!" was Jen's wise advice. "She'll buck you up and help you to keep going. But don't worry, Joy! It's you the kids like, just as you are; not any fancy picture, or stained-glass-window saint! The cream-buns-and-pillows story has endeared you to Rosamund, I know; you've gone up immensely in her affection! She's just hoping you'll be taken that way here occasionally. And you know it broke the ice with Maidlin!"

"I guessed it would. That's why I encouraged her," Joy grinned. "Here come the children! What's the row? Oh, are we late for brekker? Sitting swinging in the orchard, Jenny-Wren, and keeping everybody waiting! How can you?"

"We thought you were lost!" Rosamund and Maidlin, hatless, came racing through the orchard. "Breakfast's been ready for ten minutes, and Mrs. Shirley's down, and the post's come, and there's a great fat letter from Ceylon!" Rosamund gave all the news in one breath.

"From the President! Come on, children!" and Joy led the wild race back to the house.

That afternoon on the lawn, and that evening in the hall, and many times during the next week, Maidlin had her first lessons in folk-dancing. While Rosamund was at school and the abbey was in its morning quiet, Jen taught her morris steps and movements on the cloister garth, where she herself had learnt them from Joan, and stood over her till she could pass her circles and side-step as correct, according to the standard set up by Madam at Cheltenham. At night, Joy went to the piano,

Rosamund's books were flung aside, Mrs. Shirley came to make a fourth, and Maidlin learned "Rufty" and "Hey, Boys" and "Hit and Miss," and the mysteries of being led down the middle of a longways set, of "swing and change," of "balance," "cast," "hey," and many other curious terms.

"Now you'll do! With that much, if you remember it all, you can get through a good big bit of a party!" and Jen allowed her to rest. "Oh, 'Traveller's Joy'! *Do* you remember 'Hey, Boys' at Cheltenham, that first afternoon? Madam standing over us, and we four doing it all by ourselves, I've no doubt to the delight of the rest of the class. And all just ready to die with laughing, and she knowing perfectly well how we felt! Do you remember?"

"I nearly exploded at sight of Cicely's face! But I was wild at first. I didn't believe we could be wrong in a thing we knew so well."

"But we were, 'dreadfully wrong,' as Madam said! And we were half scared of her all the time, although it was all so fearfully funny. I know I used to keep one eye on her to see what she'd do or say next. And, of course, the first thing I did was to lose my head and run about wildly all over the place."

"Tell us about it!" Rosamund begged. "I love to hear about Cheltenham! Come on, Maidie! We'll go with them next August, shall we?"

"Ros, what a gorgeous idea! I'd love it!" Maidlin spoke fervently. "Joy, would they have us? Would we see all those jolly people again?"

Joy nodded, her fingers wandering into the new "Spring Song," which was still haunting her. "They'll all be there, of course. Cicely and Joan, too. Don't see why you shouldn't go. But you'd better work hard at your morris, or you'll find yourselves with the beginners, while *we* shall be Advanced students!"

"Swank!" said Rosamund.

"They might get the Pixie to teach them, though," Jen remarked. "She had beginners for the last week last year, Maidie, and she said—you know her, so you'll appreciate this!—once you could get them to feel they were safe with aunty, it was all right! Isn't she priceless?"

"Ros wants to see her, too," said Maidlin.

"I want to see them all! Maidie's jolly lucky. Oh, Joy! Is that a new bit? Play it all through to us! Isn't it ready yet? What a long time you take making it up!"

"Times have changed!" Joy murmured, her lips twitching, as Jen bent over the piano. "Ros and Maidie! Since when? I bet it was Rosamunda started it!"

"It's a change for the better, anyway," Jen said heartily.

CHAPTER XXIII

"SPRING GARDEN"

MRS. SHIRLEY came down the wide staircase to the entrance-hall, and smiled at the picture of the four girls in their dancing frocks, as they waited for the members of the Hamlet Club to arrive. Joy had been faithful to her first choice, and wore bright apple-green, with a white muslin collar and little white cap laid on her bronze hair. Jen's frock was of rich blue, with rosettes of bright cherry ribbon high under her arms and a full swinging skirt, the round neck and short sleeves edged with ribbon to match the rosettes. Rosamund's very short dress was of bright golden brown, "the colour of a well-baked scone," Joy had said teasingly, with white frills at the elbows and neck. Maidlin's golden frock had been made with a smooth, simple little bodice and a short full skirt coming high under her arms, and the simplest of white collars and wide cuffs, and with her hair braided in long black plaits she was a picturesque contrast to fair-haired Rosamund. Both wore white stockings and flat dancing shoes, and both, at present, had the plain white caps which they wore as "women," but which they would discard if they decided to dance as "men," to show their sex. Without any conscious thought of the pretty effect of their contrasting colours, but with the true folk-dancer's disregard for anything but enjoyment, they had arranged to be partners for a good deal of the dancing.

"Because you don't know the girls yet, Maidie, and you mustn't get left out," the invitation to make a couple had come from Rosamund. "Of course, you'll want to dance with Joy and

Jen too, and Babs will ask you, because the Queen always does. But if you haven't a partner for anything, you can count on me. I'll shove you through!"

In Joy's memory, that afternoon lived as "the party when things happened." It was the most eventful meeting of the Hamlet Club she had known, except only for the one at which she was chosen Queen, and that other night in the barn, when Cicely had made her engagement and Joan's known, and Madam and the Pixie had come to dance the Running Set to the Club for the first time.

All began happily, however, and even Maidlin forgot to be shy as the crowds of eager, bright-faced girls arrived, cycling, walking, or driving, changed their shoes and left their coats and hats indoors, and gathered on the lawn, where a morning's hot sun had dried the smooth turf, and a week of showers and sunshine had brought the spring flowers into full glory. The daffodils, the almond-trees, the deep blue scillas, the white and crimson prunis, were no more vivid than the dancing frocks of the girls, however, and their chatter drowned even that of the blackbirds and thrushes, whose astonishment at this invasion of their domain was loud and insistent at first. When Margia Lane tuned her fiddle and struck up "Haste to the Wedding," and then "Butterfly," it would have been difficult to find a gayer scene, even at a London evening party.

Mrs. Shirley smiled, and sighed for Joan, as she stood watching from the long hall window. Babs Honor—Queen Barbara—had insisted, for reasons of her own, on opening the dance with Rosamund, and was leading her down the middle. Joy had Maidlin as a partner, and was bidding her, "Lean well back and let yourself go, as you saw Madam do at the party; but keep facing me; don't twist your shoulder round!" when they came to the swing and change; and if Maidlin's skipping was a trifle uncontrolled, it was very hearty and full of enjoyment. At last she was really part of a dancing party! No longer need she look on, as on that Thursday night! Now she knew what it was all about; now she understood how to give herself up to the music and obey its command. She exulted in the thought, and in the joy of the movement, and danced well.

Jen was dancing with Nesta, one of her first partners, four years ago. But when "Rufty" was called, she came to claim Maidlin for her partner, and the long lines changed as if by magic into squares for four.

After several set dances, for eight and six, Joy called for "longways for as many as will" again, and, standing on a chair, taught the two new dances she and Jen had learned at the party, "The 29th of May" and "The Whim." These were new to the Club, and were received with delight and given a high place among favourites at once; the skipping rings of the first, and the more subdued, but more finished, balance and change, back-to-back and hey, of the second, taking the fancy of the girls by storm.

Then came tea, in groups sitting under the trees, on all the rugs and cushions the house could furnish, since no one would agree to go indoors; and after tea a time for rest and chat. Joy and Jen, making up for the interval since their last meeting with the Club and greeting friends on every hand, met near the house, and stood on the slope below the windows, looking over the pretty scene.

"Rosamunda's taking care of Maidlin and introducing her to 'dear old Meg' and everybody else. She's a jolly good sort!" Joy said warmly. "And Maidlin's thawing visibly in the atmosphere of the Hamlet Club!"

Jen nodded, but her eyes were on the almond-trees around the lawn, each a miracle of soft pink cloud, almost too faint and fairy-like to be blossom—on the sheets of daffodils spread below the green-tipped branches of lilacs and laburnums—on the snowy prunis trees, with their crimson leaf-buds just opening—on the green dancing floor, and the hyacinths around its border.

"'Spring Garden'!" she said softly. "Joy, they *ought* to dance it! But oh—think of Plaistow! Wouldn't you bring the whole of London here, if you could?"

"I've thought of it often," Joy said soberly. "But it's no use, Jen; we can't do that! We must do the little we can to help the Pixie, who's doing a lot, that's all. As for 'Spring Garden,' the girls would love a new big dance, but you'd have to give it them. I haven't even seen it."

"I? I couldn't teach the Club!"

"Why not? You teach your classes at home!"

"Oh, but they're only infants! I could never teach the Club! Why, Edna and Georgie are here, and they've been dancing since the very first start of the Club, when I must have been about ten!"

"But, my dear kid, they haven't been to Cheltenham! Or to London!" that was a conclusive argument to Joy. "You've had the real thing, from the real people. Everybody knows that. A week of Madam is worth years of our kind of pottering! And you had two weeks of her, and one of the Pixie! Get up on the chair and have a shot at it. I'm going to learn 'Spring Garden' too."

"But it's difficult, Joy! They'll never remember. I'm not sure that I've got it right myself."

"I saw you writing it down," Joy said ruthlessly. "And you know you looked it up in the book, and said it was all right. Don't funk, Jenny-Wren! You'll teach us beautifully!" and before Jen could finish her protest, she was mounted on the chair, and the girls, eager and interested, were in longways sets of eight before her.

Half-shy for once, and very doubtful of her own powers, she eyed them deprecatingly, more than half inclined to apologise for her impertinence. For a moment she hesitated, then laughed, and spoke out bravely.

"Girls, I know it's fearful cheek! But Joy wants me to try to give you a new dance. I'm the only one of us who's learnt it, you see. It's difficult, but if you'll let me try, I'll explain it as well as I can, and I believe you'll love it. I had it from a topping teacher a fortnight ago; no, not one of the ones who came here! Quite a different kind of person! But a very special kind of teacher. I thought it was lovely of her to teach us 'Spring Garden' in March; and Joy and I feel you ought to have it too. So if you'll try, I'll try too, if you'll let me, and we'll see how we get on. Longways for eight; that's right! Now listen to the tune once; then start with forwards and backwards twice."

The dance was complicated and long, for a country-dance, but Jen's orders were very clear and very definite, which was not to be wondered at, considering from whom she had learnt the dance. There were some girls present, however, who would not, or could not, take the trouble to think and remember; and for their sakes movement after movement had to be repeated again and again. Gradually Jen's calmness forsook her; her commands became more emphatic, her comments more scathing; and Joy's grin of delight deepened till she could hardly keep in her laughter. At last Jen, exasperated beyond bearing, sprang from her chair and fairly hurled herself into the midst of the offending set, scolding right and left.

"I said turn *right*, everybody! Everybody means *all* of you; don't you understand English? Edna, which *is* your right hand? Don't you know? Nesta, you were wrong, too, every time. When I say turn right, I mean turn right, and not left! I know it *feels* the wrong way, but it isn't. How could I have said it so often, if I didn't mean it? Go back to the beginning of the figure—the back-to-back square. Not the rest of you; you were all right. It's only this set; they're hopeless, I think. Now cast, as you did before; now set right and left, and cross, and turn *right* into places! No, *no*, Nesta! *That* way; right round, the longest turn!" and she took her friend by the shoulders and swung her round.

"Oh!" Nesta said blankly. "Oh, is that what you mean?"

"*Now* do you all see? Very well then! Do it once more, with the music, everybody, and do be careful, or I really shall begin to say things!—What's the matter with you, Joy Shirley?" indignantly, for Joy had collapsed on the grass, hugging herself in silent glee.

"Madam! You've got her style to a T! It was priceless! You're just her over again! Didn't you know? I could just *see* her! I nearly died! They say we all catch our teachers' little tricks! You got the wind up just as she does; that's exactly her hectic way of flying into a set and shoving them right! It was as good as old Room C, at dear old Cheltenham! Oh, Jenny-Wren, you have cheered me up this day!"

"Get up, you big silly!" Jen laughed indignantly. "We'll go on without you, if you roll about there any longer! Maidlin's waiting for you. I didn't learn this from Madam, you goat!"

"You were Madam to the life. Now be the Pixie!"—and Joy rose dramatically. "SILENCE! Now"—very winningly—"we haven't all quite got that, have we? Let's have it just once more for luck, shall we?"

"Joy, you are an idiot! We're ready, all but Joy, thank you, Margia! Be careful now, girls! Do think this time!"

"Madam's mantle has fallen on you, Jenny-Wren!" Joy murmured, as she took her place by Maidlin again.

"Now do the whole dance right through! And do think what you're doing this time!" Jen commanded, when she had taught the easier last figure; and Joy's eyes danced again at the familiar words in a very familiar tone.

Jen ignored her, though she saw well enough. But at the end she said, with deliberate intention, "Yes, that's *quite* good! It really wasn't at all bad! Try to remember that for next time!" and her eyes met Joy's mischievously. Then, from her chair, she called, "I want this set, and that set, to stand out and watch while the rest dance. Then they'll dance and you shall watch," to the dismayed victims. "Get on chairs and seats, or up on the bank and window-sills, you audience people! I want you to see the pattern you've been making. It's rather extra special."

"Jenny-Wren, what a perfectly brilliant idea!" Joy stepped up beside her and steadied herself precariously on half the chair. "Of course, we couldn't see it while we were doing it! I'd no idea it looked like that. Oh, isn't it pretty! What a topping idea, Jen!"

"It's not original!" Jen laughed. "But it is brilliant. I saw it done in town that Friday night. We were told to watch the pattern, and there was a wild rush at once for the high seats at the back of the platform. We looked right down on the class; it felt perfectly awful when our turn came and the rest looked down on us, though! Like giving a demonstration in the bottom of the Albert Hall! I was sure I should lose my head from sheer fright, as I did that first day with Madam! I didn't, though. Now you go and dance, and let us see how beautifully you can do it. That second figure is rather fascinating, isn't it?"

"It's all rather wonderful, the weaving in and out. I had no idea it was so brainy. I intend in future to watch every country dance from above, if I have to climb trees to do it! I love the way it disentangles itself. Cheers! It's a great idea!"

"But they ought to show if they're men or women! Women, do remember your caps! The first lot spoiled their effect by not showing what they were. That's better; now we can see what it looks like. Yes, it is pretty!"

"Visitors, Joy! Alice is looking for you," Maidlin came up as the girls gathered round Margia, clamouring for something simpler, something "we can do without thinking, and just let ourselves go, like 'Goddesses' or 'Mage' or a longways!"

"Bother! On a Saturday afternoon? I do call that the limit!" Joy said indignantly.

"Must you go? Won't Mrs. Shirley see them?"

"She will, but I mustn't leave it all to her. Joan doesn't like her to be worried, and visitors worry her. They don't need me here. You can carry on all right!" and Joy ran across the lawn to the house, with no very cordial feelings towards the intruders.

CHAPTER XXIV

ANOTHER QUEEN FROM THE ABBEY

"Bother! Oh, bother!" Joy exclaimed, as she glanced at the card the maid handed her. "Those people again! Are they always going to catch us at awkward times? What do they mean by coming on a Saturday afternoon, anyway?"—for the card bore the names of the old lady and her son, who had come to see the abbey on the morning after Joan's wedding.

"Their car had a breakdown, Miss Joy, and it was near our gate, so they came in to ask if Atkins could lend a hand at getting it right again, and Mrs. Shirley said the lady must come in to rest and wait."

"Oh, I see! It's not really a call. Of course, we ought to have called on them first. We were going to, in time!" Joy murmured apologetically. "But I do hate calling! I'm afraid I made aunty put it off. I'd better explain to the old lady! And I'd also better explain why I'm dressed up!" she laughed, with a glance at her loose green frock. "It's not exactly a March costume! She'll think I'm always dodging about in weird garments, considering she saw me first in my tunic, and then the other day on Belinda, in my helmet and goggles and gaiters! But perhaps she didn't recognise me that time; the man did, though! I saw his look. I expect they'll be extremely frigid and disapproving towards me, and very gracious, but rather sympathetic, to poor dear aunty!"

Mrs. Shirley had sent for tea for Lady Marchwood, and was apologising for her delay in calling. As Joy went forward to add her explanation, the grave eyes of the man standing by his mother were on her curiously; she was so very dainty in the green and white frock and the little white hood, such a spring picture against the panelled walls, so graceful and yet dignified in the easy movement her dancing had given her. Through the open window came the lilting music of "Lady Spellor," and Joy's foot was tapping unconsciously as she asked politely if the breakdown to the car had been serious, if her man had done everything to help, if they thought they were going to like the neighbourhood.

"I fear we have intruded at an awkward time," Lady Marchwood glanced at the window, where the bobbing heads of the girls could just be seen.

"Oh, that doesn't matter at all, if you'll excuse my dancing frock! We're only having a schoolgirls' party, a meeting of our folk-dance club," Joy said lightly. "Won't you come and watch? It's really rather pretty, especially on the lawn," and she led them to the window.

"I have been out of England for some years," there was a curiously wistful note in the man's voice, as he gazed intently at the moving coloured lawn, the happy girls, the flowers and trees behind. "This seems to crystallise all I've dreamed of, when I have been very far away. But we are keeping you from your dancing and your friends. Won't you go back to them?"

"Oh, I've danced enough! That's quite all right. Shall we see what they do next? It looks a wild muddle when the sets break up, doesn't it?" as the Club crowded round Margia again.

"It is quite a pretty scene," Lady Marchwood said graciously, as the tea arrived, and she and Mrs. Shirley turned back to the table.

"It's more than pretty. May I watch? I would rather have this than tea. But I must not keep you—"

"I've had mine with the girls. Yes, do watch! I must wait on your mother first, though. I'll come back," and Joy went to hand tea and cakes.

"Thought he wanted to watch country-dancing!" she said indignantly, but very much to herself, as she realised that, while she waited on one guest, the eyes of the other were following her every movement instead of looking out of the window. "He *shall* watch dancing! I'm not here on show!" and as soon as she could she went back to the window. "I'll keep the silly creature busy! Staring like that, just because I've got on a baby frock and a white cap!"

"What are they doing now? Have they had a dance since I went away?" she asked severely, knowing very well that she, having heard the music of "Goddesses" all the time, knew more about it than he, who had only been watching her.

"It's—it's something very lively!" he gave a guilty start, and looked hastily out at the lawn, where the last figure was ending in a very wild cast-off.

"It's very untidy! They're all over the place! Just look at Jen! That's romping!" Joy said severely. "She ought to know better! Jen's the tall one with the bobbed yellow curls, that you met in the crypt a fortnight ago; the one in the pretty blue frock. I nearly killed her in a motor-bike accident, seven months ago," she added defiantly. "You wouldn't think so to look at her now, would you? We thought she'd be crippled for the rest of her life."

"She seems to have made a very complete recovery," the great traveller said gravely.

"You should see her dance a morris jig! It's great; she puts so much into it. Oh, sets of eight! "Paper!" Then they'll sing! How jolly nice of them!"

The voices of the girls, as they sang for their introductions— "If all the World were Paper, if all the Sea were Ink"—put the finishing touch to the picture on the lawn, and the great man's face softened to a smile which changed it surprisingly, as he said,—

"Inexhaustible energy! One would think they would have no breath left!"

"The singing's feeble!" Joy retorted. "But after 'Goddesses,' it's no wonder. They'll go through this two or three times; yes, 'arms up to the maypole'—that's beginning again, you know. The maypole's in the middle, though you can't see it! It's a May-day dance, of course."

"Won't you go and dance with them? I feel we have spoiled your afternoon."

"Oh, I've danced heaps, thank you! I've been taught one new dance—by Jen; and I've taught the rest two others."

"It all sounds very enjoyable!"

"Oh, it *is*! You'd better learn!" Joy said mischievously, her lips twitching. "Excuse me one moment!"

She went to the garden door and called to Maidlin, who was, of necessity, watching the dance. "Maidie, as soon as they stop, get hold of Jenny-Wren, and say this to her! Say—'Jen, Joy says, if you love her, dance "Molly Oxford," as you did in the orchard one morning!' Just that. And say it's very important!"

Maidlin sped, a spot of brilliant gold, into the crowd to give the message. Jen laughed, and questioned, but could get no explanation.

"Margia! Joy says I'm to dance 'Molly Oxford'! Do you think there's anything the matter with her?"

"I should do it," Margia laughed down at her from her perch on a chair. "I expect she has a good reason. I can think of one, anyway. She wants the Club to see you're able for morris again. At Christmas you weren't fit for jigs, you know. They'd all be pleased, Jenny-Wren."

"Oh, if you think it's that, of course I will! I'm absolutely fit.

I'd do more than a morris jig to please Joy. She still feels bad about that old smash-up. All right, Margia! Have a rest, girls! I'm ordered to show you how jolly fit and well I am! Hankies, please, somebody! Any one got big morrisy ones? Good for you, Edna! And bells? Oh, cheers!" and she slipped the rings of bells up below her knees.

"She's going to do it," Joy at the window spoke softly but eagerly. "Now you'll see! Watch this; it's worth watching!" as Jen, a lone blue figure on the lawn, began to dance.

"Yes, that was *very* good! *Very* well done!" Joy spoke with deep satisfaction, as the girls on the banks below the windows broke into applause, and Jen, laughing and breathless, bobbed a curtsey and retired to rest by Margia.

"It was very fascinating; and beautiful. I've seen nothing like it."

"I'd forgotten you!" Joy said frankly. "I asked her to do it for you to see, but I'd forgotten everything but the joy of watching her. Won't she say things when she hears there were strangers looking on? She thought she was only doing it for the Club. Oh, Jen's a real folk-dancer, and jolly good, and as keen as mustard!"

"I would like to see more," regretfully, as Lady Marchwood rose to go. "Don't you invite friends to look on?"

"Well, of all the cheek! Friends!" said Joy to herself, in indignant surprise. "Not outsiders, as a rule," she said definitely. "We generally dance at school, or in our barn, near Wycombe. This is a special invitation."

"We are neighbours. I hope we must not always remain outsiders," he said tentatively. "Oh, but they are wanting you! We have trespassed on your time too long already!" as a shout went up from the lawn for "Joy! Joy!"

"I ought to go. I expect they want me to vote for the new May Queen. It's a very important occasion!" and Joy excused herself and fled, glad to cut short the discussion of the extent of their possible friendship.

She ran lightly down the dark-walled hall, unconscious that both her guests were gazing after her, one hungrily, the other with approval; and at the doorway met Queen Barbara giving out voting papers, scribbled Rosamund's name on a slip, and screwed it up and handed it back to Babs.

"A pretty chatelaine for this old house!" said Lady Marchwood to Mrs. Shirley, as she thanked her for her hospitality and begged her to call if she felt strong enough, for since her illness in the spring a year before, Mrs. Shirley had been very frail.

According to custom, Queen Babs, and two of the earlier Queens retired to count the votes, in a corner of the big hall, and Jen, Edna, and other seniors set the excited Club to dancing again, by begging Margia to play "Pop goes the Weasel." The call of the music was too strong; the girls turned from useless guessing on the result of the voting, formed their long lines again, and began running gaily round in rings of three, "popping" one under the raised arms of the other two, and repeating the movement with the waiting "second man."

"The first dance I saw the Club do!" Joy murmured. "In the old barn, when Joan and I had been to tea with Cicely for the first time. I'd just heard that Joan meant me to go to school instead of her; but none of us dreamed then that I should ever be Queen, let alone Joan! It *has* all been queer! I wonder if kid Rosamund is the new one?" and she turned to ask Mrs. Shirley if the visitors had tired her.

A letter was awaiting her on the hall table. She took it up, in curiosity, which deepened as she saw it bore the stamp of the lawyer on whom she had called with Maidlin, ten days before. She tore it open, and glanced at the first few words; then, with a dismayed cry of "Help! Oh, *no*! Not that! Oh, what *hard* lines!"

she dropped on the settle, and read the long letter through at feverish speed.

Then, clutching it in her hand, she raced through the house, forgetful of the dancing girls, the new Queen, everything; caught up the key of the abbey gate, and sped away down the shrubbery path and into the abbey, to find Ann Watson.

Ann was just showing out the last party of visitors for the afternoon, for the abbey was not open to tourists after six. They were ladies of the neighbourhood, who had brought friends who happened to be staying with them; and, knowing Joy well, they smiled and stopped to greet her.

"We heard the music, Miss Shirley. Is it a meeting of the dancing Club?"—and the strangers eyed the mistress of the Hall, in her picturesque costume, with interest and felt themselves in luck.

Joy, with a great effort, steadied herself to a polite formal reply. "Yes, Jen Robins and I invited the rest. She's still here, keeping me company. The girls are just choosing the new Queen."

"You must miss your cousin terribly. Have you good news from Mrs. Raymond?"

Ordinarily, Joy liked them well enough; but at the moment it was all she could do not to be rude. She answered as briefly as possible, then said good-bye and went into Ann's little sitting-room, and the guests had no choice but to go.

As the big gate clanged and Ann turned to see why she was wanted, Joy met her in the old cloister passage. "Ann, when did Maidlin see her father last?"

Ann gasped at the sudden question. "It's a long time, Miss Joy. Five years, I guess it'll be. She were only a little thing then. He come over and stopped with them a few days. He were to come again, before he went to Chiny, but 'twasn't possible."

"Five years! Oh, good!" Joy drew a long breath of relief, and leaned against the wall. "Then she can't remember him much. It can't break her heart, anyway. Look here, Ann! Don't faint; it won't help matters. But he's dead. I've just had a letter from the man in London. Now I've got to go and tell the kiddy. She'll come to you, I suppose, since you belong to her; she'll want somebody of her own at first! So you'd better know. They were in a very lonely corner of China, and some people started a little rebellion, and all but one of the white men were killed. One escaped, and sent home the news. But he wasn't Maidlin's father. Now be awfully good to her, if she comes to you! She'll be fearfully upset, of course; but if she hasn't seen him for five years she'll soon get over it. It's only the idea of having no one left, that will frighten her. And look here, Ann! If she says anything about that, and about being all alone, tell her he wanted her to stay in England till she was twenty-one; he wanted her education to be all English. There are people in Italy who will see to all the business for her until she's of age. It's all in the letter from the lawyer; he knew all her father had planned for her. He'd heard from him, just a few days ago, giving him all instructions, in case anything happened to himself. Now you tell Maidlin that I'm ready to do every single thing I can. She can stop with us till she's grown up, and after, if she wants to. I'd like her to feel from the first moment that she has a home, and that somebody wants her. She thinks she has only come to us for a time; tell her now it can be for always, if she likes. I'll tell her myself, of course; but you're her aunt, and she may want to come to you first. If she does, give her that message from me. Tell her I'll stand by her and see her through, as long as ever she needs me. See?"

"Oh, Miss Joy, it's that good of you!" sobbed frightened Ann. "Whatever we should ha' done without your help, I *don't* know! And that's the truth!"

"Neither do I, and that's the truth too!" Joy said to herself, as she crossed the garth soberly. "But I'm not doing it because I have to, and because there's no one else, this time. I like the kid, and I want to help. I don't mean to let her go. I hope—oh, I do hope we've made her feel we really want her! For we shall know now. This will show how she feels, when she knows it's for years, not months!" and she went still more slowly, her face very grave.

As she locked the abbey gate, a shout from the lawn startled her and reminded her of the great events in progress there. To the girls of the Club, the choosing of the new Queen was a very important moment. Looking through the bushes, Joy saw Queen Barbara leap from the chair on which she had stood to announce the result, and fly across the lawn, to fling her arms round Rosamund, who, astounded and unbelieving, was the centre of a cheering crowd.

Joy laughed a little. "How mixed up things are! It's one of the great moments of Rosamund's life; of the early part of it, anyway! And one of the saddest of Maidlin's. How pleased Madalena looks! She's shouting with the best of them; nice kid! How she's come out of her shell in the last fortnight! I hope this won't send her in again, that's all!"

The girls, in a big ring, hand in hand, were dancing "Sellenger's Round," the reigning Queen and the Queen-elect in the middle. But Rosamund's happy eyes, dazed still with surprise and delight, had discovered that Joy was not in the ring, though Jen was there, dancing as heartily as any one. Diving under the arms, and colliding with astonished Edna, as the ring went round again, the new Queen made a very undignified exit as she raced towards the house, shouting, "Joy! Joy! Where are you? Joy, I want you *quickly*! *Joy!*"

Joy caught her breath; she was worked up to a high pitch of nervous excitement, and this touched her deeply. "The kid wants *me* to know! How awfully nice of her! Wants to tell *me* first of all! I'll pretend I haven't heard, so that she can tell me— What's the hurry, Rosamunda? Stockings coming down?"

"Joy, you pig! Oh, Joy, I'm the new Queen! Isn't it simply gorgeous? I never dreamt they'd choose me! Isn't it lovely of them?" and Rosamund hurled herself into Joy's arms, which caught and held her in warm sympathy.

"Isn't it awfully nice, Joy?" Maidlin, with the same idea, had followed close on Rosamund's heels. "Aren't you pleased? Did you think they'd choose her? Won't it be fun to have the Queen living in the house with us?"

"Of course, I'm pleased, and frightfully proud!" Joy assured them warmly. "But I'd seen it coming. I thought it was very likely. I'm glad the Club has had such good sense and hasn't disappointed me."

"Oh! *I* never did! How could you?" Rosamund cried excitedly. "What made you think it was likely? I'd never dreamt of it!"

"Little things had made me think it might happen," Joy said seriously. "It's simply tophole, kid! I'm awfully glad. Go and tell aunty! Maidlin, won't we have a topping time helping her to choose her colour, and her flower, and her Maid, and everything?"

Rosamund paused on her way to the door. "I'll have Meg for my Maid, of course. I'd have you, Maidie, but you don't go to school, and it has to be somebody in the school. And besides, dear old Meg will love it, and the others will get to know her better, if she's the Maid of Honour. I'd like her to be in the procession!"

"You stick to that, Rosamunda! It's jolly decent of you to think so much about dear old Meg!" Joy said warmly. "As for flower, you've no choice really, 'Rose of the World'!"

Rosamund laughed. "I do love roses! But I can't have them at a coronation in May!"

"You can have them on your train; Margia will paint them for you. Oh, you'll have to be the Rose Queen! As for colour—"

"There aren't any colours left. It's awfully difficult to be the tenth Queen! We'll have to begin having stripes!"

"You needn't! 'Rose of the World' is a big red rose, surely! Pity you haven't Maidlin's hair and eyes! But you'll look jolly well in deep crimson, Rosamunda, with yellow and white roses on your train! You must keep away from 'Strawberry,' but now she's a proud mamma she may not come to coronations very regularly! Oh, you must be a red, red rose when you're crowned!"

"I'll think about it," Rosamund laughed, and ran in eager delight to tell the good news to Mrs. Shirley.

"Isn't it jolly? Good old Ros!" Maidlin said happily.

Joy put her arm round her, and drew her down on the settle. "Maidie, the Club doesn't need us for a few minutes. They'll be too busy congratulating Rosamund. I have to tell you something, dear."

Maidlin looked up at her with startled eyes, her sensitive instinct aware in a moment that something was the matter. Joy had never called her "dear" before, nor had she spoken in this very gentle tone, though she had always been kind.

"I've had a letter this evening, from that man we went to see in town, before the party, you know. Do you remember the last time your father came to see you?"

Maidlin's bewildered look had deepened. "I do remember, but not very well," she said honestly. "I was only nine, Joy, and— and I was rather frightened of him. It was a long time since he had been to see me. He'd been abroad, you know. Is he coming again?" There was more of dismay than of pleasure in her startled tone, as the idea occurred to her as a possible explanation of Joy's gravity. "Will he take me away?" she asked tremulously. "I don't want to go, Joy. I'd rather stay here."

Joy's arms tightened round her. "Maidlin, he isn't coming any more, dear."

Maidlin flung back her head and stared up into her face. "Joy! why?" she whispered. "Joy—oh, what was in the letter, Joy?"

"A story, Maidie," and in as few words as possible Joy told her. "All the white people in the little town got together for safety," she explained, when she had told of the sudden rising of the natives. "They were a very long way from any other white people. There were seven men, and three of them had their wives there, and there were some little children. One man was a missionary, and two were doctors, and they meant to stay there always and work for the good of the Chinese people, and so they had their families with them. The men who had no women and children, like your father, could perhaps have got away, by disguising themselves as Chinese and escaping to the coast. But that wasn't possible for the wives and children, and, of course, the fathers couldn't leave them. So the rest said they'd stay and help to defend them to the last. When the fighting was all over, one man who had managed to hide, a Frenchman, did get away, and he escaped safely and brought the news. But he knows none of the others could have got away; he—he saw what happened. Maidlin, you must always remember your father wouldn't run away, though he had the chance, because there were weaker people left, and he had to stay and protect them. It's a very fine story, Maidie, dear."

Maidlin lay in her arms, her face hidden, her shoulders shaking. "Then—there's nobody—!" she whispered brokenly, after a long silence.

"Oh, yes! You've still got your aunts! You have them as much as ever. He'll only seem a little farther away, at first, than he did before. That's all, Maidlin."

An impatient movement of Maidlin's shoulders had greeted the reference to her aunts. In it Joy found confirmation of a fear which had troubled her, that already the child had grown beyond the farm-folk who had brought her up.

Suddenly Maidlin raised her head. "Joy!"

Joy had been waiting for her to spring up and run to Ann for comfort. She said quietly, "Yes, dear?"

"I've got *you*?" It was a question, and one full of dreadful anxiety. "You won't send me away? I—I haven't any right here, but—Joy, I do want to stay!"

Joy's hug almost crushed her. "Maidlin, that's your right! And I want you to stay! That's another reason! Listen to me, kiddy!"

But while she repeated, swiftly and clearly, the directions for the future contained in the lawyer's letter, and her own plans and hopes, as outlined to Ann, her heart was singing a joyful song of its own, and she had her reward for all the efforts at understanding and patience and sympathy she had made during the last two weeks. For Rosamund, in the most joyful moment of her girlhood, and Maidlin, in her loneliness and sorrow, had both turned to her first of all. Joy would never forget that.

"So you'll stay here with me, won't you, Maidlin? And we'll make plans for you together. I think you should go to school with Rosamund, next term. You've seen the girls now, and they know you. They'd welcome you, and you'd have a very good time. And some day we'll run across to Italy and look up your friends there, and see your house, and all that. But you won't go there to live, till you're of age, for that is what he wanted."

"I'll never go away from you till you send me away!" Maidlin whispered fervently. "Oh, Joy, I am so glad I've got you! I would have been so lonely!"

"You couldn't say any other thing that would make me half so glad!" and Joy kissed her again.

"Joy, where are you?" Jen's voice called her from the doorway. "The girls want you for the last dance; they say you haven't danced in Rosamund's honour yet! Have you heard? Isn't it tophole?"

Joy put Maidlin down in the corner quickly. "I'll tell Jenny-Wren when we've got rid of the crowd. You stay here, Maidie, and I'll send them home."

"Anything the matter?" Jen looked at her with quick intuition.

"Yes, a little bit of trouble for Maidlin. But it's going to be quite all right; don't worry, Jenny-Wren!"

Rosamund came flying across the grass to meet them, the embodiment of joyous, excited life. "Joy, where's Maidie? Can't you make her say she'll come to school? For I want her for my Maid after all. Meg says she positively couldn't; she'd die of fright. I've told her she's an idiot, but she says she'd be shaky all over, and of course she is like that sometimes! So don't you think I could have Maidie?"

"I think perhaps you could," Joy laughed. "You must go and ask her, as soon as we've had one more dance, in your honour, Your Majesty! No, don't fetch Maidlin for this. She's danced enough for her first day. Go in the middle with Babs again! And don't run away as you did last time! It was most undignified! You must remember your position now, you know!"

"Oh, but that was to find you! I wanted to tell you first of all!"

"Jolly nice of you! I'm frightfully pleased about it. So's Maidie. Now, girls, 'Sellenger's Round!' And then all go home to bed!"

Girls Gone By Publishers

Girls Gone By Publishers republish some of the most popular children's fiction from the 20th century, concentrating on those titles which are most sought after and difficult to find on the second-hand market. We aim to make them available at affordable prices, thus making ownership possible for both existing collectors and new ones so that the books continue to survive. Authors on our list include Margaret Biggs, Elinor Brent-Dyer, Dorita Fairlie Bruce, Gwendoline Courtney, Monica Edwards, Antonia Forest, Lorna Hill, Clare Mallory, Violet Needham, Elsie Jeanette Oxenham, Malcolm Saville and Geoffrey Trease. We also publish some new titles which continue the traditions of this genre.

Our series '**Fun in the Fourth—Outstanding Girls' School Stories**' has enabled us to broaden our range of authors, allowing our readers to discover a fascinating range of books long unobtainable. It features authors who only wrote one or two such books, a few of the best examples from more prolific authors (such as Dorothea Moore), and some very rare titles by authors whose other books are generally easy to find second-hand (such as Josephine Elder).

We also have a growing range of non-fiction: more general works about the genre and books on particular authors. These include *Island to Abbey* by Stella Waring and Sheila Ray (about Elsie Oxenham), *The Marlows and their Maker* by Anne Heazlewood (about Antonia Forest) and *The Monica Edwards Romney Marsh Companion* by Brian Parks. These are in a larger format than the fiction, and are lavishly illustrated in colour and black and white.

For details of availability and ordering (please do not order until titles are actually listed) go to www.ggbp.co.uk or write for a catalogue to Clarissa Cridland or Ann Mackie-Hunter, GGBP, 4 Rock Terrace, Coleford, Bath, BA3 5NF, UK.